LIFE
AS WE
KNEW
IT

LIFE AS WE KNEW IT

Susan Pfeffer

SCHOLASTIC INC.

New York   Toronto   London   Auckland   Sydney
Mexico City   New Delhi   Hong Kong   Buenos Aires

ISBN-13: 978-0-545-03971-0
ISBN-10: 0-545-03971-1

12 11 10 9 8 7 6 5 4 3 2 1   7 8 9 10 11/0

Printed in the U.S.A.   40

First Scholastic printing, November 2007

Text set in Spectrum
Designed by April Ward

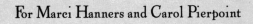

For Marci Hanners and Carol Pierpoint

LIFE
AS WE
KNEW
IT

SPRING

ONE

Lisa is pregnant.

Dad called around 11 o'clock to let us know. Only Mom had already taken Jonny to his baseball practice and of course Matt isn't home from college yet, so I was alone to get the big news.

"The baby is due in December," Dad crowed, like he was the first guy in the history of the world with a younger second wife about to have a baby. "Isn't that great! You're going to have a little brother or sister. Of course it's too soon to tell what it's going to be, but as soon as we know, we'll tell you. I wouldn't mind another daughter myself. The first one I had turned out so wonderfully. How'd you like a baby sister?"

I had no idea. "When did you find out?" I asked.

"Yesterday afternoon," Dad said. "I would have called you right away but, well, we celebrated. You can understand that, can't you, honey? A little private time for Lisa and me before letting the world know."

"Of course, Daddy," I said. "Has Lisa told her family?"

"First thing this morning," he replied. "Her parents are

thrilled. Their first grandchild. They're coming for a couple of weeks in July, before you and Jonny visit."

"Are you going to call Matt and tell him?" I asked. "Or do you want me to?"

"Oh no, I'll call," Dad said. "He's busy studying for his finals. He'll be glad for the interruption."

"It's great news, Dad," I said, because I knew I was supposed to. "Be sure to tell Lisa how happy I am for her. And you, too. For both of you."

"You tell her yourself," Dad said. "Here she is."

Dad muffled the phone for a second so he could whisper something to Lisa and then she took the phone. "Miranda," she said. "Isn't it exciting!"

"Very," I said. "It's wonderful news. I'm really happy for you and Dad."

"I was thinking," she said. "Well, I know it's way too soon and I haven't even discussed this with your father yet, but would you like to be the baby's godmother? You don't have to answer right away, but do think about it, all right?"

That's the problem I have with Lisa. Whenever I want to get mad at her, or just irritated because she really can be immensely irritating, she goes and does something nice. And then I can understand why Daddy married her.

"Of course I'll think about it," I said. "You and Daddy think about it also."

"We don't have to give it any more thought," she said. "You should see the glow on your father's face. I don't think he could be any happier."

"I couldn't," Dad said, and I could tell from his laughter that he'd grabbed the phone away from Lisa. "Miranda, please say yes. It would mean so much to us for you to be the baby's godmother."

So I said yes. I couldn't exactly say no.

After that we chatted for a while. I told Dad about my last swim meet and how I was doing in school. Mom still hadn't come back by the time I finally got off the phone, so I went online to see what's new with figure skating. The hot topic at Brandon Erlich's fan site is how good his chances are to win Olympic gold. Most people think not very, but a lot of us think he has a real shot at medaling and ice is slippery and you never know.

I think I'd like to take skating lessons again. I've missed it the past couple of years and besides, it'll give me a chance to pick up news about Brandon. He isn't being coached by Mrs. Daley anymore, but I bet she still hears stuff. And maybe Brandon's mother would show up at the rink.

When Mom got in, I had to tell her about Lisa. She just said that was nice and that she knew the two of them wanted children. She and Dad have worked really hard on making it a "good divorce." Matt says if they'd worked half as hard on their marriage, they'd still be married. I didn't tell her about how I'm going to be the godmother (assuming Lisa doesn't change her mind, which she's more than capable of doing). I feel kind of bad that I'm going to be the godmother but no one said anything about Matt or Jonny being godfathers. Of course Lisa and Matt don't get along very well, and maybe 13 is too young to be a godfather.

I hope Lisa changes her mind and I won't have to deal with it.

May 8

Not the greatest Mother's Day ever.

I'd told Mom a while ago that I'd make dinner and she decided to invite Mrs. Nesbitt. I can't say I was surprised, but I figured if Mom was having Mrs. Nesbitt over I could ask Megan and her mom, too. Only when Jonny found out it was going to be me and Mom and Mrs. Nesbitt and Megan and Mrs. Wayne, he said that was too many females in one room for him and he was going to have dinner at Tim's instead.

Mom always thinks it's a good idea for Jonny to spend time with Tim and his family because there are three boys and Tim's father is around a lot. She said if it was okay with Tim's folks it was okay with her.

I called Megan and told her to bring her history notes with her and we'd study for the test together, and she agreed.

Which is why I'm so mad at her. If she hadn't said yes, it would be one thing. But she did and I made enough meatloaf for five and salad and then right before I started setting the table, Megan called and said she had decided to stay on at her church and do something with the youth group. She'd gotten the dates mixed up. And her mother didn't feel like coming without her, so it was going to be two less for Sunday dinner and she hoped I didn't mind.

Well, I do mind. I mind because I'd been looking forward to all of us having dinner together and to studying with Megan. I also figured Mrs. Nesbitt and Mrs. Wayne would be good people for Mom to talk to about Lisa's baby. Mom may not be best friends with Mrs. Wayne, but she's funny and she would have gotten Mom laughing.

Megan is spending so much time at her church. She goes to services every Sunday and she never used to and she does stuff with the youth group at least twice a week and sometimes more and for all her talking about how she's found God, I think all she's found is Reverend Marshall. She talks about him like he's a movie star. I even told her that once and she said that's how I talk about Brandon, like it was the same thing, which it isn't at all. Lots of people think Brandon is the best skater in the U.S. right now and besides it isn't like I talk about him all the time and act like he's my salvation.

Dinner was okay except I overcooked the meatloaf so it was a little dry. But Mrs. Nesbitt's never been shy with the ketchup bottle. After a while I left her and Mom alone and I guess they talked about Lisa and the baby.

I wish it was summer already. I can't wait to get my driver's license.

I also wish I was through studying for my history exam. BORING!

But I'd better get back to it. Bad grades, no license. The Rules According to Mom.

May 11

Got a 92 on the history test. I should have done better.

Mom took Horton to the vet. He's fine. I worry a little bit about him now that he's ten. How long do cats live?

Sammi told me she's going to the prom with Bob Patterson. I know I shouldn't be jealous but I am, not because I like Bob (actually I think he's kind of creepy), but because nobody asked me. Sometimes I think no one ever will. I'll spend the rest of my life sitting in front of my computer, posting messages about Brandon Erlich and his future in figure skating.

I told Megan about Sammi and how she always gets dates and she said, "Well, the reason is there's always a man in Samantha," and after I got over being shocked I laughed. But then Megan spoiled it by becoming that new preachy Megan and she went on about how sex before marriage is a sin and how you shouldn't date just to go out with guys but because you were serious about making a lifetime commitment.

I'm 16 years old. Let me get my learner's permit first. Then I'll worry about lifetime commitments.

I went to bed in a bad mood and today everything just went worse.

At lunch today, Megan told Sammi she was going to go to hell if she didn't repent soon and Sammi got real mad (I don't blame her) and yelled at Megan that she was a very spiritual person and didn't need any lessons from Megan about what God wanted because she knew God wanted her to be happy and if God hadn't wanted people to have sex He'd have made everybody amoebas.

I thought that was pretty funny, but Megan didn't and the two of them really went at it.

I can't remember the last time the three of us had lunch together and enjoyed ourselves. When Becky was still healthy the four of us did everything together, and then after Becky got sick, we grew even closer. Megan or Sammi or I visited Becky at home or at the hospital almost every day, and called or e-mailed the others to say how Becky was doing. I don't think I could have made it through Becky's funeral without them. But ever since then Sammi and Megan both changed. Sammi started dating all kinds of guys and Megan got involved with her church. They've both changed so much over the past year and I seem to be staying who I always was.

Here I am going into my junior year of high school and these are supposed to be the best years of my life and I'm just stuck.

But the real reason why I'm in a bad mood is because I got into a big fight with Mom.

It started after supper. Jonny had gone into his room to finish his homework and Mom and I were loading the dishwasher, and Mom told me she and Dr. Elliott were going out for dinner tomorrow night.

There was this quick moment when I was jealous of Mom because even she has a social life, but it passed pretty fast. I like Dr. Elliott and Mom hasn't been involved with anybody in a while. Besides, it's always smart to ask favors of Mom when she's in a good mood. So I did.

"Mom, can I take skating lessons?"

"Just for the summer?" she asked.

"And next year, too," I said. "If I feel like continuing."

"After your ankle healed, you said you didn't want to skate again," Mom said.

"The doctor said I shouldn't even try jumping for three months," I said. "And by then there wasn't any point competing. So I stopped. But now I'd like to skate just for fun. I thought you like it that I do sports."

"I do like it," Mom said, but the way she slammed the dishwasher closed let me know she didn't like it nearly as much as I thought she did. "But you have swimming and you were planning on trying out for the volleyball team in the fall. You can't handle three sports. Two's probably a stretch, especially if you want to work on the school paper."

"So I'll skate instead of volleyball," I said. "Mom, I know my limitations. But I loved skating. I don't understand why you don't want me to."

"If I thought the only reason was because you loved it, then we'd talk about it," Mom said. "But skating lessons are very expensive and I can't help thinking you only want them so you can gossip about Brandon Erlich on the message boards."

"Mom, Brandon doesn't even skate here anymore!" I cried. "He trains in California now."

"But his parents still live here," Mom said. "And you'd want to be coached by Mrs. Daley."

"I don't know if she'd even take me on," I said. "It's about the money, isn't it? There's money to send Jonny to baseball camp this summer, but not enough money for me to have skating lessons."

Mom turned 15 shades of red and then we really went at it. Mom yelled at me about money and responsibilities and I yelled at her about favorites and not loving me like she loves Matt and Jonny (which I know isn't true, but Mom wasn't right about me not understanding about money and responsibilities) and we got so loud Jonny left his bedroom to see what was going on.

Mom came into my room about an hour later and we both apologized. Mom said she'd think about the skating lessons. She said she thought volleyball would be better on my college applications since I could join a college squad if I was good enough.

She didn't say I'd never be good enough at swimming for a college squad, which was actually kind of nice of her. I'm never going to be good enough for anything the way things are going.

And I don't much like either of my two best friends these days.

All that and a math test tomorrow I can't even pretend I studied enough for.

I wish I was in college already. I don't see how I can make it through the next two weeks, let alone two more years of high school.

May 13

Friday the 13th. Well, things weren't that bad.
The math test wasn't as hard as I thought it would be.
Mom said if I wanted, I could take skating lessons in July.

August I'll be spending with Dad, anyway. Then if I want to continue, we'll talk about it again.

Megan had lunch with her church friends (I don't like any of them) and Sammi had lunch with this week's boyfriend, so I ended up eating with some of the swim team, which was a lot more fun than listening to Megan and Sammi yell about God. Dan, who'll be captain next year, told me I had a really good crawl stroke and that if I worked at it, he could see me anchoring relays as soon as next season.

And I like Peter (he told Jonny and me to call him that; said Dr. Elliott was his name at the office). Some of the guys Mom's dated have tried too hard with us, but Peter seemed pretty casual. Not with Mom, though. He actually stammered when he was talking with her and he stumbled and nearly fell. But he laughed at himself and said he wasn't nearly that careless when he was operating on someone.

He asked if any of us had heard about the asteroid and the moon. Mom remembered something about it, because it was big news when the astronomers first announced it was going to happen. Some asteroid is going to hit the moon, and Peter heard on the radio driving over that it's going to be visible in the night sky next week. I asked Mom if we could dig out Matt's telescope and she said we should ask him, but she was sure it'd be okay.

Jonny and I didn't even argue over the computer after Mom left. There was something I wanted to watch on TV from 8 to 9 and there was something he wanted to watch from 9 to 10, so that worked out really well. The fan board is still fighting over whether Brandon'll need two quads to win the Olympics or whether he could win with just one.

It would be so amazing if Brandon won a gold. I bet we'd have a parade and everything.

It's 11 already and Mom still isn't home. I guess she and Peter are out admiring the moon.

May 15

Spent the weekend working on my English paper.
Dad called this morning.
Matt says we can use the telescope. He'll be home in a couple of weeks. He swears he'll teach me how to drive.
Jonny was named middle school player of the week.

May 16

All of a sudden this moon thing is the biggest thing ever. Either that or my teachers are as bored with schoolwork as we are.

I could understand it if I were taking astronomy. But French? Madame O'Brien made us talk about "la lune" the entire class. She's making us write a composition about it due Friday, because Wednesday night we're all going to be outside watching the asteroid hit the moon.

Sammi says every time they make a big fuss like that, for an eclipse or a meteor shower, it rains.

It isn't just Madame O'Brien who's hot for this asteroid. In English today we talked about the origin of the word lunar. Eddie made a joke about mooning, and Mr. Clifford was so excited about word origins, he didn't even get mad. He talked about slang instead and metaphors that have to do with astronomy and he gave us a new assignment, too. We can write on any topic that has to do with the moon. Due Friday, of course.

I guess Ms. Hammish thinks this moon thing is historical, because in history that's what we talked about. How people throughout history have looked at the moon and comets and eclipses. Actually, that was kind of interesting. I never really thought about how when I look at the moon it's the same moon Shakespeare and Marie Antoinette and George Washington and Cleopatra looked at. Not to mention all those zillions of people I've never heard of. All those Homo sapiens and Neanderthals looked at the very same moon as me. It waxed and waned in their sky, too.

Of course Ms. Hammish wasn't satisfied with inspiring us like that. She gave us an assignment, too. We can write either an essay about astronomy in the past and how it affected someone in history (like if they saw a comet and it scared them or prophesized something) or an article about what's going to happen Wednesday night.

Either way it's due on Friday.

I don't understand teachers. You'd think they'd talk to each other and at least one of them would realize how unfair it is to give us all assignments due on Friday. I wouldn't mind if I could figure out how to double up on them, write my history essay and translate it into French (which I could maybe do if my French was good enough, which it isn't). But I don't see how to do two for the price of one, so I think I'll have to write three separate papers (and one in French) and hand them all in on Friday.

I'll really be sick of the moon by then.

This moon thing is supposed to happen around 9:30 Wednesday night, and Mom was interested enough that we watched the news tonight. They said asteroids hit the moon pretty often, which is how the moon gets its craters, but this one is going to be the biggest asteroid ever to hit it and on a clear night you should be able to see the impact when it happens, maybe even with the naked eye but certainly with binoculars. They made it sound pretty dramatic, but I still don't think it's worth three homework assignments.

Mom watched the local news, too, which she almost never does because she says it's too depressing, and they're predicting a really nice night. Clear skies and temperatures in the low 60s. They said in New York people are organizing parties for Central Park and on apartment rooftops. I asked Mom if we could have a party, and she said no, but people on our road will probably be out watching and it'll be like having a block party.

I don't know how interesting it's really going to be, but compared to everything else in my life, at least it's something different.

May 17

I got an 82 on my math test. There were at least four questions I should have gotten right but made careless mistakes on.

I know for a fact that Sammi's mother hasn't looked at a test result of hers in years, and Megan's mom has always worried about who Megan hangs out with, but I don't think she cares all that much about her grades. I had to get stuck with the mother who works at home and has plenty of time to check things out and hover and demand to see tests.

We didn't have a big fight over it (I did pass, after all), but Mom gave me one of her famous You Shouldn't Be So Careless lectures, which I get at least once a week and sometimes more than that if the mood strikes her.

Mom said since I'm prone to carelessness, etc., it might be a good idea if I got a head start on all my moon papers, especially since they didn't have to be about whatever is going to happen tomorrow.

She suggested writing about the 1969 moon landing, so I Googled it, and I found out lots of people didn't really care that there were men walking on the moon. They all watched <u>Star Trek</u> (the original, old lousy-special-effects Beam Me Up Scotty

<u>Star Trek</u>) and they were used to seeing Captain Kirk and Mr. Spock hopping around the universe so real people walking on the real moon wasn't as exciting.

I think that's funny. Men were walking on the moon for the very first time in history and people preferred watching Dr. McCoy say, "He's dead, Jim," for the thousandth time.

I wasn't exactly sure how to turn that into a paper, so Mom and I talked about it, about how fiction can have more power than reality and how in 1969 there was a lot of cynicism because of Vietnam and the sixties and all that and there were people who didn't think men were really on the moon and thought it was a hoax.

I think I'll do my French paper on what happens tomorrow night, because my French isn't good enough for stuff like hoaxes and cynicism. For English I'm focusing on how fiction can be more exciting than reality and for history I'll focus on how people in the '60s were cynical about what the government told them.

I told Mom that Sammi said it was sure to rain tomorrow night because it always rains when something important is supposed to happen in the sky and she laughed and said she had never known a more pessimistic 15-year-old.

I'll be at Dad's when Sammi turns 16. I have a feeling if she has a party, it'll be all boys, so it probably won't matter.

Around 10, something kind of odd happened. I was working on my paper and Mom was arguing with Jonny about going to bed, when the phone rang. We never get calls that late, so we all jumped. I got to the phone first and it was Matt.

"Are you okay?" I asked him. Matt never calls that late and he pretty much never calls on a weekday night.

"I'm fine," he said. "I just wanted to hear your voices."

I told Mom it was Matt. Jonny took the kitchen phone and

she used the one in her bedroom. We told him what was going on (I complained about my three moon papers), and he told us about what he has left to do at school. Then he and Mom talked about the arrangements for him to get home.

This was all perfectly normal stuff, but it didn't feel right. Jonny hung up first and then Mom, and I managed to get Matt to stay on a minute longer.

"Are you sure everything's okay?" I asked him.

He paused for a moment. "I have a funny feeling," he said. "I guess it's this moon business."

Matt's always been the one to explain things to me. Mom had her writing and Jonny, and Dad was at work (for as long as he was here), so Matt was the one I turned to. I don't think he's psychic and maybe it's just because he's three years older than me, but whenever I've had a question he's seemed to know the answer.

"You don't think anything is going to go wrong?" I asked him. "It's not like the meteor is going to hit us. It's just the moon."

"I know," he said. "But things might get a little crazy tomorrow night. Phone lines might get tied up, people calling each other. Sometimes people panic even if there's no reason."

"You really think people are going to panic?" I asked. "Around here, it just seems like an excuse for teachers to give us even more work."

Matt laughed. "Teachers never need an excuse for that," he said. "Anyway, I figured I'd find you all home tonight and it'd be a good chance for me to say hello."

"I miss you," I said. "I'm glad you're coming home."

"Me too," he said. He paused for a moment. "Are you still keeping that journal of yours?"

"Yeah," I said.

"Good," he said. "Be sure to write about tomorrow. You'll probably enjoy reading all the details twenty years from now."

"You just want me to keep a record of all your clever sayings," I replied. "For your many biographers."

"Well, that, too," he said. "See you in a few days."

When we hung up, I couldn't figure out if I felt better because he'd called or worse. If Matt's worried, then I'm worried.

But maybe all Matt is worried about is getting through his papers and exams.

TWO

May 18

Sometimes when Mom is getting ready to write a book she says she doesn't know where to start, that the ending is so clear to her that the beginning doesn't seem important anymore. I feel that way now only I don't know what the ending is, not even what the ending is tonight. We've been trying to get Dad on his land line and cell phone for hours and all we get are the kind of rapid-paced busy signals that mean the circuits are tied up. I don't know how much longer Mom'll keep trying or whether we'll talk to him before I fall asleep. If I fall asleep.

This morning seems like a million years ago. I remember seeing the moon in the sunrise sky. It was a half moon, but it was clearly visible and I looked at it and thought about how tonight the meteor was going to hit it and how exciting that would be.

But it wasn't like we talked about it on the bus going to school. Sammi was complaining about the dress code for the prom, nothing strapless, nothing too short, and how she wanted a dress she could wear when she went clubbing.

Megan got on the bus with some of her church friends and they sat together. Maybe they talked about the meteor, but I think they just prayed. They do that on the bus sometimes or read Bible verses.

The whole school day was just normal.

I remember being bored in French class.

I stayed for swim practice after school, and then Mom picked me up. She said she'd invited Mrs. Nesbitt to watch the meteor along with us but Mrs. Nesbitt had said she'd be more comfortable watching at home. So it was just going to be Jonny and Mom and me for the big event. That's what she called it: the big event.

She also told me to finish my homework early so we could make a party of it after supper. So that's what I did. I finished two of my moon assignments and did my math homework and then we ate supper and watched CNN until around 8:30.

All CNN talked about was the moon. They had a bunch of astronomers on and you could see how excited they were.

"Maybe after I'm through playing second for the Yankees, I'll be an astronomer," Jonny said.

I'd been thinking the exact same thing (well, not about playing second for the Yankees). The astronomers looked like they loved what they were doing. You could see how excited they were that this asteroid was going to make a direct hit on the moon. They had charts and computer projections and graphics, but basically they looked like big kids at Christmas.

Mom had gotten out Matt's telescope and she'd found the really good pair of binoculars that had somehow hidden themselves last summer. She'd even baked chocolate chip cookies for the event, so we carried a plate out and napkins. We decided to watch from the road, since we figured we'd have a better view from up front. Mom and I brought out lawn chairs, but Jonny decided to use the telescope. We didn't know exactly how long the hit was going to take or if there'd be something exciting to see afterward.

It seemed like everyone on the road was out tonight. Some of the people were on their decks having late barbecues, but most everyone else was in front of their houses, like we were. The only one I didn't see was Mr. Hopkins, but I could tell from the glow in his living room that he was watching on TV.

It was like a big block party. The houses are so widespread on our road, you couldn't really hear anything, just a general happy buzz.

When it got closer to 9:30, things got really quiet. You could sense how we were all craning our necks, looking toward the sky. Jonny was at the telescope, and he was the first one who shouted that the asteroid was coming. He could see it in the night sky, and then we all could, the biggest shooting star you could imagine. It was a lot smaller than the moon, but bigger than anything else I'd ever seen in the sky. It looked like it was blazing and we all cheered when we saw it.

For a moment I thought about all the people throughout history who saw Halley's Comet and didn't know what it was, just that it was there and frightening and awe inspiring. For the briefest flick of a second, I could have been a 16-year-old in the Middle Ages looking up at the sky, marveling at its mysteries, or an Aztec or an Apache. For that tiny instant, I was every 16-year-old in history, not knowing what the skies foretold about my future.

And then it hit. Even though we knew it was going to, we were still shocked when the asteroid actually made contact with the moon. With our moon. At that second, I think we all realized that it was Our Moon and if it was attacked, then we were attacked.

Or maybe nobody thought that. I know most of the people on the road cheered, but then we all stopped cheering and a woman a few houses down screamed and then a man screamed, "Oh my God!" and people were yelling "What? What?" like one of us knew the answer.

I know all those astronomers I'd watched an hour earlier on CNN can explain just what happened and how and why and they'll be explaining on CNN tonight and tomorrow and I guess until the next big story happens. I know I can't explain, because I don't really know what happened and I sure don't know why.

But the moon wasn't a half moon anymore. It was tilted and wrong and a three-quarter moon and it got larger, way larger, large like a moon rising on the horizon, only it wasn't rising. It was smack in the middle of the sky, way too big, way too visible. You could see details on the craters even without the binoculars that before I'd seen with Matt's telescope.

It wasn't like a big chunk of it flew off into space. It wasn't like we could hear the sound of the impact, or even that the asteroid hit the moon dead center. It was like if you're playing marbles and one marble hits another on its side and pushes it diagonally.

It was still our moon and it was still just a big dead rock in the sky, but it wasn't benign anymore. It was terrifying, and you could feel the panic swell all around us. Some people raced to their cars and started speeding away. Others began praying or weeping. One household began singing "The Star Spangled Banner."

"I'm going to call Matt," Mom said, like that was the most

natural thing in the world to do. "Come on in, kids. We'll see what CNN has to say about all this."

"Mom, is the world coming to an end?" Jonny asked, picking up the plate of cookies and ramming one into his mouth.

"No, it isn't," Mom said, folding her lawn chair and carrying it to the front of the house. "And yes, you do have to go to school tomorrow."

We laughed at that. I'd been wondering the same thing.

Jonny put the cookies away and I turned the TV back on. Only there was no CNN.

"Maybe I'm wrong," Mom said. "Maybe the world really is coming to an end."

"Should I try Fox News?" I asked.

Mom shuddered. "We're not that desperate," she said. "Try one of the networks. They'll have their own set of astronomers."

Most of the networks were off, but our local channel seemed to be carrying NBC out of Philly. Even that was weird, because we get New York City feeds.

Mom kept trying to get Matt's cell phone, but without any luck. The Philly news broadcasters didn't seem to know much more than we did, although they were reporting some looting and general panic in the streets.

"Go check how things are outside," Mom told me, so I went back out. I could see the glow from Mrs. Nesbitt's TV set. There was still some praying going on in someone's backyard, but at least the screaming had stopped.

I forced myself to look at the moon. I think I was afraid I'd see it had grown even bigger, that it really was lumbering its way to earth to crush us all to death, but it didn't seem to have gotten any larger. It was still off, though, still tilted in a funny way, and still too large for the night sky. And it was still three quarters.

"My cell phone is out!" someone screamed a few doors down, and she sounded the way we'd felt when we saw CNN was gone. Civilization had ended.

"Check your cell phone," I told Mom when I came back in, so she did, and hers wasn't working, either.

"I guess cell phones are out in this part of the country," she said.

"I'm sure Matt's okay," I said. "Why don't I check e-mails? Maybe he sent us one from his laptop."

So I went online, or rather I tried to go online, because our Internet connection was dead.

"He's fine," Mom said when I told her. "There's no reason to think he isn't fine. The moon is right where it belongs. Matt'll call us when he has the chance."

And that was the one thing Mom said all evening that turned out to be true. Because about ten minutes later, the phone rang, and it was Matt.

"I can't talk long," he said. "I'm at a pay phone and there's a line of people waiting for me to finish. I just wanted to check in and let you know I'm okay."

"Where are you?" Mom asked.

"In town," he said. "When we realized our cells weren't working, some of us drove to town just so we could phone in. I'll talk to you tomorrow when things aren't so crazy."

"Be careful," Mom said and Matt promised he would be.

I guess it was around then Jonny asked if we could call Dad, and Mom started trying to reach him. But the phone lines were crazy all over. I asked her to call Grandma in Las Vegas, but we couldn't get through to her, either.

We sat down in front of the TV to see what was happening to the rest of the world. The funniest thing was that Mom and I both jumped up at the exact same moment to get the chocolate chip cookies from the kitchen. I beat her to it, and brought the plate in. We all started devouring them. Mom would eat a cookie, sit still for a few moments, then get up and try Dad or Grandma. Jonny, who's really good about limiting the number of sweets he eats, just kept ramming cookies into his mouth. I would have eaten an entire box of chocolates if there'd been any in the house.

The TV connection went in and out, but we never got cable back. Finally Jonny thought to bring out a radio, and we turned that on. We couldn't get any of the New York stations, but Philly was coming in strong.

At first they didn't seem to know much more than we did. The moon got hit, like we'd been told it would. Only something had been miscalculated.

But before some astronomer could come on and explain to the rest of us just what had gone wrong, there was a bulletin. First we heard it on the radio, and then we got enough TV reception to see it as well, so we turned the radio off.

Whoever was broadcasting the news must have heard it over his little earphone, because he actually turned pale and then said, "Are you sure? Has that been confirmed?" He paused for a moment to listen to the reply, and then he kind of turned to face the camera.

Mom grasped my hand and Jonny's. "It'll be all right," she said. "Whatever it is, we'll get through this."

The newsman cleared his throat, like taking an extra few seconds was going to change what he had to say. "We are receiving reports of widespread tsunamis," he said. "The tides. As most of you know, the moon controls the tides. And the moon, well, whatever happened this evening at nine thirty-seven PM—and we don't know just what really did happen, but whatever it was—the tides were affected. Yes, yes, I got that. The tides seem to have swelled far beyond their normal boundaries. The reports coming in are from people in airplanes who happened to be flying overhead at the time. Massive flooding has been reported all over the eastern seaboard. There has been some confirmation of this, but these reports are all preliminary. Sometimes you hear the worst and it doesn't prove that way at all. Wait a second."

I quickly thought about who I knew on the eastern seaboard. Matt's in Ithaca and Dad's in Springfield. Neither one was anywhere near the ocean.

"New York City," Mom said. "Boston." She has publishers in both cities and goes there on business.

"I'm sure everybody's fine," I said. "You'll go online tomorrow and send everybody e-mails and make sure they're okay."

"All right, we are getting some confirmation," the newsman said. "There are confirmed reports of tidal waves twenty feet or higher in New York City. All power there has been lost, so these are very sketchy reports. The tides don't seem to be stopping. AP is reporting that the Statue of Liberty has been washed out to sea."

Mom started crying. Jonny was just staring at the TV like it was broadcasting in a foreign language.

I got up and tried Dad again. Then I tried Grandma. But all I got was the busy-circuit signal.

"We're getting an unconfirmed report that all of Cape Cod has been flooded," the newsman said. "Again, this is unconfirmed. But the AP is reporting that Cape Cod,"—and he paused for a moment and swallowed—"that Cape Cod has been completely submerged. The same seems to be true of the barrier islands off the Carolina coast. Just gone." He stopped again to listen to whatever was being said through his earpiece. "All right. There is confirmation of massive damage to Miami. Many deaths, many casualties."

"We don't know what he's saying is true," Mom said. "Things get exaggerated. Tomorrow morning we may find out all this didn't really happen. Or if it did, it wasn't nearly as bad as they thought it was. Maybe we should just turn the TV off now and wait until tomorrow to see what really happened. We may be scaring ourselves for no reason whatsoever."

Only she didn't turn the TV off.

"There's no way of knowing the number of deaths," the newsman said. "Communication satellites are down. Telephone lines are down. We're trying to get an astronomer from Drexel to come to our studio and tell us what he thinks is happening, but as you can imagine, astronomers are pretty busy right now. All right. We seem to be getting a national feed again, so we're cutting to our national news bureau for a live update."

And there, suddenly, was the NBC anchorman, looking reassuring and professional and alive.

"We're expecting word from the White House momentarily," he said. "Early reports are of massive damage to all the major cities on the eastern seaboard. I'm coming to you from Washington, D.C. We have been unable to make contact with our New York City headquarters for the past hour. But here's the information as we have it. Everything I'm going to announce has been verified by two sources."

It was like one of those lists on the radio to let you know which schools were having snow days. Only instead of it being school districts in the area, it was whole cities, and it wasn't just snow.

"New York City has suffered massive damage," the anchor said. "Staten Island and the eastern section of Long Island are completely submerged. Cape Cod, Nantucket, and Martha's Vineyard are no longer visible. Providence, Rhode Island—in fact, most of Rhode Island—can no longer be seen. The islands off the coast of the Carolinas are gone. Miami and Fort Lauderdale are being battered. There seems to be no letting up. We've now had confirmation of massive flooding in New Haven and Atlantic City. Casualties on the eastern seaboard are believed to be in the hundreds of thousands. Naturally it is far too early to tell if that number is excessive. We can only pray that it is."

And then, out of nowhere, was the president. Mom hates him like she hates Fox News, but she sat there transfixed.

"I am broadcasting to you from my ranch in Texas," the president said. "The United States has suffered its worst tragedy. But we are a great people and we will place our faith in God and extend a helping hand to all who need us."

"Idiot," Mom muttered, and she sounded so normal we all laughed.

I got up again and tried the phone with no luck. By the time I got back, Mom had turned the TV off.

"We're fine," she said. "We're well inland. I'll keep the radio on, so if there's any call for evacuation, I'll hear it, but I don't think there will be. And yes, Jonny, you have to go to school tomorrow."

Only this time we didn't laugh.

I said good night and went to my bedroom. I've kept the clock radio on, and I keep hearing reports. The tides seem to have pulled back from the East Coast, but now they're saying the Pacific is being affected also. San Francisco, they say, and they're afraid for LA and San Diego. There was one report that Hawaii is gone and parts of Alaska, but no one knows that for sure yet.

I looked out my window just now. I tried to look at the moon, but it scares me.

THREE

May 19

I woke up around 6 to the sound of the phone ringing. I threw on my robe and went to Mom's room.

"It's your father," she said, and handed me the phone.

Right after Mom and Dad split up, I got it into my head I'd never see him or hear from him again, and every time he called, I'd get this ridiculous sensation of relief. I felt the exact same way, like a hundred-pound weight had just flown out of my stomach.

"Are you okay?" I asked. "And Lisa? Is she all right?"

"We're both fine," he said. "Your mother says everything is fine where you are and that you heard from Matt last night."

"That's right," I said. "We tried and tried to reach you and Grandma last night and the circuits were all busy."

"I reached her late last night," Dad said. "She's fine. A little shaken up, but that's natural enough. We're lucky, Miranda. We all seem to have made it, no problem."

"I feel like it should have been a dream," I said. "Like maybe I'm still dreaming and when I wake up none of it will have happened."

"That's how we all feel," he said. "Your mother says school

hasn't been canceled. I guess the idea is for us to get on with our lives and be grateful that we can."

"All right," I said. "I can take a hint. Give my love to Lisa, okay? Tell her I was thinking about her and the baby."

"I will," he said. "I love you, honey."

"I love you too, Daddy," I said. I gestured to Mom to see if she wanted the phone back, but she shook her head, so I hung up.

"How late did you stay up?" I asked. "Did anything else happen?"

"I went to bed around the same time you did," she said. "I saw you turn your light out. I didn't sleep very well, though, kept waking up and turning the radio on, that kind of thing."

"Did the tides stop?" I asked. "Did the flooding stop?"

"They stopped, they started," Mom said. "It's very bad." She kind of laughed. "Very bad doesn't really describe it. Catastrophic. They don't know how bad the damage is yet, how many countries were affected."

"Countries?" I said. Somehow I'd forgotten there were other countries, that we shared the moon with other countries.

"I don't know," Mom said. "They don't know. Nobody knows. Holland was decimated; they're pretty sure about that. Australia: Most of the cities there are on the coast, so it was very badly hit. The tides just went mad. They think the asteroid was denser than they'd assumed it would be, so the collision was bigger. They think the moon got knocked off kilter, got pushed a little closer to the earth. At least that was the theory around five."

"But it's not going to crash into earth," I said. "We're okay, right? We don't live that close to the ocean."

"They're sure it won't crash into the earth," Mom said. "At least not in the foreseeable future. Beyond that, I don't think anybody's predicting anything."

It was funny. I was actually glad school was still on, like that proved we'd be okay. I left Mom and took a shower, and by the time I dressed and went downstairs, Mom had already started breakfast and I could hear Jonny moving around.

Mom made pancakes, which she never does on a school day. I didn't think I'd have any appetite, but I ate more than my share. So did Jonny. I don't remember seeing Mom eat any, but there was some batter left, so maybe she made some for herself after we left.

When I went outside to wait for the bus, I looked up, and I could see the moon in the morning sky. It was still bigger than it should have been, and it didn't seem quite as washed out as it usually looks in the daytime. I stopped looking at it, and concentrated on the dogwoods instead.

On the bus, all anybody talked about was what happened last night. Not that anyone really seemed to know or understand. A couple of the kids seemed to think it was cool, and a couple of girls were crying the whole trip.

I sat next to Sammi, but she didn't say much. Megan didn't get on the bus, and neither did her church friends. The bus was only half full.

I hated the kids who were acting like it was all a big joke.

There were a lot of kids missing from homeroom, too, but most of the teachers seemed to have shown up. We'd just started history when the first lightning bolt landed. It flashed so brightly the whole classroom seemed illuminated. The thunder followed, loud enough to shake the building. At least one kid screamed, and I was just glad it wasn't me.

Ms. Hammish tried to pretend the storm wasn't happening, but there was no way we could avoid talking about the moon. She asked how many of us knew someone who lived on one of the coasts, who might have been affected.

All our hands went up.

"I don't actually know someone who lives there," Michelle Webster said. "But I feel like I do, because all the stars live in Hollywood or in New York, and I know I don't know them, but I feel like I do."

A lot of the kids said they felt that way too.

I guess Ms. Hammish was going to tell us that was a normal way to feel, but then a lightning bolt hit one of the trees right outside the school grounds. The tree burst into flames, and then we lost our electricity.

A lot of kids started screaming then. Michelle began sobbing, real hysterical sobs, and other kids started crying, too. Sarah pulled out her cell phone to call home maybe or 911 but she couldn't get a connection and she threw the cell phone across the room. The thunder kept rolling, and the tree began to smolder from the fire and the rain.

It was weird. There was all this craziness going on around me, and Ms. Hammish was trying to calm everybody down, only we could hardly hear her, because the thunder was so loud, and kids all over the school were screaming, so it wasn't just our classroom, and I didn't feel anything. I wasn't screaming or crying. I was just noticing things, how the winds had picked up, and branches were flying around outside, and how the storm didn't seem to be letting up any.

Ms. Hammish must have decided it was a tornado, because she told all of us to get up and go into the hallway. I don't know how many of the kids heard her, but I did, and I got up and started walking around the classroom, lifting the other kids out of the seats, until they all figured out what we were supposed to do. By the time we'd evacuated the room, there were lots of kids sitting on the hallway floor, and we joined them.

I kind of missed being able to see the storm. I didn't feel like it was a tornado. I felt like the world was coming to an end, and I was going to miss all the action, because I was going to be sitting on the hallway floor when it did.

And then I thought, Well, that's typical, I can't even get any action when the world's coming to an end, and I started laughing. It wasn't hysterical laughing (it really was funny that the world was coming to an end and I still couldn't get any action), but once I started, I couldn't stop. Other kids were laughing, too, so the hallway consisted of kids laughing and kids crying and kids screaming and teachers walking around and checking classrooms to make sure they were empty. The hallway was completely dark, except for the flashes of lightning we could see from the classroom windows.

I managed to stop laughing, but then I thought, at least nobody's singing "The Star Spangled Banner," and I started laughing all over again. The phrase "By the dawn's early light" got stuck in my mind, and I kept hearing it over and over again. "By the dawn's early light." "By the dawn's early light." I wondered how many people had sung "By the dawn's early light" yesterday and were dead today.

We were in the hallway for almost an hour. It's hard to stay hysterical for that long, and by the time the hour was over, and the storm had died down, almost all the kids were quiet, except for one girl who kept screaming, "I don't want to die!"

Like any of us did.

We went back into our second-period classrooms, even though it was already fourth period. It was still raining with thunder and lightning, but the winds had calmed down, and the lightning was farther away. Some of the kids who'd been crying were just shaking. The electricity still wasn't on, and with the lightning not striking so close or so frequently, things were actually darker in the classroom. The sky was still a mean gray, and I think we all felt like the storm could come back at any moment full tilt and we'd be back in the hallway. Ms. Hammish didn't tell us to go to our fourth-period classes. We all just sat there instead.

I couldn't totally shake "By the dawn's early light" from my head, and I was kind of wishing Ms. Hammish would distract us with a history lesson, when in walked Mom.

She was soaking wet and looked wild and determined. I thought, something's happened to Matt, and that stomach weight came right back like it had never been gone.

"Come on, Miranda," Mom said. "Get your books and let's get going."

Ms. Hammish stared at her, but she didn't say anything. I got my books and followed Mom out of the classroom.

I thought, If I don't ask what happened, it won't have happened, so I kept quiet as we left school. Mom didn't say anything, either. The rain was pouring, and the thunder was still pretty loud, and I thought the world really is coming to an end, and Mom wants me home when that happens.

We ran to the parking lot, and Jonny opened the door for me. I jumped in, and I was surprised to see Mrs. Nesbitt sitting in the passenger seat. I could see Mom not wanting Mrs. Nesbitt to be alone when the world ended, but I couldn't figure out why she had to be driven somewhere first.

"Here, Miranda, take this," Mom said, and she handed me an envelope. I looked inside it and saw ten $50 bills.

Mom started the car. I looked at Jonny, who just shrugged.

"When we get to the supermarket, I want Jonny to go to the pet food department," Mom said. "Jonny, you know what Horton'll eat. Get kitty litter, too, and put the bags on the bottom of the wagon. Get the biggest bags that'll fit there. Fill the wagon with as many bags of dry food as you can."

"Horton likes canned," Jonny said.

"Get the little ones," Mom said. "The expensive kind. As many as you can throw into the empty spaces. Fill the wagon as high as you can possibly can. And Mrs. Nesbitt, when you get the paper goods, don't forget Tampax for Miranda and me. Lots of boxes."

"Thanks for reminding me," Mrs. Nesbitt said.

"What's going on?" I asked. "Would someone please tell me?"

"It's just in case the world's coming to an end," Jonny said. "Mom wants us to be ready."

"I went to the bank this morning," Mom said. "And I filled the gas tank and gas was already at five dollars a gallon. I went to the supermarket and the electricity went out and there was chaos there, so they just said a hundred dollars for each wagon no matter what was in it. I had a lot of cash on me, so I filled a wagon and then I went back and got Mrs. Nesbitt and then Jonny and you so we could each get wagons to fill."

"You don't really think we're going to need this stuff?" I asked. "Everything's going to get back to normal soon, isn't it?"

"Not in my lifetime," Mrs. Nesbitt said.

"We don't know," Mom said. "But kitty litter doesn't go bad. If it turns out I'm wrong and I've wasted all this money, fine. I'd just as soon the world gets back to normal. But in case it takes a while, we might as well have toilet paper. Miranda, you're going to canned vegetables and fruits. You know what we like."

"Mom, we don't eat canned vegetables," I said.

"We do now," she said. "Canned vegetables. Fruits. Soups, too. Lots of cans of soup. Find the cartons in the back of the car and put them on the bottom shelf of the cart. Fill those cartons up too. Get as much as you can in the wagon."

I stared out the window. The rain was still falling and occasional flashes of lightning could be seen in the distance. The electricity was still out, so corners with traffic lights were crazy, with cars stopping and starting and not knowing what exactly to do. I saw a lot of trees had fallen, and cars were driving over the smaller branches that littered the streets.

Mom just plowed through.

"What about desserts?" I asked. "If the world comes to an end, I'm going to want cookies."

"We're all going to want cookies if the world comes to an end," Mrs. Nesbitt agreed. "And chips and pretzels. If the world is coming to an end, why should I care about my blood pressure?"

"Okay, we'll die fat," Mom said. "Grab what you can grab and ram it into your wagons. But remember if we actually need this stuff, we're going to be a lot more grateful for a can of soup than for a box of stale cookies."

"Speak for yourself," Mrs. Nesbitt said.

"Get Progresso," Mom said. "They don't need water."

"Mom," I said. "We have water."

"Which reminds me," she said. "After you pay for your first wagons, put the stuff in the car and go back. Jonny, you get water. As many bottles as you can fit in. Mrs. Nesbitt, you get whatever you think you're going to want. Miranda, you go to health and beauty aids. Get aspirin and peroxide and Band-Aids."

"Great," I said. "The world's coming to an end, and we're fixing it with Band-Aids."

"Vitamins," Mom said. "Get lots and lots of vitamins. And

laxatives. Calcium. Vitamin D. This is so hard, trying to remember everything we might need."

"Or might not," I said. "Mom, I love you, but I think this is crazy."

"So we'll all get vitamin D for Christmas presents," Mom said. "Just do it, okay. Jonny and Mrs. Nesbitt and I have car keys, so wait for one of us to show up, and we'll put your stuff in with theirs. Okay?"

"Sure," I said, because I decided it was better to humor her.

"After we finish our second loads, we'll see what it's like," Mom said. "Then we'll see if it's worth it to go back in."

She pulled into the supermarket parking lot and I got a real sense of the madness going on. There were people racing for carts, people screaming, and two guys punching each other out.

"Jonny, get a wagon for Mrs. Nesbitt first," Mom said. "Everyone stay calm, and remember you have cash. That's all they're taking, and we have a real advantage there. Work fast. Don't debate. If you can't decide between two things, take both. Pack the carts as high as you can manage. If you have any problems, go to the car. Don't try to find anyone in the store. Okay? Are you ready?"

We all said we were. Jonny looked like he actually meant it.

Mom found a parking spot toward the back of the lot, and there were two carts there. We raced out of the car and grabbed them. Mrs. Nesbitt and I each took one and went into the store together.

The supermarket reminded me of the hallway at school this morning, and maybe because I'd just been through all that, the store didn't scare me as much as it ordinarily would have. So what if people were screaming and crying and fighting. I plowed through people and raced to canned vegetables.

I realized I'd forgotten the cartons for the bottom of the wagon. There was nothing I could do about that, except put as many cans on the bottom as I could and hope for the best.

Except for the total terror I was feeling in the pit of my stomach, it was kind of fun, like those game shows where someone wins five minutes at the supermarket except there were dozens of other winners and we were all there at the same time.

I didn't have much time to look around, but it seemed like most of the people were buying meats and produce, and there weren't that many people fighting over the canned carrots. I even lucked out with the soups: Campbell was a lot more popular than Progresso, which made my life easier.

When I filled the cart as full as I could possibly manage, I wheeled it to the checkout lines only to discover people were simply throwing cash at the poor terrified cashiers. I took two $50s out, tossed them in the same general direction, and then since nobody seemed to be bagging, I pushed the cart out of the store and made my way back to the car.

It was actually raining harder, and the storm seemed to be closer. Not as bad as it had been this morning, but bad enough. I was relieved to see Mrs. Nesbitt standing by the car, waiting for me.

We threw all the cans into the car, and put the jars in a little more carefully.

Mrs. Nesbitt grinned at me. "All my life I've been well behaved," she said. "It's about time I got to push people around and not apologize."

"Mrs. Nesbitt, you little devil," I said.

"Ready for round two?" she asked. I said I was, and we made our way back to the store.

Except that some guy tried to steal the cart from Mrs. Nesbitt. "I need it!" he yelled. "Give it to me."

"Get your own!" she yelled right back at him. "This is war, man."

I was afraid the man thought that was exactly what it was. I didn't know what else to do, so I rammed my wagon into his back and caught him by surprise. That gave Mrs. Nesbitt just enough time to pull away from him. I raced away, also, and didn't look back.

Compared to battles in the parking lot, the store almost seemed comfy. I went to health and beauty aids and found it fairly empty. I guess the rest of the world hadn't realized they were going to need vitamin D.

The great thing about ransacking painkillers was I knew I was getting more than $100 worth of stuff. I filled the cart to overflowing, stopped one more time at canned goods, and then over to baked goods, where I put boxes and boxes of cookies on the cart's bottom shelf. I even remembered Fig Newtons, since Matt likes them.

This time I found Mom unloading her stuff in the car. She'd bought enough tuna fish and salmon and sardines to last us for two lifetimes.

The back of the van was as much a madhouse as the store, since there weren't bags for anything. Mom was trying to unload as best she could, but things kept falling out, and I spent as much time grabbing stuff from the pavement as Mom did unloading.

A man came over to us. He had a wagon, but he looked desperate. "Please," he said. "Please help me."

"You have a wagon," Mom said.

"I need you to come in with me," he said. "My wife is seven months pregnant, and we have a two-year-old and I need diapers and baby food and I don't know what else. Please come in with me so I can use your cart. I beg you, for my wife and my babies."

Mom and I both looked at him. He looked like he was in his late twenties and he seemed sincere.

"Miranda, go back into the store and just use your best judgment," Mom said. "I'm going with this man." We finished ramming stuff into the van, and then the three of us went back in.

I felt better catching a glimpse of Mrs. Nesbitt as we walked in. She was at gourmet foods. I guess she figured she might as well go in style.

I also found Jonny finishing up at the water section. He seemed to be enjoying himself.

I went over to juices and selected juices that were in cans or cartons. In a million years, I never thought we'd be drinking canned juice, but bottles were just too hard to deal with. I also got some of that last-forever milk.

By that point, a lot of the shelves were nearly empty, and people were starting to fight over single boxes of things. There were broken eggs on the floor, and spilled liquids, so just walking around was getting tricky.

There was still some room in my cart, so I went over to snacks and got a couple of boxes of pretzels. I spotted canned nuts, and threw lots of those in. Baked goods seemed pretty empty, so I filled the wagon with cartons of salt and bags of sugar and, just for the hell of it, a bag of chocolate chips.

I threw my $50s to the cashier and made my way to the van. The parking lot was getting nastier, and the rain was still falling hard. Jonny was there, but as soon as Mom showed up she told both of us to go back in and ransack the shelves for anything we could find. There really wasn't much left in the store, but I managed to fill the cart with lima beans and brussels sprouts and other end-of-the-world delicacies.

When we finally all got into the van, Mom wouldn't let any

of us talk until she maneuvered her way out of the lot. By that point we were too exhausted to make conversation anyway.

Mom started driving home. The roads were even worse than they had been. At one point Jonny and I had to get out of the van and clear a big branch off the road. A couple of other people showed up and helped us, but I was scared until we got back into the van and Mom started driving again.

We were halfway home when Mrs. Nesbitt said, "Stop at that strip mall."

"You think?" Mom said, but she pulled into the parking lot. It was practically empty.

"Jonny, you go to the pet supply store," Mrs. Nesbitt said. "I'm going to the gift shop. Laura, you go to the nursery."

"Good idea," Mom said. "I'll buy vegetable flats. We'll have fresh produce all summer."

That didn't leave much for me, so I went to the antiques store. I don't know why, but then again, I didn't know why Mrs. Nesbitt was so insistent on going to the gift shop. It wasn't like Hallmark put out Happy End of the World Day cards.

The great thing about the antiques store was I was the only customer. There still wasn't any electricity, and the lightning flashes were still a little too close for comfort, but it was the only place I'd been to in hours that didn't seem like a madhouse. The woman behind the counter even said, "Can I help you?"

I didn't want to give away our secret, that we were stocking up for the end of the world, just in case it gave her any ideas. So I said no, thanks, and kept looking.

I still had $200 in my envelope so I knew I could buy pretty much anything we needed, if I could only figure out what we might need. Then I saw three oil lamps. I grabbed them and went up front.

"We have scented oil to go with them if you're interested," the woman said.

"I'll take all of them," I told her.

"We should be getting electricity back soon," the woman said. "At least that's what I heard on the radio."

"My mom is worried," I said. "This'll just make her feel better."

The store had an old-fashioned cash register, so she was able to ring up my purchases. I handed over two $50s and actually got change.

I was the first person at the car. I stood there, getting even wetter, until Jonny showed up. "Horton's never going to go hungry," he said.

There was hardly room for all the stuff he'd bought, but we rearranged everything we could. Then Mrs. Nesbitt came out, carrying bags and bags.

"I bought every candle in the store," she said. "Gift shops always have candles."

"Mrs. Nesbitt, you're a genius," I said. "I got oil lamps."

"We're both geniuses," she said.

We got in the van and waited for Mom. When she showed up, she had a dozen flats. I had no idea how we were going to fit them in, but it turned out to be easy. Mrs. Nesbitt sat on my lap, and we used up all her space with flats of tomatoes and cucumbers and string beans and strawberries.

"The more we harvest, the longer the canned foods will last," Mom said. "Okay, is there anything anyone didn't buy that we might need?"

"Batteries," I said. The transistor radio in the shop had made me think of them.

"Matches," Mrs. Nesbitt said.

"That convenience store should have them," Mom said. "And it doesn't sell gas, so it should be pretty quiet."

She was right. There was only one other car in the lot. Mom bought all their batteries and boxed matches and bars of soap. She even bought a coffee cake and a box of donuts.

"Just in case the world ends tomorrow," she said. "We might as well enjoy today."

We dropped Mrs. Nesbitt off at her house and we all carried food and supplies for her. We didn't fuss over which can of soup belonged to who or whether she was entitled to more candles. We just divvied stuff up, so that she had plenty. We kept the cat food and the vegetable flats. I made sure she had one of the oil lamps and oil to go with it.

It took a long time to get her stuff out, and a longer time to unload the car when we finally got home. Mom got shopping bags and we filled them and put everything in the dining room, except for the donuts. Those we ate as soon as we were finished.

"I'll sort things out later," she said. "Thanks, kids. I never could have done this without you."

And then she started crying.

That was two hours ago. I don't think she's stopped crying yet.

FOUR

May 20

No school today.

The electricity came back on around 4 this morning. It's still dark and cloudy outside, so it felt good to be able to turn lights back on.

Horton has been acting like a maniac the past couple of days. He seems to wake up with a start from his naps and he's been running around all night long, hopping from bedroom to bedroom. He raced onto my bed around midnight and yowled at me—which woke me up, naturally. Then he sniffed my face to make sure it was me. We both fell asleep, but he woke me up again around 2, when he began running through the house, meowing like crazy. Exactly what none of us needs right now.

There was an e-mail from Matt waiting for us. He's fine, everything there is fine, although they're having blackouts, also, and school remains on schedule. He says it's tricky taking finals with limited light, but the professors all say that'll be taken into account when they're marked. He's still planning to get back here on Wednesday.

Mom let Jonny and me each have half an hour on the Internet. I used part of my time to go to Brandon's fan site. There was a thread where we were all supposed to say where we live and how conditions are. A lot of names were missing, some of them I know from people who live around New York or on the West Coast. There were 14 PMs waiting for me. Twelve people asked how I was and if I'd heard anything about Brandon. The other two just asked if I'd heard anything about Brandon.

With all that had been going on, I'd forgotten that Brandon's training in LA now. I guess no one has heard from him or seen any reports about him.

I posted about how things were in northeastern PA, but added I hadn't seen or heard about Brandon. It's not like I run into his parents or Mrs. Daley every day, but I guess I've made it sound like I'm closer to them than I really am. Or maybe everyone's just desperate to hear how Brandon is, to make sure he's still alive.

I've got to believe he is.

Mom and Jonny and I spent most of the day putting the food and supplies away. I don't know what Horton's complaining about. Jonny got him enough food to last for years. Mom was almost laughing at herself when she looked at all the food she made us get. With the electricity back on, things seem a lot more normal. And with the day so cloudy, you can't really see the moon hovering.

Uh-oh. The lights are flickering. I hope we're not about to lose

May 21

The president was on TV tonight. He didn't say much that we didn't already know. Tsunamis and floods. Untold numbers of people dead, the moon out of its orbit, etc. Monday is a national day of mourning, and we should all pray a lot.

He did say, and he didn't look too happy about it, that we needed to prepare ourselves for even worse. Jonny asked Mom what that could mean, but Mom said she didn't know, but she guessed the president did only he didn't want to tell us because he was an evil jerk.

That was the first normal-sounding thing Mom's said in days, and we all laughed.

The president said that almost every offshore oil refinery was gone, and that it was believed most of the oil tankers had been lost at sea. I guess that was part of what's going to be worse.

Mom said later that didn't just mean oil companies would gouge us, but that there might not be enough gas and oil to heat all the houses in the winter. But I don't think that's true. It's only May now, and there's got to be time to get oil over here. They can't let people freeze to death.

When the president finished, he said that the governors of every state would follow, and we should watch to see what our governor had to say.

Then the governor came on, and he didn't look too happy about things, either. He said there'd be no school throughout the state Monday or Tuesday, but that school should resume on Wednesday, although some districts might not be able to. He said the state was looking into the possibility of rationing gas, but as of the moment, he asked for an honor system. Only get gas if you have less than a quarter tank. He also said that if any gas stations were found to be overcharging, they'd face serious consequences. Mom laughed at that.

He didn't know when the blackouts would stop. We weren't alone, he said. Just about every state had reported some power outages.

Jonny was upset because the governor didn't say anything

about the Phillies and the Pirates. The Phillies were in San Francisco on Wednesday and no one had mentioned if they made it out okay.

Mom said the governor has a lot of things on his mind and a lot of things he has to tell us, but then she paused and said, "You know, he <u>should</u> have told us if the Phillies and the Pirates are okay. I bet the governor of New York told everyone how the Yankees and Mets are."

I thought about saying no one makes any announcements about how figure skaters are, but it didn't seem worth the effort.

I'll feel better when Matt is home.

May 22

Jonny asked this afternoon if we could go to McDonald's or someplace. The electricity has been so on and off the past few days that Mom emptied the freezer and we've finished everything that was in it.

So Mom said we might as well try, and we got in the van and went food hunting.

The first thing we noticed was that gas had gone up. It's $7 a gallon now, and there were lines at all the gas stations.

"How much gas do we have in the tank?" I asked.

"We're okay for a while," Mom said. "But I think we'll switch over to Matt's car next week. This thing gets zero mileage."

"When do you think gas prices will go down?" I asked. "They can't stay this high forever."

"They'll go up before they go down," Mom said. "We'll have to be very careful about where we drive to. No more hopping in the car and just going someplace."

"I can still go to baseball practice, can't I?" Jonny asked.

"We'll see about carpooling for that," Mom said. "We're all in the same boat here."

When we got to the road with McDonald's and Burger King, we saw there was hardly any traffic. We drove up to McDonald's, only it was closed. So were Burger King and KFC and Taco Bell. All the fast food places were closed.

"Maybe they're just closed because it's Sunday," I said.

"Or because tomorrow's a national day of mourning," Jonny said.

"They're probably just waiting for the electricity to run full time," Mom said.

It felt weird, though, seeing them all closed, the same kind of weird when you see the moon and it's just a little too big and too bright.

I guess I always felt even if the world came to an end, McDonald's would still be open.

Mom drove around some more, and we found a local pizza place that was open. The parking lot was jammed, and there were about a dozen people standing outside just waiting to get in.

Mom dropped Jonny and me off and we got in line. Everybody was pretty friendly, and there was a lot of talk about what places were closed and what were open. The mall was closed, but one of the supermarkets was still open, even though it didn't have much stuff left.

Jonny asked if anyone had heard anything about the Phillies, and it turned out one of the guys in line actually had. The Phillies had played a day game on Wednesday and the game was over before the asteroid hit. They'd taken a charter flight to Colorado, and apparently they were all okay.

I asked if anyone knew Brandon's family or Mrs. Daley, just

in case anyone had heard anything about Brandon, but no one did.

There were a lot of rumors going around, like we should be prepared not to have electricity for the entire summer, and some people had heard that the moon was going to crash into the earth by Christmas. One man said he knew someone on the school board and they were thinking about canceling the rest of the school year, and all the kids standing in line cheered, Jonny included. I guess as rumors go that's a lot better than the moon's going to crash into the earth, but I don't think either one is likely to happen.

Not that I know what is.

By the time Mom got back to us, we were almost in the shop. She looked kind of excited, but she wouldn't tell us why.

It took another half hour before we actually got to place our order, and by the time we did, there wasn't much left. But we were able to get a plain pizza and some garlic rolls. I don't think I've ever been so excited about food.

We walked back to the car and when we got in Mom said she'd found a bakery that was open, and she'd bought cookies and cake and a couple of loaves of bread. Nothing was fresh, but it was still edible.

We stopped off at Mrs. Nesbitt's and brought her over for our feast. The electricity was on so we reheated the pizza and the garlic rolls and they tasted great. For dessert, we had chocolate cake, and Jonny drank one of those weird never-go-bad milks I'd bought. The rest of us drank ginger ale. Horton hung around hoping for treats.

"This may be the last meal like this we have for a while," Mom said. "We shouldn't count on pizza and burgers and chicken until things get back to normal."

"There was rationing during World War Two," Mrs. Nesbitt said. "That's probably what they'll do now. We'll pool our ration points and we'll be fine."

"I wish I trusted the president," Mom said. "I just can't imagine him handling this."

"People rise to the occasion," Mrs. Nesbitt said. "We have, after all."

Just then the electricity went off. Only somehow it felt funny and we all laughed. Mom got out the Monopoly game and we played until there wasn't enough sunlight left. Mom drove Mrs. Nesbitt home and I went to my room, where I'm using a combination of candlelight and flashlight to write by.

I wonder when we'll get electricity back for good. It's going to be an awfully hot summer without air conditioning.

May 23

The national day of mourning meant that there were memorial services on the radio. Lots of clergy, lots of politicians, lots of sad songs. They're still not giving a number for how many people died, but maybe that's because people are still dying. With so much coastline lost, the oceans keep rolling in and destroying more land and more buildings, and people who didn't want to evacuate or who couldn't because the highways are all jammed have been drowning.

Mom says we're still plenty inland and have nothing to worry about.

The electricity came on for an hour this afternoon. There was an e-mail from Matt saying he was still planning on getting home Wednesday.

I know it's dumb of me, but I keep thinking that once Matt gets home, everything'll be okay. Like he'll push the moon back into place.

I wish there was school tomorrow. I keep thinking about cafeteria lunches and how I always complained about them and how much I want to eat one now.

May 24

The electricity came on around 9 this morning and Mom grabbed Jonny and me and we drove around looking for any stores that might be open. We did find one supermarket that was open, only it just had school supplies and pet toys and mops.

It was so strange, walking around this big store and seeing all those empty shelves. There were only a couple of employees there, and a security guard, although I can't imagine what he was protecting.

Mom didn't think we'd be hungry enough to eat pencils, so we left without buying anything.

A lot of the appliance stores had boarded-up windows. There was broken glass in the parking lots, so I guess they'd been looted. I don't know why, since there isn't any electricity to run the flat-screen TVs or anything else, for that matter.

It was funny seeing which stores were still open. The really expensive shoe store had boarded-up windows but it was open. Mom said the world might be coming to an end, but she still wasn't going to pay a hundred bucks for a pair of sneakers.

The sporting goods store was closed and its window was boarded up and someone had painted in giant letters: NO MORE GUNS OR RIFLES.

Mom still has cash left and I could tell she wanted to buy something. She's started to look at all the soups and vegetables and peroxide at home and feel proud of herself.

We finally found a clothes store that was open. There was a cashier, but no one else. It was the kind of store we never go to ordinarily, small and not well lit, and everything looked dingy.

Mom bought two dozen pairs of socks and underwear. She asked if they had any gloves, and when the cashier found them hidden away in a drawer, Mom bought five pairs.

Then she got this scary I-just-had-a-brilliant-idea look that I've noticed more and more the past few days, and asked if they had any thermal underwear.

I practically died of embarrassment and Jonny didn't look too happy, either, but when the cashier dug out the long johns, Mom bought them, too.

The cashier got into it, then, and started pulling out scarves and mittens and winter hats. Mom went berserk and bought everything, whether it would fit any of us or not.

"You could open your own store now," the cashier said, which was probably her way of saying, "Thank God I found someone even crazier than I am and maybe she'll buy everything and I can go home."

We carried bagloads of stuff back to the van. "What are we going to do with kids' mittens?" I asked Mom. "Give them to Lisa for her baby?"

"You're right," Mom said. "Baby things. I should have remembered." And she went right back into the store, and when she came out, she had armloads of baby shirts and baby overalls and baby socks and even a baby coat.

"No brother or sister of yours is going to go cold this winter," she said.

That was kind of sweet of her, but I think she's gone crazy. I know Lisa and she'd never want a baby of hers to wear the clothes that store was selling.

Actually, it should be kind of funny to see Mom make the big presentation to Lisa and Dad. I guess she'll do it when she picks up Jonny at baseball camp and takes us to Dad's for August. Of course by then Lisa's parents will have visited and the baby will have enough clothes for a lifetime. And there Mom'll be, handing over all those socks and things and Lisa'll be trying to act like she's grateful.

Maybe if the store stays open, Mom'll be able to return all the stuff. I know I don't plan on wearing long johns next winter.

May 25

Mom and Matt should have been home by now. We have electricity, so Jonny's watching a DVD, but he's nervous, too.

It was a long, weird day and it's already feeling like a long, weird night. For the first time in a week the sky is completely clear and you can really see the moon. It's so big and bright it feels like we don't need lights on, but we have them all on anyway, just about every light in the house. I don't know why Jonny and I feel like having them all on, but we do.

School started again today and that didn't make things feel right, like I thought it would. The bus was only about half full. Megan was on, but she was sitting with her church friends, so we just said hello. Sammi was nowhere to be seen.

It's funny how over the past few days I haven't felt like calling them. The phone's worked most of the time, but we haven't gotten many phone calls or made many. It's like we were so occupied with taking care of ourselves we didn't feel we could handle anybody else's lives.

School looked exactly the same as it did last week, but it didn't feel the same. There were a lot of absentees and a lot of teachers were missing, too, and there weren't substitutes for them, so classrooms doubled up and we all had extra study halls.

No one had done any homework since last week and no one seemed to know what we should be doing. Some of my teachers had us doing our regular work and others had us talking about what was going on.

It was funny, what we'd talk about and what we wouldn't. Mom told Jonny and me not to tell anyone about how we'd practically bought out the supermarket last week. She says it's better if people don't know what we have stored away, like someone is going to break into the kitchen and steal our cans of soup. Or the long johns. Or the two dozen bags of kitty litter.

I don't know if other people weren't saying what their mothers had bought, but a lot of kids didn't seem to be saying a lot of things, if that makes any sense.

Instead of fifth period, we went to the auditorium. Usually we have to have two assemblies, because we wouldn't all fit otherwise, but there were so many kids absent, there was room for all of us.

It wasn't really an assembly, not the kind with a program, anyway. Mrs. Sanchez stood on the stage and made announcements.

She started by saying how grateful we should be that we were all safe and sound and she thanked all the teachers for everything they'd done, which was pretty funny, seeing as so many of them weren't there.

Then she talked about how what had happened wasn't just a local crisis, even though we might feel that way, since we didn't have electricity we could count on, and McDonald's wasn't open. She smiled when she said that, like it was supposed to be a joke, but nobody laughed.

"This is a crisis the whole world is going through together," she said. "I have complete faith in our ability as Pennsylvanians and Americans to be able to pull through."

A few kids laughed at that, even though we obviously weren't supposed to.

Then she got to the part about how we were all going to have to make sacrifices. Like we haven't been making sacrifices for a week already. Like the supermarkets were miraculously going to reopen and gas wasn't going to cost $9 a gallon.

There would be no more after-school activities. The class play, the prom, the senior trip all were canceled. The swimming pool was no longer available. The cafeteria would no longer serve hot lunches. Starting on Tuesday, there'd be no more bus service for the high school.

It's funny. When she said the stuff about the prom, a lot of kids started yelling and I thought what babies they were. But when she said the pool was closed, I yelled, "No!" and by the time she told us about no more buses, pretty much all the kids were yelling and booing.

She just let us. I guess she knew we couldn't be stopped. When the bell rang, she got off the stage, and the teachers all told us to go to our next class, which we mostly did.

Some kids went into the classrooms, though, and started breaking windows. I saw cops come in and drag kids out. I don't think anyone was hurt.

I really missed Sammi at lunch. Megan joined me, though. Her eyes were all bright and shiny, kind of the way Mom's have been getting when she sees something else to stockpile.

"This is the first time in a week that I've left Reverend Marshall," she said. "We've been sleeping at the church, just getting an hour or two of sleep each day so we can keep praying. Isn't it wonderful, what God is doing?"

There was a part of me that wanted to tell Megan to shut up and another part of me that wanted to hear what God was doing that was so wonderful. But mostly I wanted a hot lunch.

"What does your mom say about all this?" I asked. Megan's

mom used to like Reverend Marshall, but she's never been as crazy about him as Megan.

"She doesn't understand," Megan said. "She's a good woman, really she is, but she lacks faith. I pray for her soul, just the way I pray for yours."

"Megan," I said, like I was trying to grab the friend I'd loved for years and bring her back to reality. "There are no more hot lunches. Half the time there's no electricity. I live five miles from school and gas costs nine dollars a gallon and we can't use the pool anymore."

"Those are just earthly concerns," Megan said. "Miranda, admit your sins and embrace Our Lord. You won't care about hot lunches and the cost of gas in heaven."

She could be right. The problem is I don't see Mom or Dad or Lisa or Matt (especially Matt—I think he's a Buddhist these days) or Jonny admitting their sins and embracing anybody even if it means a ticket to heaven. And I don't much want to be in heaven if they're not there with me (okay, I could manage without Lisa).

I considered trying to explain that to Megan, but it would have been like trying to explain to Mom that I wasn't going to wear long johns no matter what the moon did to us. So I left Megan and went to where the swim team was and groaned and moaned along with them.

Dan said he heard from his mother who knows just about all the coaches in the area that all the schools in Pennsylvania have closed their pools and so have the ones near us in New York. It's because without electricity the filters can't run, and without the filters the water isn't sanitary. So no more meets for the time being.

Karen mentioned the pool at the Y, but a couple of the kids

said the Y was closed. The town has a pool, but it's outdoors and it isn't heated, and even if they have it working, it won't do us much good until the end of June.

So I mentioned Miller's Pond. There were actually kids who didn't know about it. I guess they live in the new developments and don't know about things at my end of town. It's still too cold to be swimming at the pond, but once it warms up enough, it's all natural and doesn't need a filter. And it's pretty big.

So we agreed we'd start swimming at Miller's Pond weekend after next. I guess that gives me something to look forward to. And I think Dan was impressed that I came up with a solution.

Now if I could only solve the hot lunch situation. It's amazing how much I miss the cafeteria macaroni and cheese.

I hear Matt and Mom! Matt's home!

May 28

Things seem so much better now that Matt is home. He's been throwing batting practice to Jonny (I've been catching) and that makes Jonny happy. He and Mom went through everything in the house, all the food we bought, and all kinds of stuff Mom's grandparents had hidden away in the attic and cellar, yarn and a crochet hook (Mom says she hasn't crocheted in years, but she thinks it'll all come back to her if she works at it) and mason jars and canning equipment and a manual can opener and an egg beater and the sorts of things kitchens had in the olden days.

He and Mom spent all day yesterday organizing the food so we know how much tuna we have and how many canned peaches. I think we have enough stuff to last forever, but Mom says she'll be relieved when the supermarkets open again. Just to hear her say she thinks they will cheers me up.

Matt and I haven't had a chance for a real talk yet. He doesn't really know any more than I do about what happened and what's going to happen, but I still feel like if I hear it from him, I'll believe it more.

School was better by Thursday. A lot more kids showed up (including Sammi) and more of the teachers, too.

The high school is 5 miles from here, which Mom says is walkable on a nice day. Jonny's lost his bus service to the middle school, and that's a little farther away, so Mom's been trying to work out a car pool. Matt got out all our bikes and he's spending the weekend getting them in shape. I used to bike a lot, and I guess it's as good a way as any to get around (I'll certainly get to school faster by bike than by foot).

Peter showed up this evening, which was a nice surprise, especially for Mom. He brought us a bag of apples that one of his patients had given him. He and Mom couldn't go out anywhere so the two of them baked an apple crisp for all of us. We had pasta with marinara sauce for like the tenth time this week, so the hot dessert was a treat. Matt got Mrs. Nesbitt, so it was really an event, six for dinner, with a main course and a dessert.

Of course by the time we were ready to eat the electricity had gone out again. It was out most of the day, but we're used to that by now. We had electricity for an hour during school yesterday and it was like none of us knew what to do about it. At home, when the electricity goes on, we rush to the TV and turn it on. We could listen to the radio all the time, but Mom wants us to preserve batteries so we only listen in the morning and in the late evening.

It's such a weird way to live. I just can't believe it's going to stay like this much longer. On the other hand, I'm already starting to forget what normal life felt like, clocks that were on time, and lights that went on with the flick of a switch, and

Internet, and streetlights, and supermarkets, and McDonald's, and . . .

One thing Matt did say to me was that no matter what the future is, we're living through a very special time in history. He said that history makes us who we are, but we can make history, also, and that anyone can be a hero, if they just choose to be.

Matt's always been my hero, and I think it's a lot harder to be one than he's saying, but basically I know what he means.

But I still miss ice cream and swimming laps and feeling comfortable looking at the night sky.

May 29

The electricity came on this morning around 9 and Mom did what she always does when we realize it's back on. She started a load of laundry.

It was only on for about 15 minutes, and it stayed off all the rest of today.

About 10 minutes ago, we all woke up because of this strange roaring sound. We all raced toward the sound, which turned out to be the washing machine going back on.

Who knew the rinse cycle could be so scary?

Mom says she's staying up until the clothes can go in the dryer. She doesn't think the electricity will stay on long enough to dry the clothes completely, but she figures it's worth a shot.

I really wish we had electricity at 2 PM rather than at 2 AM. But I guess I should think of Mom as a hero of the all-night laundry.

May 30

I don't always know how long the power has been off. It went on in the middle of the night, but by the time I woke up this morning, it was off again.

We're spending more and more time outdoors, just because it's nicer outside and the sun provides natural light. We're all used to seeing the moon now, so that isn't bothering us like it used to.

But we leave a light on in the living room window, so when the electricity does come back on we can go inside and do what we need to do. Today it came on around 1 and we raced in.

Mom went on the Internet, which kind of surprised me. Usually she vacuums or starts a load of laundry. She's given up changing the time on the clocks.

But this afternoon she skipped all that and went to the Internet. She had heard on the radio this morning that they were starting to list the names of the dead.

She found the names of most of the editors she worked with, and her agent, and a lot of writers she'd met over the years. She found two friends from college and one friend from a long time ago, before we moved here, and Dad's best man and his family. She also found a couple of second cousins and their kids. In less than 10 minutes, she found over 30 names. But one good thing: She checked on Mrs. Nesbitt's son and daughter-in-law and their kids and didn't find them on any list.

I asked her to look up Brandon and she did but couldn't find him. Of course there are still millions of people unaccounted for, but at least there's still hope he's alive. I don't get to go on the board very much, but when I do, no one seems to have heard anything. I can't help thinking that's a good sign.

There were names of people I know that I could have looked up: kids I went to summer camp with, and kids I know from swimming, and old friends from elementary school who moved to New York or California or Florida. But I didn't try to find them. They weren't everyday parts of my life anyway, and it feels wrong somehow to find out if they're dead when I didn't much think about them while they were living.

Jonny looked up baseball players. A lot of them were listed as known dead and a lot more were listed as missing/presumed dead.

Matt looked up kids from his high school class. Only three were listed as dead, but a bunch were listed as missing/presumed dead.

As a test, he looked us up, but none of our names were on any of the lists.

And that's how we know we're alive this Memorial Day.

May 31

The first day without bus service. So naturally it poured.

It wasn't scary rain like it was that other time. No big thunderstorm, no tornado winds. Just good old-fashioned pouring rain.

Matt ended up driving Jonny and me to school. Mom stayed home to take advantage of electricity and work on her book. I hadn't really thought about how hard it must be for Mom to get any writing done without a computer. Or without an agent, or editors, or publishers.

Over half the kids were absent and Jonny says there were even fewer kids at the middle school. Most of our teachers were there, though, and we actually got a lot of work done. And we had electricity until nearly 2, so even though it was dark outside, the school was really kind of cheerful. Empty but cheerful.

When Jonny came home today, he told us they'd announced that all standardizing testing had been canceled. I've begun wondering what they're going to do about our finals, which should start in two weeks. We haven't really gotten any schoolwork done, and no one is assigning homework because there's never any way of knowing if there'll be any light to work by.

Peter said over the weekend that he'd heard a rumor that they might just close school next week and promote all of us and hope things are back to normal by September.

I don't know if I want that or not. Except the part about back to normal by September. I know I want that.

FIVE

We all got notices at school today to take home. It said there would be no final exams this semester and our grades would reflect only those tests we'd taken before May 19. We'd be told what our grades are tomorrow in class. If we wanted to raise our average in a course, we were to talk to our teacher next week and see if there was a way of doing that. School would officially close on June 10 and reopen on August 31, unless we heard otherwise.

They're still planning to have graduation, though. Outdoors, with a rain date.

It feels weird to think there aren't going to be any finals, but it's not like I've been studying for them. It's not like I've done any schoolwork in weeks.

I feel bad for kids who are on the cusp, though: One good grade and they won't flunk the course. Sammi for one. I know she's been just below passing in French all year. And I've seen her cram for a final and ace it, which was probably what she planned on doing this year.

She probably doesn't care, though. Actually, except for

some of the Really Bright Ivy League types, I doubt anyone cares.

I got my grades and they're all pretty much as I expected. My math grade was dragged down by those stupid tests (or by those tests where I was stupid), so I know I'm going to have to talk to Mom this weekend about what to do.

All they served for lunch today was peanut butter and jelly sandwiches on stale white bread. We each were allowed one sandwich.

I don't want to whine about being hungry, because I know compared to a lot of kids, I'm eating okay. For breakfast we have cereal with powdered milk. It doesn't taste the same as real milk, but it's still something and it's thanks to Mom, who bought boxes of the stuff on Crazy Shopping Day.

And even if I'm sick of tuna or pasta or canned chicken, I can't say we're not eating supper. So it's not exactly the end of the world for me if lunch consists of a peanut butter and jelly sandwich. I know I should be grateful we're getting that much. Everyone knows the reason school is closing so early is because they're running out of food for us and they don't know what to do about it.

I had lunch with Megan and Sammi and Dave and Brian and Jenna. Megan didn't eat with her church group, which was a nice change of pace. Half the swim team wasn't at school.

We stood in line and got our sandwiches and people were griping and moaning and it wasn't very pleasant. We went to our table, and even though we should have nibbled on our sandwiches to make them feel like a full meal, we gulped them down. Three bites and 25 minutes to kill.

Except for Megan. She tore her sandwich in two roughly equal parts and took dainty-lady bites. She finished her half sandwich in more time than it took us to eat our whole ones, and then she asked if anyone wanted the other part of her sandwich.

Everyone (except me) said yes.

She looked around the table and gave the half sandwich to Dave. I have no idea why she picked him, but he didn't ask. He just ate his half sandwich fast, before anyone else had a chance to get to it.

I don't know why this bothers me, but it does.

June 4

Mom and I discussed my grades. I'll be getting a 95 in English, a 94 in history, a 90 in French, a 91 in biology, and a 78 in math.

"I could ask to retake a math test," I said. "If I do well on the test, I'd at least pull my grade up to an eighty."

"What's the point?" Mom said.

I was so glad she wasn't mad, I just said okay and changed the subject. But this evening it hit me. I found Matt and we sat outside under the bean tree. Mom calls it a big weed, but it's so beautiful when it flowers, and it's the last tree to lose its leaves in the fall so I love it.

"Matt, does Mom think we're all going to die?" I asked. I could never ask her that, because I know she'd lie if she did.

Matt was quiet for longer than I would have liked. What I wanted him to do was laugh and say of course not and everything was going to be okay once they got the electrical systems back online and figured out a way of getting oil here so the trucks could start transporting food again.

"Mom's concerned," he said instead. "We all are."

"That we're going to die?" I asked, and my voice got shrill. "Like we're going to starve to death or something?"

"I don't think Mom's worried we're going to starve to death," he said. "She has the garden going, and we still have plenty of canned goods. Everything could be back to normal by this fall; maybe a little sooner, maybe a little later. We're okay for food until then if the garden stays healthy. And even if things don't get exactly back to normal, that doesn't mean things won't improve. Mom's an optimist and so am I."

"So why did she say it doesn't matter about my math grade?" I asked. "When has Mom ever not cared about our grades?"

Matt laughed. "Is that what this is all about?" he asked.

"Matt, this isn't funny," I said. "I'm not a kid, but Mom's more likely to talk to you than to me. What does she think is going to happen? You're with her all day. She's got to be talking to you."

"Right now her main concern is Jonny and baseball camp," he said. "She wants Jonny to have as normal a summer as possible. Who knows what next summer will be like? And . . ." He paused for a moment. "Look, this is strictly between you and me, okay?"

I nodded.

"If Jonny's at camp, then Mom doesn't have to feed him," Matt said. "And when you and Jonny spend August with Dad, Mom won't have to feed either of you. Mom's eating less already. She doesn't have breakfast and she only eats lunch if I make her. Which I do about half the time. With school letting out two weeks early, that means lunch for you and Jonny for two extra weeks. Right now that's more important to Mom than your math grade."

I couldn't say anything. I looked at the sky. Sunset was just beginning. That used to be my favorite time of day, but now at sunset the moon is so large it looks like it's about to hit us. I almost never look at the sky anymore.

"Look," Matt said, and he grabbed my hand and held it. "If things get back to normal, no college in the world is going to care about your seventy-eight. They'll know how crazy things were this spring. A seventy-eight in tenth-grade math won't keep you from getting into college."

"And if things don't get back to normal?" I asked.

"Then it won't matter, anyway," he said. "Promise me you won't tell Mom what we talked about?"

"I promise," I said.

"And don't start skipping meals," he said. "We need you to be strong, Miranda."

"I promise," I said.

But I can't help thinking that I'm not strong. Would I give up food for Jonny if it comes to that? Is that what Megan did at lunch on Friday?

Will things ever be normal again?

June 5

Mrs. Nesbitt drove over around 5 today. I don't remember the last time I saw her look that happy or excited.

Even a visit from Mrs. Nesbitt is something different these days. The electricity is out pretty much all day and most of the night, so it's not like we can watch TV or go online. There isn't any homework to do, and no one feels like socializing.

"I have a wonderful treat," she said, and she carried in a bowl covered with a dish towel.

We crowded around to see what she had to show us. She

pulled away the towel, like a magician pulling a rabbit out of a hat, but all we saw were washcloths. She laughed at the expressions on our faces. Then she carefully unwrapped the washcloths. And there were two eggs.

They weren't very big, but they were still the most beautiful eggs I've ever seen.

"Where did you find them?" Mom asked.

"One of my old students brought them to me," Mrs. Nesbitt said. "Wasn't that sweet of him? He has a farm about ten miles out of town and he still has feed for his chickens, so they're still laying. He brought two eggs to me and to a few other people. He said he has enough for his family if they're careful and they decided we might like a special treat. I couldn't possibly enjoy them by myself."

Eggs. Real honest-to-goodness, actual eggs. I touched one, just to remind myself of what an eggshell felt like.

First Mom took two potatoes and an onion, and chopped them up and fried them in olive oil. Just the smell of fried potatoes and onions was enough to make us giddy. While they were cooking we discussed all possible egg dishes. By a vote of 4–1, we picked scrambled. We stood around and watched as Mom put in some powdered milk and beat those eggs. Of course we don't have any butter, and we decided against cooking oil, so Mom used a little spray-on stuff and a nonstick pan.

We each took equal amounts of the eggs and potatoes and onions. I watched Mom, to make sure she didn't cheat herself of any. We got a couple of teaspoons' worth of scrambled egg, and we nibbled to make it last longer.

Then Matt jumped up and said he also had a special treat he had been saving, but tonight seemed like as good a time as any. He ran to his room, and when he came back he had a chocolate bar.

"I found this in my bag when I unpacked," he said. "I don't know how old it is, but chocolate doesn't go bad."

So we each had a piece of chocolate for dessert. I'd almost forgotten how much I love chocolate, how there's something about it that makes life a little more wonderful.

After supper, we sat around and sang. None of us has much of a voice, and we didn't all know the same songs, but Horton was our only audience and he didn't mind. We sang for more than an hour and we laughed and Mrs. Nesbitt told us stories about Mom when she was a little girl.

It almost felt like we were happy again.

June 6

At lunch today, Megan did the same business with her PB&J sandwich. This time she gave her second half to Sammi.

If she keeps it up, she'll be the most popular girl in high school.

I waited for her after school and yanked her away from her church friends. "Why aren't you eating all your lunch?" I asked.

"I'm not hungry," she said.

I love Megan and she isn't fat, but I've seen her pack away double burgers and extra fries with a milkshake. I looked at her, really looked at her, and noticed she'd lost weight, maybe 10 pounds. The thing is we're all losing weight so it's easier not to notice. It's kind of like the moon: If I don't look I can pretend it's still the same.

"Are you eating at all?" I asked her.

"Of course I am," Megan said. "I just don't need to eat much anymore. God sustains me. Food doesn't."

"So why are you even eating half your sandwich?" I asked. I don't know why. It wasn't a rational question, so there was no reason to expect a rational answer.

"I figured people wouldn't notice if I ate half," she said.

"They notice," I said. "I notice."

"It's only for a couple more days," she said. "Next week no one will see what I'm eating and what I'm not."

"They can't possibly be telling you at your church not to eat," I said.

Megan gave me one of those pitying looks that always make me want to slug her. "Reverend Marshall doesn't have to tell us how much to eat," she said. "He trusts us to hear God's voice."

"So God's the one telling you not to eat?" I said. "What? He called you up and said, 'Split the peanut butter and jelly sandwich with the poor unfortunates'?"

"I'm starting to think you're the poor unfortunate," Megan said.

"And I'm starting to think you're crazy," I said. That's something I've been thinking for a while now, but haven't said out loud.

"Why?" Megan asked and for a moment she really was angry like she used to get when we were 12. But then she bowed her head, closed her eyes, and moved her lips, in prayer I guess.

"What?" I said.

"I begged God for forgiveness," she said. "And if I were you, Miranda, I'd ask for divine forgiveness, also."

"God doesn't want you to starve to death," I said. "How can you believe in a God that would ask that of you?"

"But He isn't asking," she said. "Honestly, Miranda, you're making an awfully big deal over half a sandwich."

"Promise me you won't stop eating," I said.

Megan smiled and I think that was what scared me the

most. "I'll get my sustenance as God wishes me to," she said. "There are lots of different ways of being hungry, you know. Some people are hungry for food and others are hungry for God's love." She gave me a look then, pure Megan, to let me know which camp I fell into.

"Eat your sandwich tomorrow," I said. "Indulge me. If you insist on starving, at least wait until Saturday when I won't have to watch."

"You don't have to watch now," she said, and walked away from me to join her church friends again.

June 7

I dreamed last night of Becky. She was in heaven, which looked an awful lot like the Jersey shore, the way I remember it from summers ago, when the tides behaved themselves and the Atlantic was the world's most glorious swimming pool. Becky looked like she had before she got sick, with those long blonde braids. I was always so jealous of her hair when we were young.

"Is this Heaven?" I asked her.

"Yes, it is," she said. Only then she closed a giant gate, so I was on one side and she and the ocean were on the other.

"Let me in," I said. "Did Megan tell you not to let me into Heaven?"

Becky laughed. I haven't thought about Becky's laugh in a long time. She used to giggle all the time and whenever she did, she'd get me laughing. Sometimes we'd laugh for five straight minutes with no idea what we were laughing about.

"It's not Megan's fault," she said. "It's yours."

"What did I do wrong?" I asked. Well, whined, really. Even in my sleep, I thought I could have worded it better.

"You can't enter Heaven because you're not dead," Becky said. "You're not good enough to be dead."

"I will be. I promise," I said, and then I woke up. I was shaking, the dream disturbed me so much. It wasn't like it was a nightmare. It was just, I don't know. I don't know the words to describe what it felt like to be locked out of Heaven, to be so desperate that I longed to die.

School is a complete waste of time. The only classes I have are English and history; all my other teachers have vanished. In English, Mr. Clifford reads out loud, short stories and poems. Ms. Hammish tries to put things in historic perspective for us, but half the time someone in class starts crying. I haven't cried in school yet, but I've come awfully close. When we're not in class, we wander around the school building and exchange rumors. One kid said he knew where there was a Dairy Queen still in business but he wouldn't tell us where. Another kid said she heard that we were never getting electricity back, that the scientists were working on perfecting solar energy. And of course lots of kids say the moon's getting closer and closer to earth and we'll all be dead by Christmas. Sammi seems convinced of that.

At lunch today, Megan tore her sandwich in two, and gave half of it to Sammi and half to Michael.

She looked at me when she did and winked.

June 8

Lately I've been trying not to know what's going on. At least that's the excuse I've been giving myself for not caring about all the stuff that's happening outside of my little section of Pennsylvania. Who cares about earthquakes in India or Peru or even Alaska?

Okay, that's not fair. I know who cares. Matt cares and Mom cares and if there were any baseball players involved,

Jonny would care, too. Knowing Dad, he cares. Mrs. Nesbitt, too.

I'm the one not caring. I'm the one pretending the earth isn't shattering all around me because I don't want it to be. I don't want to know there was an earthquake in Missouri. I don't want to know the Midwest can die, also, that what's going on isn't just tides and tsunamis. I don't want to have anything more to be afraid of.

I didn't start this diary for it to be a record of death.

June 9

The next to last day of school, whatever that means.

One day this week when we had electricity, someone took advantage of it to print a few hundred flyers, telling us if we wanted to bring in blankets and food and clothes for the people in need in New York and New Jersey, we should do so on Friday.

I liked getting that sheet. I liked the idea of helping someone. I guess we can't get stuff down to the people in Missouri because gas is up to $12 a gallon and there aren't that many gas stations still open.

I put the sheet in front of Mom, who was sitting at the kitchen table staring out the window. She's been doing that more and more lately. Not that there's much else she can be doing.

The flyer caught her eye. She read it all the way through, then picked it up and tore it into two pieces, then four, then eight. "We're not giving anything away," she said.

For a moment I really wondered if she was my mother, and not some pod person who'd taken over her body. Mom is always the first to give stuff away. She's the queen of food drives and blood drives and teddy bears for foster kids. I love that about her, although I know I'll never be half as generous as she is.

"Mom," I said. "We can spare a blanket or two."

"How do you know that?" she asked. "How can you possibly know what we're going to need this winter?"

"This winter?" I said. "Everything'll be back to normal by winter."

"And what if it isn't?" she said. "What if we can't get any heating oil? What if the only thing that keeps us from freezing to death is a single blanket, only we don't happen to have it because we gave it away in June?"

"Heating oil?" I said. I felt like a total idiot, only able to parrot her. "There'll be heating oil by winter."

"I hope you're right," she said. "But in the meantime, we're not giving anything away to anybody who isn't family."

"If Mrs. Nesbitt felt that way, we wouldn't have shared her eggs," I said.

"Mrs. Nesbitt is family," Mom said. "The poor unfortunates of New York and New Jersey can get their own damn blankets."

"Okay," I said. "I'm sorry I brought it up."

That was the moment when Mom was supposed to snap back to herself, when she was supposed to apologize and say the stress was getting to her. Only she didn't. Instead she went back to staring out the window.

I tracked Matt down, which wasn't hard, since there's nothing for him to do, either. He was lying on his bed, staring at the ceiling. I guess that's what I'll be doing starting next week.

"Heating oil," I said to him.

"Oh," he said. "You know about that?"

I wasn't sure whether to say yes or no, so I just stood there and shrugged.

"I'm surprised Mom told you," he said. "She must figure if we can't get any, you'll find out by fall, anyway."

"We can't get any heating oil?" I said. Just call me Ms. Parrot.

"So she didn't tell you," he said. "How'd you find out?"

"How are we going to survive without heating oil?" I asked.

Matt sat up and faced me. "First of all, maybe the oil reserves will be back by fall," he said. "In which case we'll pay whatever it costs and get the oil. Second, people survived for millions of years without heating oil. If they could, we can. We have a woodstove. We'll use that."

"One woodstove," I said. "That keeps the sunroom heated. And maybe the kitchen."

"And that's going to leave us a lot better off than people without a woodstove," he said.

It seemed silly even to me to suggest electric heat. "How about natural gas?" I asked. "Practically everyone in town heats with natural gas. The gas company supplies it. Couldn't we convert the furnace to gas?"

Matt shook his head. "Mom already spoke to someone at the gas company. They're making no guarantees about having any gas next winter. We're lucky we have the woodstove."

"This is ridiculous," I said. "It's June. It's eighty-five degrees outside. How can anybody possibly know what it's going to be like in the winter? Maybe the moon will warm things up. Maybe the scientists will figure out how to turn rocks into oil. Maybe we'll all have moved to Mexico."

Matt smiled. "Maybe," he said. "But in the meantime, don't tell Jonny, okay? I'm still not sure how you figured it out, but Mom doesn't want any of us to worry any more than we have to."

"How much do we have to?" I asked, but Matt didn't answer. He went back to staring at the ceiling instead.

I went to the linen closet and counted our blankets. Then I went outside and waited for the warmth of the sun to stop me from shivering.

The last day of school. The last peanut-butter-and-jelly-on-increasingly-stale-white-bread sandwich.

Actually today it was an open-faced sandwich. I guess the cafeteria has run out of bread, which is as good a reason to end the school year as any.

Megan cut her open-faced peanut butter and jelly sandwich into four pieces. She offered me one, but I said no.

"I'll take her share," Sammi said. "I'm not too proud to beg."

"You don't have to beg," Megan said, and gave Sammi two pieces. Brian and Jenna got the other pieces.

Sammi looked like a pig, eating one and a half sandwiches.

After lunch, most everyone went home. There wasn't much point staying in school once the food was gone.

I went home, changed into my swimsuit, and went to Miller's Pond. The weather's been warm enough for swimming for a couple of weeks, but the pond is still pretty cold. Swimming laps and shivering kept me from thinking about hungry I was.

But when I got out of the pond and dried myself off, I began thinking about the peanut butter and jelly jars. Were there any left? Did the cafeteria run out of bread but still have peanut butter and jelly stockpiled away? Did the teachers get the leftovers, or the janitors, or the cafeteria staff? Did the school board get the peanut butter and jelly? Was there more peanut butter left or more jelly? Maybe there wasn't any jelly left, just peanut butter, or maybe there were jars and jars of jelly but no peanut butter. Maybe there was even a lot of bread left, only they just weren't going to give it to the students.

For supper tonight we had a can of tuna fish and a can of green peas. I couldn't stop thinking of peanut butter and jelly.

SUMMER

SIX

Dad called. Or rather he called and got through. He's been trying to call, he said, several times a day for the past two weeks. We all believed him because we've been trying to call him and never get through.

It was great to hear his voice. He said he and Lisa were fine, and there were no problems with her pregnancy. He said the supermarkets in Springfield were all closed, but the two of them had a fair amount of food in the house. "So far so good."

Mom also got a call from Jonny's camp today, and they're still planning on being open. So the plan remains for Jonny to go to camp, and then Mom and I'll drive up there, get him, and she'll drive us to Springfield. Dad asked Matt if he'd be coming, also, but Matt said he thought Mom would need him around in August so he'd be staying home.

I know that hurt Dad, even though it's probably true and Dad probably knows that. Anyway Dad said maybe Matt could come along for the drive and at least see him and Lisa. We could all have dinner together. For a moment we forgot that all the restaurants are closed. For a moment, things were normal again.

Matt said that sounded like a good plan to him, and Mom said she'd enjoy having the company on the drive home.

Jonny asked if Dad had heard anything about the Red Sox. Dad said he thought they were okay, but he really didn't know. I feel like Dad should have known Jonny was going to ask, and he should have been able to answer. He could have lied, after all, and said they were all fine.

Although knowing what a Yankee fan Jonny is, maybe Dad should have just said Fenway had floated out to sea.

June 12

Peter dropped by this afternoon, bringing us a can of spinach.

"I know it's good for me," he said. "But I really can't stand the stuff."

Mom laughed, like she used to. "Stay for supper," she said. "I promise I won't serve spinach."

"I can't," he said. "I shouldn't be taking time off now, but I needed to escape, if only for an hour."

We all sat in the sunroom, happy to have a visitor. But it was obvious Peter wasn't relaxing.

Finally Mom said, "If this is a house call, at least tell us what we're sick with."

Peter laughed, but it was the kind of halfhearted laugh I'm used to hearing these days. "You're not sick with anything," he said. "But I did want to tell you to start using Off or any other kind of insect repellent you might have. And if you still know a place where you can buy some, do. Pay whatever it costs, but get it."

"Why?" Jonny asked. I don't think Mom or Matt or I really wanted to know.

"I've seen three cases of West Nile virus in the past week," Peter replied. "I'm hearing from other doctors that they're seeing cases, too. I've heard rumors of malaria. Friend-of-a-friend stories, but that doesn't mean they're not true."

"Mosquito-borne illnesses," Matt said.

"Exactly," Peter said. "The mosquitoes seem to be happy, even if no one else is."

"I know I have some Off left over from last summer," Mom said. "But I don't know how long it'll last."

"Cover yourself up," Peter said. "Wear socks and long-sleeved shirts and pants when you're outside. No perfume. And if you even think you feel a mosquito, swat at it."

All of which I'm sure is very good advice, but I still plan on swimming at Miller's Pond. I don't know what I'll do if Mom tries to stop me.

June 15

It rained for the past couple of days, bad thunderstorms. No blackouts, though. No electricity at all, so no blackouts.

This morning the electricity came on for a few minutes, and when it did, Jonny said, "Hey, it's a black-on."

This is what passes for humor around here.

Actually it was kind of cozy in the rain. We couldn't go anywhere, so we stayed in and read books and played games and pretended not to worry. It was like being snowed in only without any snow.

But today the sun was shining and even though the moon glow is disconcerting in the daytime, the sun was still a pleasant relief. No humidity, temperature in the high 80s, just about perfect weather.

So without telling Mom, I slipped my bathing suit on, put

on jeans and a shirt over it, and went to Miller's Pond. I got there around 10, and there were already a few other people there, taking advantage of the good weather.

Dan was among them, and it was great to see him. We swam laps, raced (he won, but not by much), and played water tag with a few other swimmers.

It felt like summer vacation.

After we got out of the water, we dried ourselves off in the sunlight. It's a little marshy around Miller's Pond, and we had to swat at mosquitoes, but even that felt like summer.

Dan and I talked as we laid in the sun. First we tried to talk about unimportant stuff, but of course these days there isn't much unimportant stuff.

"Next year I'll be a senior," he said. "Assuming there's school next year. Assuming there's a next year."

"There'll be a next year," I said. At that moment, it was impossible to think otherwise.

Dan grinned. "I notice you're not guaranteeing there'll be a school," he said.

"With my luck, there will be," I said, "and my grades from this year'll count."

"My parents and I were going to look at some colleges this summer," he said. "Check out some schools on the way to my grandparents'. They live in Florida." He paused for a moment. "Lived," he said. "We saw their names on a list."

"I'm sorry," I said.

"They liked it down there," he said. "They kept real busy. We think it probably happened fast with the first tsunamis. Their place was right on the ocean, so that's probably what happened."

"My mother's parents have been dead forever," I said.

"Since Mom was a little girl. Her grandparents raised her, right where we live now. My dad's mother is in Las Vegas, and we're pretty sure she's okay."

"I try not to think about it," he said. "What'll happen next, I mean. But of course I do. And I get so angry. I know it's nobody's fault, but the government should have done something."

"Like what?" I asked.

"It could have warned people," he said. "It could have evacuated people from the coastlines. Even if it turned out to be a false alarm. And there's got to be something they could do about electricity. And gas prices. And food. Somewhere there's got to be supplies of food that aren't getting to us."

"I guess I don't think it does much good to be angry," I said.

We both swatted at mosquitoes and suddenly we laughed. It was balletic, swatting in unison. And then Dan said the most amazing thing.

"If there is a world," Dan said, "and if there is a school, would you go to the prom with me next year?"

"I insist on a corsage," I said. "And a limo."

"A stretch," he said. "And orchids."

"You in a tux," I said. "Me in a formal gown."

"We'll be King and Queen of the prom," Dan said.

"I'd be honored, your majesty," I said.

Dan bent over and kissed my hand. Our faces met and we kissed, really kissed. It was the most romantic moment of my life, and it would have been even more romantic if some little boy hadn't yelped, "Oooh, kissing, yuck," which ruined the mood.

Dan walked me home and we kissed again at the back door. "It's a date," he said.

"I'll see you before then, won't I?" I asked. "The prom won't be for another year."

He laughed. "Meet me at the pond tomorrow," he said. "At ten if it isn't raining."

"I will," I said, and we kissed good-bye. It was a completely magical moment, so naturally it was spoiled by Jonny.

He opened the door, caught a glimpse of Dan, and said, "Mom's on the warpath. Better talk to her."

I found Mom in the sunroom. "Where were you?" she shouted.

"Out," I said. One of the great all-time answers: Out.

"I know that. Where out? What have you been doing?"

"Swimming," I said. "At Miller's Pond. Which I intend to keep doing all summer long, so don't give me any lectures about mosquitoes, okay?"

I don't think I've ever seen Mom look so angry. For a moment, I actually thought she was going to hit me, which she's never ever done.

I'm not a complete idiot, so I apologized. "I'm sorry," I said. "What exactly did I do wrong?"

"You left here without telling me where you were going or how long you'd be gone," Mom said.

"I didn't realize I had to," I said. "I've gone out without telling you for years now."

"These are not normal times," she said, but I could see she'd calmed down if only a little. "I thought you were old enough to realize that."

"And I thought I was old enough to go out in broad daylight without it being some kind of crisis," I said.

"Age has nothing to do with it," she said. "How would you feel if you turned around and couldn't find me and had no idea where I'd gone or why or when I'd be back? Think about that, Miranda. How would you feel?"

So I did think about it, and my stomach clenched up. "I'd be terrified," I admitted.

Mom half smiled. "Good," she said. "I'd hate to think you wouldn't miss me."

"Mom, I'm sorry," I said. "The truth is I was afraid you'd tell me I couldn't go. And I wanted to so much. So I snuck out. I really am sorry."

"Why would I tell you you couldn't go?" she asked.

"Because of the mosquitoes," I said. "West Nile virus and malaria and all that."

"Oh yeah," Mom said. "All that."

I took a deep breath and waited for Mom to tell me never to leave the house again. But she didn't say anything.

"Well?" I said, so she could say no and I could yell at her and we could get into a really bad fight.

"Well what?" she said.

"Can I go to Miller's Pond?" I asked.

"Of course you can," she said. "I'd love to wrap you and Matt and Jonny up in swaddling clothes and protect you from everything but I know I can't. You're all entitled to have some fun. For you that means swimming. For Jonny it's baseball, and for Matt it's running."

"What is it for you?" I asked.

"Gardening," Mom said. "Even if my crop is vegetables this year and not flowers. I'm not stopping gardening just because there's a chance I'll get West Nile virus. I don't expect you to stop swimming. Were there other people at the pond?"

"Quite a few," I said. "Including Dan from my swim team."

"Good," she said. "I'd prefer to think there are people there, for safety's sake. Just let me know from now on when you're going."

"I love you," I said. I couldn't remember the last time I'd said that to Mom.

"I love you, too, sweetie," she said. "Are you hungry? Would you like some lunch?"

I thought how strange that was, that Mom was asking me if I wanted lunch, not what I wanted for lunch. "I'm not that hungry," I said. "Maybe I'll have something later."

"All right," she said. "I'll be in the garden if you want me. There are some weeds out there with my name on them."

I went to my bedroom and stripped out of my still-damp bathing suit and put on a T-shirt and shorts. I thought about Mom and about Dan kissing me and about how hungry I really was and how long I could go without eating. I thought about mosquitoes and the prom and the end of the world.

And then I went out and helped Mom with her weeding.

June 16

Dan and I swam. We also kissed. I like them both so much, I'm not sure which I prefer.

June 17

Mom came home from the post office today with a smile on her face. They aren't doing home deliveries anymore, so Mom goes into town a couple of times a week and picks up the mail at the post office. The only mail is letters (which people are writing more of since there's no other way of communicating). Oh yeah, and bills. The bills never stop. But no junk mail or catalogs. Just letters and bills and there's no way of knowing how long that'll last.

I saw Mom talking to Jonny about something, and then this evening she told us what.

"I got a letter from Jonny's baseball camp," she said at supper (salmon, canned mushrooms, and rice). "They're opening on schedule. They have enough food for a couple of weeks, and they plan to stay open at least that long. But there's a catch."

"Catch," Matt said to me. "That's baseball talk."

I thumbed my nose at him. "What's the catch?" I asked.

"The people who own the camp have a farm that adjoins it," Mom said. "In addition to playing ball, the boys are going to work at the farm. They'll get fresh milk and eggs and vegetables."

"Wow," I said, and I meant it. I still think about those two eggs Mrs. Nesbitt brought over. "That's great. Congratulations, Jonny."

"Yeah, it'll be okay," he said. I guess he'd rather just play baseball.

I looked at Mom and she was practically glowing with happiness. For two weeks, maybe even longer, Jonny was going to have food, and not just canned stuff. Eggs and milk and vegetables. For two weeks, there'd be one less person to worry about.

No wonder Mom was smiling.

June 19

Father's Day. We tried to reach Dad a few times, but no success. We can still sometimes get through on local calls, but I can't remember the last time we had any luck with long distance.

I wonder if Dad was trying to call us or if his feelings were hurt because we didn't call, or if he even thought about us. Maybe it's for the best that Lisa is pregnant.

I know that's dumb. I'll be seeing Dad in a few weeks, spending a month with him and Lisa and Jonny in Springfield. He probably thinks about us as often as we think about him.

More, probably. Sometimes a day goes by and I realize I haven't thought about him at all.

June 21

It's dawn and I'm writing now because I just woke up from a nightmare and it's too late to go back to sleep and too early to get out of bed.

The whole day was just one of those days. It's so hot, over 90 every day for the past week and the nights aren't much cooler. Half the time the electricity comes on in the middle of the night, and it never stays on much more than an hour, so the house barely cools down even with the central air on. Mom actually got a letter from the electric company last week apologizing for the inconvenience. Mom says that's the first time a utility company has ever apologized to her.

The best part of every day is swimming at the pond. When I'm in the water I feel as though nothing bad has happened. I think about the fish, how they don't know what's going on. Their world is unchanged. Actually it's probably better now to be a tuna or a sardine or a salmon. Less chance of ending up as somebody's lunch.

The mosquitoes are getting worse or maybe people are just more worried about West Nile, but there are fewer people at the pond. This would be good for Dan and me except Karen and Emily from the swim team have started swimming at the pond the same time we're there.

It makes the swimming more fun, since we race and offer advice and play really vicious games of swim tag, but it makes the after-swimming a lot less fun, since Dan and I can't just escape into the woods for a little private time.

I don't know why Karen and Emily are showing up then, if it's a coincidence or if Dan told them that's when we swim.

I miss the kissing. I miss the ridiculous sensation of having a boyfriend and being on a date. I wonder if I'll ever have a real date again. Everything's closed: the restaurants and movie theaters and the skating rink. Dan may have his license, but nobody just drives anymore, and he lives on the other end of town.

This is all just dumb. But I guess it's one reason why I had my nightmare.

Peter showed up this evening. He brought us a jar of mixed nuts. Mom stared at it like it was a five-course Thanksgiving dinner: turkey and stuffing and mashed potatoes and sweet potatoes and string beans and salad and soup and pumpkin pie. Or maybe that's what I thought when I saw the jar.

"I'm allergic to peanuts," Peter said, almost apologetically. "Someone gave me these months ago, and it's been sitting in my cupboard."

Mom invited him to stay for dinner, and in his honor she made quite the feast. She took a can of chicken and put some golden raisins in it and it almost passed for chicken salad, if you think of chicken salad being canned chicken and golden raisins. She also served beets and string beans with pearl onions. For dessert we each had a fig and a date.

"This is as close to a date as I'm getting," I said and everyone laughed a little too long.

When Mom put out the string beans and pearl onions, Jonny asked if it was Christmas. I have to admit, the onions seemed like overkill to me, too. I noticed Mom didn't eat very much of anything and neither did Peter, although he pretended like it was the best meal he'd ever had. That left more food for Matt and Jonny and me and we certainly ate it all.

Peter always brings death with him, along with spinach or nuts. He said he'd seen 20 cases of West Nile during the week and five deaths from it. He also said two people had died from food allergies.

"They're so hungry they're taking their chances eating foods they're seriously allergic to," he said.

He and Mom went outside after supper and sat on the swing. I could hear murmured conversation from them, but I didn't try to eavesdrop. It must be horrible to be a doctor now. Before Peter cured people. Now they just die.

Peter left before sunset. He bikes over and with the streetlights gone, it's dangerous to be out after dark. Besides, with no electricity, everyone pretty much goes to bed once the sun sets.

"We're keeping farmer's hours now," Mom says. She's stopped reminding us we can use our flashlights only to get undressed and into bed. We're all starting to sense how important our supply of batteries is.

Maybe it was because of the swimming and maybe it was because of my date joke, but I dreamed that Dan and I were on a real date. He picked me up at the house, and he gave me a corsage, and we got in a car and drove to an amusement park.

We had a wonderful time. We rode the merry-go-round and the Ferris wheel and we were on this amazing roller coaster that went down at 100 miles an hour, only I wasn't scared, I loved it, and as we flew down, we kissed. It was incredibly exciting.

"I'm hungry," I said, and the dream shifted and Dan wasn't there anymore. I was in a tent and it had long tables overloaded with food. There was so much to choose from, southern fried chicken and real tuna salad and pizza and vegetables and fruit. Oranges the size of grapefruits. Even ice cream.

I decided to have a hot dog with all the trimmings. I slathered mustard and ketchup and relish and sauerkraut and chopped onions all over it. I was just about to take a bite when I heard someone say, "You can't eat until you pay."

I turned around and saw there was a cashier. I found my pocketbook and went to give her the money, when I realized the cashier was Becky.

"You can't pay with money," she said. "This is Heaven and you have to die before you can eat the hot dog."

I looked around the tent some more. Everyone there was someone I've known who's died, like Mr. Nesbitt or Grandpa or Mom's grandparents or my seventh-grade math teacher, Mr. Dawkes. Angels were serving the food. Even Becky was wearing white and had wings.

"I really want the hot dog," I said. "But I don't want to die."

"You can't always get what you want," Becky said.

"Don't be careless," Mr. Dawkes said, which was what he always said when he'd hand back a test and I'd made a lot of careless mistakes. Which was really pretty funny, since he died when he ran through a red light on Washington Avenue.

I remember begging for the hot dog and Becky taking it away from me and eating it herself. I never wanted anything as much as I wanted that hot dog.

I woke up with my throat burning and a taste of bile in my mouth. I don't even like hot dogs all that much.

What I'd really love are pancakes, the kind Mom used to make for special occasions. Pancakes with butter and hot maple syrup. Now that I think about it, we have pancake mix and maple syrup. I wonder if we really could have pancakes. I wonder if waking up alive is enough of a special occasion.

When Mom gets up, I'll ask her about the pancakes, but not about what constitutes a special occasion. I think Mom wants us to think we'll wake up every morning for years to come.

Maybe Mom's right. It's a beautiful sunrise. We are all still alive, and I'm really not ready for Heaven. Not as long as I can swim in Miller's Pond and go on make-believe dates with Dan and dream about the possibility of eating pancakes slathered in maple syrup.

June 22

The best day in ages.

For starters, Mom made pancakes. Okay, they weren't pancakes as we all remembered them, but close enough. Water instead of milk, dried egg whites instead of eggs (which made them fluffier and less heavy), no butter, but lots of maple syrup.

We loved them. Mom smiled like I haven't seen her smile in weeks. Jonny asked for seconds, and Mom made them for him, for all of us, really, since we ate like pigs. Mom sent Matt to get Mrs. Nesbitt so she got to eat pancakes, also.

It was amazing not to feel hungry and not to crave more or different.

Then after I'd fully digested (Mom insisted on that) I went to the pond. Dan was already there, and so was Emily, but Karen didn't show up. The day was a little grayish, but still murky and humid and hot, and the water felt great. We swam and raced and had a good time, and then, oh happy day, Emily had to leave to do something back at her house, so Dan and I were alone. (Okay, there were a half dozen other people at the pond, but we didn't know them so we were alone in that way.)

We continued to swim for a while longer, and then we got out of the water, toweled off (not the sort of day where you dry yourself off in the sun), and took a little walk through the woods surrounding the pond.

It was wonderful. We held hands, we hugged, we kissed. We talked, too, and sometimes we didn't do anything, just stood quietly and let the trees and the birds surround us.

Underneath everything, I wonder if Dan would even know I was around if things were normal. Sure he was nice to me at school and at practice sessions, but there's a big difference between saying I have a good crawl stroke and holding me tight in the forest while we kiss.

If anybody ever reads this diary, I will absolutely die.

Dan walked me back home, but he didn't come in. It was lunchtime, and there's an unspoken understanding that you don't drop in at mealtimes (Peter doesn't seem to understand this, but he always brings food).

When I went into the kitchen, there was a strange, pleasant smell that I couldn't quite identify, and then I saw Mom punching a lumpy white thing. She was positively grinning as she punched.

"I'm baking bread," she said. "The pancakes made me think about just what we have, and I remembered buying yeast. I put it in the fridge and I forgot about it, but there it was. I'm using water instead of milk, but that's okay. We're going to have fresh baked bread."

"You're kidding," I said. It seemed too good to be true.

"I have enough yeast for six loaves," Mom said. "I'm baking two today, one for us, and a half loaf for Mrs. Nesbitt and a half for Peter. As soon as we're finished with our loaf, I'll bake another. There's no point holding off. We'll eat bread for as long as we can. And then I'll check out non-yeast recipes and we'll have something breadish until I run out of flour. I just wish I'd thought of it sooner."

"We can save some of it for the fall," I said. "After Jonny and I get back from Springfield."

And just because it was that sort of day, as soon as I said it, the phone rang. It's been so long since I heard that sound, I practically had a heart attack. I answered the phone, and it was Dad. Jonny and Matt were at the park, so they didn't get to talk with him, but I did.

It was so great hearing his voice. He's fine and Lisa is fine and she saw her obstetrician and the baby is fine. Dad says he tries our number and Grandma's and Lisa's parents' three times a day. He spoke to Grandma a couple of days ago and she's fine. Lisa reached her parents about a week ago, and they were okay, also.

He said he can't wait to see us and he was sure we'd be able to manage. Springfield hasn't had any food deliveries in the past couple of weeks, but he and Lisa had stocked up on stuff when all this first happened, and they have some friends who've left Springfield to go south and let them have all their canned goods and boxed foods. Besides, he'd heard that the local farmers were planting crops and that some trucks were on the roads again and things couldn't stay this way forever.

Just hearing Dad say all that and smelling bread in the kitchen made me feel a lot more optimistic.

Mom was so proud when the loaves came out of the oven. They were golden brown and tasted much better than store-bought bread. Matt biked over to Mrs. Nesbitt's and to Peter's office and gave them their goodies.

We had peanut butter and jelly on fresh baked bread for supper tonight. Open-faced sandwiches because we sliced the bread so thick.

Mom says if we keep eating like this we'll end up fat and malnourished, but I don't care. It was wonderful.

Then, because when good things happen they just keep on happening, we had electricity and it came on at 7 PM, a time when we could actually use it. And it stayed on for 3 whole hours.

Mom did three loads of laundry and got two of them dry. I vacuumed the whole house. We ran all the dishes through the dishwasher. We ran the central air and cooled the house off. Just for the hell of it, Matt toasted a slice of bread and we all nibbled on it. I'd forgotten how great toast is: crunchy on the outside and soft on the inside.

A couple of days ago, Matt had gone into the attic and brought down a real old black-and-white TV set with a built-in antenna. Mom says the antennas were called rabbit ears, which I think is pretty silly.

With the electricity on, we turned on the TV set, and got two stations. We can't get any TV reception on our other sets—our cable reception is completely gone.

Just seeing a picture on TV was exciting. One station was religious. The other station showed reruns of <u>Seinfeld</u> and <u>Friends</u>. Guess which station we watched!

Watching sitcoms was like eating toast. Two months ago, it was so much a part of my life I didn't even notice it. But now it feels like Santa Claus and the Easter Bunny and the Tooth Fairy and the Wizard of Oz all rolled into one.

We have clean sheets to sleep on, a clean house, clean clothes, clean dishes. We spent the evening laughing. It wasn't 90 degrees in the house when we went to bed. We aren't hungry. We're not worried about Dad. I know what it feels like to be kissed by a boy.

If I could, I would relive this day over and over. I can't imagine a more perfect one.

June 24

I'm so angry at Mom I could scream. And it doesn't help that she's as mad at me as I am at her.

The day started out great, too. The sun was shining, perfect swimming weather. There was enough bread left for each of us to have a slice for breakfast. Mom brought in a few strawberries from the garden, and we each had two.

I went to the pond and I didn't even mind that Karen and Emily were there. We swam, we raced, we had fun.

I guess they've figured out something's going on with Dan and me, because when we got out of the pond, they made themselves scarce. Dan and I took our walk in the woods. When we're together like that, I feel as though everything is going to work out. I like to think I help him feel that way, also.

Dan walked me home and we ran into Mom in the driveway. "I'm off to get gas," she said. "Dan, would you like a lift into town?"

Dan said yes, and I asked if I could go, too. Mom said sure. We'd be picking up Mrs. Nesbitt, also. She wanted to go to the library.

There are two gas stations in town that still have gas. The way it works is you get in line and then you prepay. It's $12 a gallon, or $35 for 3 gallons, exact change only, and a maximum of 3 gallons. It usually takes about an hour to get the gas, and then you drive to the other gas station and get 3 gallons there. Then if you have the time and the money, you go back to the first gas station and start all over again.

So while Mom is waiting in line, there's plenty of time to go to the library or do anything else you want to do. A lot of times

Mom drops Matt and Jonny off at the park, and they find a pickup game of baseball, while Mom does the gas lines. But since we were all sure it was going to rain, they decided to skip the trip, so there was room for Mrs. Nesbitt and Dan and me.

Mom got into the gas line, and Mrs. Nesbitt, Dan, and I walked over to the library. There's very little that's still open in town, so the library has gotten real popular. Of course it's not the same way it used to be, either. With no electricity, things are pretty dark, and they can't scan the books, so you're on an honor system. Four books to a customer, and they trust you to return them as soon as you can.

We have lots of books at home, but Mom's been urging Matt and Jonny and me to use the library as much as possible. I guess she's afraid it won't stay open that much longer.

We all found books to take out. I put Mrs. Nesbitt's and my books in my book bag. Dan and I kissed in the stacks, and then when we left the library, he started walking toward his home and Mrs. Nesbitt and I started back to the gas station to keep Mom company while she waited.

Only, as we were walking, we saw a long line in the elementary school playground. There were maybe 50 people in the line, and we noticed a couple of state troopers standing around, making sure people stayed in place.

I ran over to see what was going on. "They're giving away food," a man told me. "One bag per household."

I waved Mrs. Nesbitt over and got her a place in the line. "I'm going to get Dan," I told her. "We'll meet you back here."

So I ran, and I do mean ran, toward Dan's home. It didn't take me long to find him and explain what was going on. We both ran back to the playground. By the time we got there, Mrs. Nesbitt was about 20 people ahead of us. I knew we couldn't just cut in line and join her, but we yelled so she knew we were there.

It wasn't bad in the line, maybe because the troopers saw to it that we behaved ourselves. Any kids who might have been whining played with the slides and swings instead and it was fun watching them have a good time. We were all excited about getting food, even if we didn't know what exactly to expect. It kind of felt like Christmas shopping.

Every now and again one of the troopers would explain the rules to us. One bag per household. All the bags were identical. Make any trouble and no bag. No cost but a thank-you would be appreciated.

Even when it began to rain, we didn't mind. It was a gentle summertime kind of rain, and since it's so humid, we hoped that the rain would clear things up and the weather would turn nice again.

Dan and I held hands and giggled and enjoyed being to-gether. We edged forward and we cheered when Mrs. Nesbitt fi-nally got into the school. We cheered again when she emerged carrying a bag.

We finally got in ourselves. There were other troopers in the school, clearly guarding the bags. It was scary seeing them with real guns.

But everyone was very well behaved. When you got to the front of the line, you had to show an ID that had your address on it. Luckily, Dan and I both had our library cards with us. We were each handed a plastic bag, and told to leave, which we did. When we walked out, we saw the troopers were telling people not to get in line; the supplies were running out.

We found Mrs. Nesbitt standing just outside the playground. "There's rice," she said. "And beans and all kinds of goodies."

I was so excited that I flat-out kissed Dan right in front of Mrs. Nesbitt. Not that she seemed shocked. Dan gave me a hug and said good-bye. "My mom is going to be so happy," he said, which pretty much summed it up.

"Maybe there'll be more," I said. "Maybe this is the start of better times."

"Let's hope so," he said. He gave me one more kiss and then he started back to his house.

I took Mrs. Nesbitt's bag and we began walking back to the gas station. I couldn't get over how excited Mom was going to be when she saw I was bringing food.

It was about a half-mile walk to the gas station, and the gentle rain had become heavy with distant thunderstorms. I told Mrs. Nesbitt I wished I had an umbrella for her, but she just laughed.

"I won't melt," she said.

When we got to the gas station, we couldn't find Mom's car, which meant she was already on her way to the second gas station. That added another five blocks to the walk, and Mrs. Nesbitt and I were drenched by the time we finally found her, but it didn't matter. Rice and beans and powdered milk and salt and boxed soup mix and dehydrated vegetables and corn flakes and lime Jell-O.

Mom only had a ten-car wait by the time we got there. I was so wet anyway, I volunteered to get out and pay, which I did. It feels so funny to go into the convenience store and see completely empty shelves and signs saying, CASHIER IS ARMED AND TRAINED TO SHOOT.

I guess Mrs. Nesbitt told Mom all about the food and the line while I was paying for the gas. All I know is Mom was in a great mood before I left the car, and she was very quiet by the time I got back in.

I don't know if Mom felt 6 gallons was enough for one day or if she wanted to get Mrs. Nesbitt home because she was so wet, but we drove straight back and dropped Mrs. Nesbitt off. Any effort Mom might have made to seem social while Mrs. Nesbitt was still in the car ended as soon as it was just the two of us.

"What?" I said when we were finally alone. "What did I do this time?"

"We'll discuss it inside," she said. Her teeth were so clenched she could have been a ventriloquist.

We walked into the kitchen and I flung the book bag and the grocery bag on the table. "I thought you'd be happy," I said. "We have all this food now. What did I do wrong?"

"Sometimes I just don't understand you," she said, like I was the mystery creature. "You saw everyone standing in line, and what did you do?"

"I got in the line," I said. "Wasn't that what I was supposed to do?"

"You left Mrs. Nesbitt and went to get Dan," Mom said. "That seems to be the part you're forgetting."

"Right," I said. "I ran to get Dan and then we got right in the line."

"And what if they'd run out of food by the time you got back?" Mom asked. "What would have happened then?"

"Then we wouldn't have gotten all this great stuff," I said. "Rice and beans and lime Jell-O. I didn't know they were going to run out of food so soon. Besides, what difference does it make? They didn't run out of the food and he got food to take home and so did I and so did Mrs. Nesbitt. I don't see what you're so mad about."

"How often do I have to explain this to you?" Mom asked. "Family is all that matters. Dan has to worry about his family and you have to worry about yours. And before you even begin to say something about Peter, he's brought us food every time he's come here and the least I could do is give him some bread in return."

I would have brought up Peter, too, if she hadn't. Even I knew better than to say Mrs. Nesbitt wasn't family.

"There was enough for all of us," I said.

"Pure luck," Mom said. "I will not have Jonny or Matt or you starve because you want to include a friend. This isn't the time for friendships, Miranda. We have to watch out only for ourselves."

"That's not how you brought us up," I said. "Whatever happened to share and share alike?"

"Sharing is a luxury," she said. "We can't afford luxuries right now."

For a moment, Mom seemed terribly sad instead of angry. I saw an expression in her eyes I remembered from when she and Dad split up.

"You think we're going to die," I said.

Any sadness immediately evaporated and rage took its place. "Don't you ever say that to me again!" she yelled. "None of us is going to die. I will not allow that to happen."

I actually reached out to comfort her. "It's okay, Mom," I said. "I know you're doing everything you can for us. But Dan and I have something wonderful. Like you and Peter. Something special. Otherwise I never would have told him about the food."

But Mom was anything but comforted. There was a look on her face, a look of horror, almost like the way she looked that first night. "Are you sleeping with him?" she asked. "Are you lovers?"

"Mom!" I said.

"Because if you are, you'd better never see him again," she

said. "I'll forbid you to go to the pond. I won't let you leave this house alone again. Do you understand me? I can't let you risk getting pregnant." She grabbed my shoulders and pulled me to an inch of her face. "Do you understand that!"

"I understand!" I yelled right back into her face. "I understand that you don't trust me."

"If I don't trust you, I certainly don't trust Dan," she said. "The two of you cannot be left alone. I forbid it."

"Just try to forbid it!" I screamed. "I love Dan and he loves me and nothing you say or do is going to stop us."

"Go to your room now!" Mom said. "And don't think about coming out until I tell you to. NOW!"

I didn't need any encouragement. I raced to my room and slammed the door as loud as I could. And then I cried. Big howling sobs.

I'm not Sammi. I'm not an idiot. Sure, I'd love to make love with Dan. I'd love to make love with someone before this whole stupid world ends. But even though I told Mom that Dan and I love each other, I know we don't. Not the kind of love that I want to feel for the first man I make love with.

Half the time I can't even figure out what Dan is feeling. I would have thought he'd try to go further with me, but he hasn't. We kiss, we hug, that's it.

And there's Mom acting like we're animals in heat.

It's so unfair. I haven't seen Sammi or Megan since school ended. Dan's practically the only friend I have left in the world. Even if we aren't lovers, even if we aren't boyfriend and girlfriend, he's still the only person I see who isn't family or Peter. I laugh with him. I talk to him. I care about him. And Mom makes it sound like that's something bad, like I can't have friends anymore, like family is the only thing that matters from now on.

If that's how the world is supposed to be, I hope it does end soon.

I hate Mom for making me feel this way. I hate Mom for making me feel that for every good day, there have to be 10 or 20 or 100 bad ones.

I hate Mom for not trusting me. I hate Mom for making me even more scared.

I hate Mom for making me hate her.

I hate her.

June 25

Except for going to the bathroom (and I only did that when I thought no one would see me), I stayed in my room all yesterday. I kept the door shut, and in a fit of rebellion even I realized was dumb, I read by flashlight for four hours.

Matt knocked on my door this morning. "Breakfast is ready," he said.

"I'm never eating again," I said. "More food that way for you and Jonny."

Matt entered the room and closed the door behind him. "Stop being a baby," he said. "You made your point. Now go to the kitchen and eat breakfast. You might want to kiss Mom good morning while you're at it."

"I'm not talking to her until she apologizes," I said. It's funny. I was still angrier than I was hungry. Or maybe I just knew that even after breakfast I'd still be hungry, so what was the point.

Matt shook his head. "I thought you were more mature than this," he said. "I expected better from you."

"I don't care what you expect," I said, which was a total lie. I care desperately what Matt thinks of me. "I didn't do anything wrong. Mom attacked me for absolutely no reason. Why aren't you telling her you expected better from her?"

Matt sighed. "I wasn't here," he said. "I only have Mom's version of what went on."

"Did she happen to mention that she was horrible?" I asked. "That she acted like I was some kind of criminal? Or did she leave that stuff out?"

"If you mean did she burst into tears and say she felt terrible for all the things she said to you, then the answer is no," Matt said. "But she did say how terrible she felt that you were going through all this. Miranda, Mom is holding on by the skin of her teeth. She has the three of us to worry about and Mrs. Nesbitt. And you know Mom. She's worried about Dad, too, and Lisa and her baby, and Peter. She's worried sick about Peter. He's working twelve-hour days, seven days a week, and she has no idea if he's eating anything."

I thought I was going to start crying again, which I didn't want to do. "Mom thinks we're all going to die," I said. "Doesn't she? Do you? Is this all for nothing? Are we all just going to die?"

"Mom doesn't think that, and neither do I," Matt said. I could tell he'd thought about it a lot, and that it wasn't just a glib answer. "That's not the same as saying the worst is over, because I don't think it is, and Mom doesn't think so, either. If things stay the way they are, then we have a real chance. All the scientists are working on making things better. That bag of food yesterday proves that things are improving."

"But this has to be the worst," I said. "How could things get any worse than they are now?"

Matt grinned. "You don't really want me to answer that, do you?" he asked.

We both laughed as I shook my head.

"Mom's more worried about Mrs. Nesbitt than she is about us," Matt said. "Mom's asked her to move in with us, but Mrs. Nesbitt has it in her head that it would be an imposition. Which only makes things harder for Mom."

"I know Mom doesn't want us to die," I said. I thought really hard about what I wanted to say so it would come out right. "But I think maybe she doesn't want us to live, either. We should just hide in our rooms and not feel anything and if we get rescued, great, but if we don't, well, maybe we'll live a little longer. If you can call that living. I know Mom tells you things she doesn't tell me, but am I wrong? Because I really feel that way more and more. I'd like to be wrong, because it scares me if Mom feels that way. But I don't think I am."

"Mom can't guess the future any better than you or me or Mrs. O'Leary's cow," Matt said. "Horton could be on CNN, assuming there still is a CNN, and have as much of a chance of being right as anybody else. But she thinks, and I do too, that we're in for some very hard times. Times worse than what we're going through now. And the way she sees it, the better we take care of ourselves now, the better chance we'll have when things get worse. So yeah, she probably does seem overprotective right now. I know she's scared to send Jonny off to camp, but she's absolutely determined to do that, and not let him know how worried she is. So don't you tell him, either."

"I won't," I promised. "Mom doesn't have to worry about me. I'm not stupid, Matt. But I don't want to have to stop feeling. I really think I'd rather die than stop feeling."

"No one's asking that of you," he said. "And Mom doesn't want you to stop swimming or to stop seeing Dan. She's happy when you're happy. But she wouldn't want Dan to be the only friend you see under any circumstances. Why don't you visit Megan or Sammi? I could use some good Sammi stories."

The truth of the matter is I hardly even think about Sammi or Megan. It's like they're a part of the world that's already ended for me. But since I'd just finished a big speech about feelings, I didn't think I could confess that. So I nodded and told Matt I'd get dressed and make things up with Mom.

But when I saw Mom in the kitchen, I didn't feel like getting all kissy-kissy with her. And I could see she wasn't all that eager to get kissy-kissy with me, either. She and Jonny were both sitting at the table, looking kind of glum.

Without even thinking about it, I said, "Jonny, you want to go to Miller's Pond with me this morning?"

Jonny's face lit up and I could see I'd said the right thing as far as Mom was concerned. "That'd be great," he said.

I have no idea why Jonny hasn't just invited himself along. It's not like I own Miller's Pond. But Jonny's been playing baseball or at least practicing with Matt. And Matt's been running when he hasn't been playing ball. Maybe they figured swimming was mine and they'd keep away from it.

Jonny put his trunks on under his jeans while I was eating breakfast, and as soon as we were both ready, we walked together to the pond. With my luck, of course Emily and Karen weren't there, so Dan and I lost good alone time.

But it was worth it to see how happy Jonny was in the water. There were a couple of kids he knew from middle school and the three of them played together. Then we all swam together, played water polo and imitation relay races. It was another one of those hot sunny days, so we all laid around after swimming and let the sun dry us off. Dan, it turns out, is a big Phillies fan, and he and Jonny talked baseball, which made Jonny even happier.

I've been so involved in my own problems, I haven't thought much about what all this is doing to Jonny. Until I saw how excited he was talking with Dan about all-time great second basemen, I hadn't realized just how bored he's been. He's had Matt, and Matt's been great with him, but this time of year when Jonny isn't playing ball, he's watching it on TV, or following it on the Internet.

Jonny's passionate about baseball the way I used to be about skating. I'm really glad his baseball camp is going to be open. He deserves a couple of weeks of doing what he loves best.

I guess because Jonny was with me, Dan didn't walk me home. That was okay, because it gave me more of a chance to talk with Jonny.

"I've been thinking about something," he said, and I could tell it was something really important to him. Right away that meant it wasn't anything good. "You know how I'm planning on playing second for the Yankees?"

Since Jonny's been planning on that since birth, I wasn't exactly surprised to hear it, so I just nodded.

"I know Mom's doing her best," Jonny said. "But I don't think I'm eating a well-balanced diet. Protein and stuff like that. I'm five five and I don't know how much taller I can get if I don't start eating hamburgers and roast beef."

"We're eating better than lots of other people," I said.

"Better than people here," Jonny said. "But what if there are thirteen-year-old guys in Japan or the Dominican Republic who are eating hamburgers and who are growing? I don't see how I can reach six feet on canned tuna. What if I end up five feet six?"

I would have laughed except he looked so serious. Besides, I knew Matt wouldn't have laughed. Matt doesn't laugh at my idiotic questions.

"You taking your vitamins?" I asked.

Jonny nodded.

"Well, they'll help," I said. "Look, Jonny, I don't know what things are going to be like tomorrow, let alone years from now. Even if things get back to normal and baseball is just like it is now, like it was last year I mean, players years from now may all be shorter than they used to be. Or maybe there'll be less competition for you because, well, because there just won't be that many second basemen around. I don't think things are great in the Dominican Republic or Japan. The guys your age may not grow to six feet, either, or have the time to work on their baseball the way you do."

"You mean you think they're all dead," Jonny said.

"Not exactly," I said, suddenly appreciating how well Matt's been handling me lately. "What I think is the whole world is going through rough times now, not just Pennsylvania. And there are probably boys in the Dominican Republic and in Japan who are worrying the same way you are. Only I don't know if they have vitamins or canned tuna. And I do know one thing. It's like Dad always says. The only way you can be the best at something is to be the best you can be. If you're the best second baseman you can be, you stand as good a chance as anyone at playing second for the Yankees."

"Do you hate all this?" Jonny asked.

"Yes," I said. "And I miss hamburgers, too."

When we got home, I saw Mom in the kitchen, flour and yeast and measuring cups all spread out on the counter. The kitchen must have been 100 degrees between how hot it was outside and the oven being on.

"Can I help, Mom?" I asked. "I'd like to learn how to bake bread."

Mom smiled at me. Really smiled. Smiled like I was her long-lost daughter, the good one, who she thought was gone forever. "I'd like that," she said.

So we baked and sweated together. I like punching the dough. I told myself it was the moon and punched it senseless.

SEVEN

July 2

Mom drove Jonny to baseball camp today. She came back really excited because she found a gas station near Liberty that was selling 5 gallons of gas at a time for $75. That's more than it costs here, but the stations here are down to a 2-gallon maximum, and Mom said it was worth the extra money to get so much gas at once.

One of the things I don't ask Mom is how much longer her cash is going to last. Then again, the only thing left to spend it on is gas, so I guess it doesn't much matter.

The temperature was near 100 and we haven't had electricity for the past 3 days. Matt decided it was time to chop down a tree. He sent me out to gather kindling. That seems dumb to me, but at least in the woods there was shade. And it's a lot easier to gather kindling than it is to chop a tree.

After I'd gathered 4 bags I brought them to the house. Matt was still working on the tree. At the rate he was going, it's going to take a week to chop down that tree.

I asked him if he wanted any help, and he said no.

But I didn't feel like I could just sit someplace reading while he was working. And frankly there wasn't that much I could do around the house. I weeded the vegetable garden, since Mom does that daily, and I washed the dishes, and then just to prove I was good for something, I scrubbed the bathrooms and washed the kitchen floor.

Matt came in and took a drink of water. "Very impressive," he said. "Got any other plans for the day?"

I was a little scared to admit I didn't, so I just mumbled.

"Why don't you visit Sammi and Megan?" he asked. "Have you seen them since school ended?"

I hadn't. Of course they haven't come to visit me, either.

But just to keep Matt from harping on it, I decided to pay calls. It felt very Jane Austen—y to do that. None of her heroines had phones or computers and nowadays neither do I.

It took 15 minutes to walk to Sammi's and I sweated the whole way. I wasn't too happy when I got there to find no one was home.

For a moment I wondered if her whole family had packed up and left (some families are doing that, moving down south because things are supposed to be better there), but there was laundry on the clothesline. Funny to think of Sammi's mom hanging clothes on the line. Of course that's what we're doing now, but Sammi's mother was never exactly the domestic type.

There didn't seem any point in staying around waiting for someone to show up, so I walked over to Megan's. I knocked on the door and Megan's mom opened the door right away.

She looked beyond happy to see me. It gave me a déjà-vu feeling. It was the same kind of look I used to get from Becky's mom.

"Miranda!" Mrs. Wayne said, and she pulled me into the house. "Megan'll be so glad to see you. Megan, Miranda's here!"

"Is she in her room?" I asked.

Mrs. Wayne nodded. "She hardly leaves it," she said. "Except to go to church. I'm so glad you're here, Miranda. See if you can talk some sense into her, please."

"I'll do my best," I said, but we both knew nothing I could say was going to change Megan's mind. I've never been able to change Megan's mind about anything.

Megan opened the door to her bedroom and she seemed genuinely happy to see me. I checked her out carefully. She's lost some weight, but not as much as I'd been afraid.

What did scare me, though, was how she glowed. She positively radiated inner joy. No way that makes sense these days.

"How are you?" she asked, and she seemed genuinely interested in everything I told her. And I told her most everything, about how Dan and I were seeing each other almost every day, and how Jonny was on his way to camp, and how Matt was chopping a tree. I didn't tell her about what food we still had because you don't talk about that anymore.

Once we finished with me, I asked her how she was. If anything, she got even more radiant. She was practically radioactive.

"Oh, Miranda," she said. "If only you could know the true happiness I'm feeling."

"I'm glad you're happy," I said, although frankly I thought she was crazy, and bad as things are, I'm still not glad when people are crazy.

"You could be happy, too, if you only embraced God," she said. "Admit your sins, cast out Satan, and offer your heart to God."

"You getting to church much?" I asked. Megan had listened to me rattle on about Dan, the least I could do is listen to her rattle on about Reverend Marshall.

"I go every day," Megan replied. "Mom knows I go every morning, but she gets angry at me if I don't come back by afternoon. And I don't want Mom to be angry, because I want to see her in Heaven. Sometimes, though, at night when she's asleep, I slip out and go back. No matter when I go, the Reverend is there. He's praying day and night for all us sinners."

Somehow I doubt he's praying for me, and if he is, I'm not sure I want him to. But at least if Megan was going to church, she was getting out of the house.

Still some questions had to be asked. "So are you eating anymore?" I asked. Funny how anymore can mean two different things.

"I eat, Miranda," Megan said, and she smiled at me like I was an idiot child. "It would be suicide if I stopped eating altogether. It's not God's will that anyone should commit suicide."

"Glad to hear it," I said.

She gave me a look of such pity I had to turn my face away. "You're like how I was," she said. "After Becky died."

It's a funny thing. We were all so close to Becky, Megan and Sammi and I, but we hardly talked about her after she died. That's when we started going our separate ways, like Becky, and even her illness, was the glue that held us together.

"What about her?" I asked. I wondered if Megan dreamed about Becky like I do, three or four times a week lately.

"I was so angry," Megan said. "Angry at God. How could He let someone like Becky die? With so many awful people in the world, why was it Becky had to be the one to die? I actually hated God. I hated everyone and everything and I even hated God."

I tried to remember what Megan had been like. It was a little over a year ago, so it shouldn't have been too hard. But that whole time was so awful. Becky had been sick for so long, and then it looked like the treatments were working, and then out of nowhere she died anyway.

"Mom was scared for me," Megan said. "And Reverend Marshall had just started preaching here, so she took me to see him. I screamed at him. How could God do that to Becky? How could He do that to me? I thought Reverend Marshall would tell me to go home and I'd understand when I was older, but he didn't. He said we could never truly understand God's will. We have to trust God, have faith in Him, and follow the rules He gave us without ever understanding Him. The Lord is my shepherd, Miranda. Once Reverend Marshall made me understand that, all my doubts and all my anger went away. God has His own reasons for what we're suffering. Maybe when we're in Heaven we'll understand, but until then all we can do is pray for His forgiveness and obey His will."

"But His will can't be for you to starve to death," I said.

"Why not?" she asked. "His will was for Becky to die. Death can be a blessing, Miranda. Think how much suffering Becky's been spared."

"But you can't pray to die," I said.

"I pray to accept God's will without any doubts," she replied. "I pray to be worthy of His love. I pray for eternal life in Heaven. I pray for you, Miranda, and Mom and Dad and even for Dad's other family. And I pray as Reverend Marshall says we should, for the souls of all the poor sinners, that they should see the light and be spared the eternal flames of hell."

"Thank you," I said, for lack of anything better to say.

Megan stared at me with pity. "I know you're not a believer," she said. "And I see the unhappiness in your eyes. Can you say you're happy, Miranda? Can you say you're at peace with the world?"

"No, of course not," I said. "But I don't think I should be. Why should I be happy when there isn't enough food and people are getting sick and I can't even turn on the air conditioning?"

Megan laughed. "All of that is so unimportant," she said. "This life is no more than the blink of an eye compared to life everlasting. Pray with me, Miranda. The only thing that's keeping me from true happiness is knowing that people I love aren't saved."

"Well, no one says you can be happy about everything," I said. "I know I should be glad for you, Megan, but frankly I think you're crazy. And if Reverend Marshall is making you this way, I think he's evil. This life, this everyday existence, is the one gift we're given. To throw it away, to want to be dead, to me that's the sin."

The Megan who used to be my best friend would have argued with me. And then we would have laughed. This Megan got down on her knees and began to pray.

When I got home, I went back into the woods and got three more bags of kindling. Maybe I'll end up in the eternal flames of hell, like Megan says. But until that happens, I intend to stay warm from the flames of a woodstove.

July 3

After supper tonight, Mom said, "I was thinking about this on the drive home yesterday. How would you feel if we cut back to two meals a day?"

I think even Matt was startled, because he didn't say sure right away.

"Which two?" I asked, like it would matter.

"We'd definitely keep eating supper," Mom said. "It's important for us to have one meal together. But we could decide every day if we wanted breakfast or lunch. I know I'd skip breakfast. I've never been much of a breakfast person."

"I skip lunch sometimes at school," Matt said. "It wouldn't be that big a deal for me to skip it."

"Of course it's voluntary," Mom said. "We're nowhere near running out of food. But I thought while Jonny is away, maybe we could all do with a little less."

I pictured Jonny on the farm, eating eggs and drinking milk and, for a second, I really hated him. "It's fine, Mom," I said. "I'll skip a meal. I'll live."

I wonder what it's going to be like with Dad and Lisa. I'm starting to develop real fantasies about Springfield. I picture a kitchen full of food, a working refrigerator, farmers' markets with fresh produce and eggs and pies and cookies and chocolate fudge. I imagine air conditioning and TV and Internet and 80-degree weather and indoor pools and no mosquitoes.

I'll settle for any one of those things. Well, any one of those things and fudge.

July 4

Happy Independence Day.

Ha!

Horton kept us up all night wailing in front of Jonny's bedroom door. He's gotten very sulky and only ate half of his food yesterday (and Mom didn't even have to ask him to).

No electricity for the past three days. The temperature has been hovering around 100 degrees and it doesn't get much cooler at night.

I dreamed heaven was an ice palace, cold and white and beckoning.

I skipped breakfast today and I was hungry when I went swimming. I'll try skipping lunch tomorrow. All the time I spent with Dan (not enough and Emily was there practically on top of us the entire time), all I could think about was food. How much I missed breakfast. What I was going to eat for lunch. How many more loaves of bread we were going to be able to bake before we run out of yeast.

I think about Jonny getting three meals a day, real food, farm food, and how Mom pulled this two-meal business on us only after he left, and I get so angry. It's like she thinks Jonny's needs come first. Got to get him his nourishment if he's going to reach 6 feet. Just to be on the safe side, give him some of Miranda's.

I hope this bad mood is just because it's the Fourth. That was always one of my favorite holidays. I love the parades and the fair and the fireworks.

This year Matt brought Mrs. Nesbitt over for supper, and after we ate, we sat on the front porch and sang patriotic songs. Horton screeched right along, and it was hard to say which one of us sounded worse.

This is without a doubt the worst summer of my life and there are still two months to go.

July 6

No electricity for the past 5 days. None of us wants to say it, but we're all thinking maybe we'll never have electricity again.

It was 97 this afternoon. Mom is making us drink lots and lots of water.

Matt's still chopping down trees and I'm still gathering kindling. It's hard to imagine ever being cold again.

I think brunch is going to work best for me. I go swimming in the morning and then when I come back, I eat my meal. That way I don't have to watch Matt eat breakfast or watch

Mom eat her half lunch and feel guilty when I'm eating more than she is.

Right after I got back from swimming, the electricity came on. We haven't had any in almost a week, and we were jubilant at its return.

Mom always leaves a load of most-needed-to-be-washed clothes in the washing machine, and she turned it on right away. I grabbed the vacuum cleaner and started on the living room floor. Mom got the dishwasher going and the central air (it was 92 degrees when I woke up this morning). Matt turned on the rabbit ears TV, but all he got was an emergency broadcasting signal, whatever that means.

After ten glorious minutes, the electricity went off. Everything stopped, the vacuum and the air conditioning and the washer and the dishwasher and the freezer that would have made us ice cubes for the first time in a week.

We stood around, actually stood around, waiting for the appliances to turn themselves back on. Mom stared at the washer; I held on to the vacuum.

After about 15 minutes, I gave up and put the vacuum cleaner away. Mom unloaded the dishes from the dishwasher, rinsed them off, and put them away.

She held off on the laundry until mid-afternoon. Then she and I unloaded it, carried the soapy wet clothes to the bathtub, and spent what felt like hours rinsing them out and wringing them so they could get hung on the clothesline.

So help me, 15 minutes after we got them hung, there was a thunderstorm. I thought Mom was going to start crying (I sure felt like it), but she was okay until Matt finally made his way back in. He spends all his time chopping wood, and I guess he wasn't going to let a little thunder and lightning get in his way.

Mom totally blew it. She screamed at him for staying in the woods during a thunderstorm. Her face turned so red I was afraid she'd have a stroke. Matt yelled right back. He knew what he was doing, every minute counted; if he'd been in any danger he would have come right in.

Then the electricity came back on. We all ran out, took the clothes off the line, and shoved them into the dryer. Mom started a second load in the washing machine. We turned on the air conditioning, and Matt went online to see if anything was there (just a week-old listing of the dead and the missing).

This time the electricity stayed on for 40 minutes, long enough for the second load of laundry. It had stopped raining, so Mom hung it on the line.

The ice cubes weren't frozen all the way through, but they still were a wonderful luxury in our glasses of water. The house cooled down and outside it was less muggy.

Mom and Matt are still speaking to each other. Horton is still demanding to know where we hid Jonny.

I can't decide which is worse, no electricity or unreliable electricity.

I wonder if I'll ever have to decide which is worse, life as we're living or no life at all.

July 9

The temperature is 102, there's been no electricity since Saturday, and I have my period. I would kill for a chocolate chocolate-chip ice-cream cone.

Here's the funny thing about the world coming to an end. Once it gets going, it doesn't seem to stop.

I woke up this morning and immediately sensed that things were different. It's hard to explain. It was cooler than it has been (which is good), but the sky was this weird gray color, not exactly like it was cloudy or even foggy. More like someone had pulled a translucent gray shade over the blue sky.

I went downstairs to the kitchen because I could hear Mom and Matt talking. Mom had boiled water for tea, and even though I don't much like tea, it still gives me the illusion of having something in my stomach so I made myself a cup.

"What's going on?" I asked, because it was pretty obvious something was.

"We hadn't wanted to worry you," Mom began.

I don't know what raced through my mind first. Jonny. Dad. Lisa's baby. Mrs. Nesbitt. Grandma. Electricity. Food. Mosquitoes. The moon crashing into earth. Everything flooded in. I know how terrified I must have looked, but Mom didn't change her expression. No reassuring smile, no laugh at my overreaction. Matt looked every bit as grim. I steeled myself for the worst.

"We thought this was a possibility," Mom said. "Matt, Peter, and I, but the scientists didn't say anything about it, at least not that we heard on the radio. I guess we hoped we were exaggerating. Worrying about things that weren't really going to happen."

"Mom, what happened?" I asked. At least it didn't seem to be anything personal. The radio wouldn't care what happened to Jonny or Dad.

"You know the moon is closer to the earth than it used to be," Matt said. "And that's changed the gravitational pull."

"Of course," I said. "That's why the tides changed. And that's what caused all the earthquakes."

"What we were concerned about—what seems to be happening now—is volcanoes," Mom said.

"Volcanoes?" I said. "There aren't any volcanoes in Pennsylvania."

Mom managed half a smile. "Not that we know of," she said. "We're not in any direct danger from volcanoes, any more than we've been in direct danger from the tsunamis or the earthquakes."

Of course there's been plenty of indirect danger. In case I needed any more reminding, a mosquito landed on my left arm. I killed it before it killed me.

"Okay," I said. "So how can volcanoes make things any worse?"

I was hoping Matt would laugh or Mom would tell me not to be so self-pitying, but instead they both looked grim.

"What is it?" I asked. "Things can't get worse. What can a volcano do that hasn't already happened?"

"A lot," Matt said, almost angrily. I don't know if he was angry at me or at the world. "The moon's gravitational pull is forcing magma through the volcanoes. From what we heard on the radio last night and this morning, there are dormant volcanoes erupting everywhere. It's been going on for a few days now and there's no guarantee it's ever going to stop. The earthquakes haven't. The floods haven't. The eruptions may not, either."

"We don't know what's going to happen," Mom said. "But right now there's more volcanic action than there ever has been."

"I still don't get how that's going to affect us," I said. "You said there are no volcanoes here. Have lots of people died?"

"Lots," Matt said. "And lots more are going to. And not just people who live near volcanoes, either."

"Matt," Mom said, and she put her hand on his arm. I think that scared me most of all. Matt's done nothing but comfort me since he got home, and now he needed Mom to comfort him.

"Look outside," Matt said. "Just look at that sky."

So I did. It was that funny shade of gray.

"When a large enough volcano erupts, it clouds the sky," Matt said. "Not just a mile away and not just a hundred miles away. Thousands of miles away, and not just for a day or two, either."

"The concern is that the volcanic ash will cover the sun most places on earth," Mom said. "Like it seems to be doing already here. And if it lasts long enough . . ."

"Crops," Matt said. "No sunlight, no crops. Nothing grows without sunlight."

"Oh, Mom," I said. "Not the vegetable garden? How can that be? We're nowhere near a volcano. I'm sure we'll get the sun back."

"They're starting to issue warnings," Mom said. "The scientists on the radio. They say we should be prepared for major climatic changes. Drought's a real possibility, and record cold temperatures. It's already cooling off here. It was eighty-eight when I went to bed last night, and it's seventy-two now. But feel how muggy it is. It hasn't cooled off because of a thunderstorm. It's cooled off because the sunlight can't penetrate the ash in the sky."

"But it can't last all that long," I said. "A week? A month? Is there something we can do to keep the garden growing?"

Mom took a deep breath. "I think we have to assume it's going to last longer than that," she said. "And we should prepare for the worst, very little sunlight, very weak sunlight for several months. A year, maybe longer."

"Longer?" I asked, and I could hear the hysteria in my voice. "Longer than a year? Why? Where's the nearest volcano? What the hell is going on?"

"There's a volcano at Yellowstone," she said. "It erupted yesterday. Phoenix and Las Vegas are drowning in ash."

"Las Vegas?" I said. "Is Grandma okay?"

"There's no way of knowing," Matt said.

I pictured Springfield, my Springfield, with its food and its electricity. "Are things better east of us?" I asked.

"Miranda, this isn't a local problem," Mom said. "It's not just one volcano. A half dozen erupted yesterday alone. Nothing like this has ever happened before. Wind currents will affect things and no one can predict the wind. Maybe we'll be lucky. Maybe something good will happen that we can't imagine just now. But we have to prepare for the worst. You and I and Matt and Jonny have to prepare for the worst. We have to assume frosts in August. We have to assume no power and no food coming in and no gas for the car and no oil for the furnace. Up till now we've been playacting survival, but from now on we have to take it seriously."

"Playacting!" I cried. "You think this has all been a game to me?"

"Look," Matt said, and I couldn't tell which one of us he was trying to calm down. "The smartest thing we can do is assume things are going to get a lot worse. Mom and I were talking about precautions we can take now so that if it's a rough winter, we'll be in better shape."

"Like eating less," I said. "Because we can't be sure of the garden."

Matt nodded. "I'm not crazy about the idea, either," he said. "But we do have to discuss the possibility."

"I can cut down to one meal a day," Mom said. "I'm too upset to be hungry these days, anyway. But I don't want you kids doing that. Not unless we really have to."

"Maybe we could fast one day a week," I suggested. "Or I could skip brunch, say, every other day."

"Those both sound like good ideas," Matt said. "I could eat breakfast Mondays, Wednesdays, and Fridays, and Miranda could eat brunch Tuesdays, Thursdays, and Saturdays, and we could both fast on Sundays. But Mom, if you're eating only one meal a day, you really shouldn't fast."

Mom looked like she was going to cry. "I'll be fine," she said instead. "I think we need to store up as much water as we possibly can. As long as we have running water, we might as well use it, but we need to conserve as much as possible."

"The well might run dry?" I asked.

"It's a possibility," Matt said. "Any water we don't use now could come in handy six months from now."

"I'm also concerned whatever rain we get will be polluted," Mom said. "We should boil our drinking water from now on. We've never had any problems with our well water, but if the air is badly polluted, we shouldn't take chances."

"What about the pond?" I asked. "I can keep swimming, can't I?"

"I think so," Mom said. "For the time being. Of course if the temperature really plummets, it might get too cold."

"It's July," I said. "How cold can it get?"

"That's what we don't know." Matt said. "But I guess we're going to find out."

Just to prove everybody wrong, Mom and Matt and all the

scientists, I went swimming this morning. Only two other people showed up, and none of us stayed very long.

Even though I knew the water was just as clean as it had been yesterday, I still felt dirty when I got out of the pond. It wasn't cold outside, but it was so clammy that I couldn't stop shivering. Just yesterday I'd been wishing things would cool off, and now that they have, I miss heat so much. I even miss seeing the moon.

Today's a Saturday, so I ate brunch. Tomorrow we'll fast. I wonder how that will be, but I guess we'll get used to it.

I hope Grandma's okay.

I guess the lists of the dead are about to get a lot longer.

EIGHT

Mom changed the rules so I can eat brunch on Mondays. She says it isn't fair for me to fast on Sundays and then not eat until Monday night. Of course she isn't eating until Monday night, but we're not supposed to notice.

Fasting wasn't as bad as I thought it would be. I got real hungry around lunchtime, but it wore off as the day went along. I guess I'll get used to it.

It's hard to be sure, but I think things are getting grayer.

Peter dropped by this afternoon. We told him our plans and he thought they were good ones. He especially approved of boiling the drinking water.

I asked him about swimming.

"It's probably better if you stopped," he said. "The people with town water are telling me it's discolored and there are concerns about how much longer it's going to last. All that takes electricity, and we know how well the power plants are working these days."

"But what does that have to do with the pond?" I asked.

"It's hard to predict what people will do if they don't have running water," Peter said. "They might start taking their dirty clothes to the pond to wash them there. Or they might start bathing there. There's a possibility the pond will become a breeding ground. Nowadays it's better to be safe than sorry."

At least he didn't list the symptoms of cholera. That, for Peter, showed real restraint.

I think I'll go swimming tomorrow, anyway. Maybe Dan will show up. Maybe the sun will shine.

July 12

No Dan. No sun. No electricity. No word from Jonny or Dad.

July 13

Matt's stopped running. It took me five days to realize that. I finally asked and he said he'd stopped on Saturday, partly because he's worried about air quality and partly to conserve strength.

The days seem a lot shorter than just a week ago. At least it's getting darker sooner. Mom lets us use one of the oil lamps in the sunroom every evening. It doesn't cast enough light for all of us to read, so Matt and I take turns sitting near it. Mom found a bag of old yarn in the attic and she's crocheting at night, so she doesn't need much light.

I'm using the flashlight to write this now. I know I should stop. Batteries don't last forever.

July 14

I did something so stupid today. I could kill myself, I'm so angry and upset.

We were sitting around this evening, doing our let's-share-the-dim-light routine, and around 9 Mom announced we'd used up enough oil for one night and we should go to bed.

We've been on a sunrise to sunset pattern for a while now, but with that horrible gray covering over the sun, our timing is off. You can still tell if the sun is up, but there are no dramatic changes. Gray at 6 AM, gray at 6 PM.

And I don't know why, but I just didn't feel like going to bed. Maybe it's the nightmares I've been having the past couple of days. Becky pushing me into a volcano, stuff like that.

I said I was going to sit on the porch before going to bed, and since sitting on the porch doesn't use up any energy, Mom had no reason to say no. So I went out onto the porch and sat there for a while, maybe half an hour. Certainly long enough that when I went back in, Mom and Matt were already in their rooms.

Only when I decided to go in, I forgot about Horton. Horton goes outside in the daytime, but we're not allowed to let him out anytime after sunset. Even when we had electricity, that was the rule. Horton stays in at night.

I guess Horton's as confused about what's day and what's night as the rest of us. He raced out as soon as I opened the door.

I went back out and called for him, but he wasn't interested. I stayed on the porch for an extra hour, calling for him, and hoping he'd come back on his own, but there's no sign of him.

I'd better not use up any more flashlight battery. I just hope he's on the doorstep, complaining about being forced to spend the night outside, when I get up tomorrow.

July 15

No Horton.

I alternated between gathering kindling and looking for him. Mom and Matt searched also, but none of us saw him.

Mom says I shouldn't feel bad, that it could have happened with any of us, but I know it's my fault. I am so careless. I've always gotten into trouble because I'm careless, but most of the time I've only hurt myself.

I don't know what Jonny will do if he gets home and Horton isn't back.

July 16

Still no sign of Horton.

Mom and I had a big fight.

"We haven't heard a word from Jonny in two weeks! And all you can think of is that damned cat."

"Jonny's fine!" I yelled right back at her. "Jonny's eating three meals a day. You waited until he left before you put us on our starvation diets. You think I didn't notice that? You think I don't know which one of us you're betting on?"

I still don't believe I said that. The thought's crossed my mind, but I haven't even written it here, it's so horrible. What if Mom truly believes only one of us is likely to make it? I know she wouldn't choose herself.

But would she really pick between Matt and Jonny and me? Will a point come where she asks two of us to give our food to the third?

The thing is I know if it comes to that, Matt wouldn't take the food. And Mom's got to know that also. And when I do think about this, and I try so hard not to, I think Mom guesses I couldn't make it on my own, that no female could.

Which leaves Jonny.

I hate thinking like this. I hate myself for being so upset about Horton that I took it out on Mom. I hate being so selfish that it never even occurred to me Mom was worried about not hearing from Jonny.

I've stopped worrying about not hearing from Dad. I just imagine a month away from here, from Mom. A month in

Springfield where for some reason the sun shines brightly and the electricity works all the time and I'm never hungry.

July 17

Three days and none of us have caught a glimpse of Horton.

Even Mrs. Nesbitt's been looking, since Horton sometimes wanders down to her house. She thought maybe she saw him yesterday, but she isn't sure, and Matt says we shouldn't assume she really did.

"People see what they want to see," he said.

Mom and I haven't talked since our horrible fight yesterday, which makes suppertime even more fun. After supper, I go searching for Horton until it's too dark to see anything, let alone a gray tabby. Then I sit on the porch and will him to come home.

Matt came out on the porch. "Horton might show up tonight," he said. "But we'd better start dealing with the possibility he isn't coming back."

"I think he's going to," I said. "I think he just went searching for Jonny. When he gets hungry enough, he'll come back. It isn't like anyone else is going to feed him."

Even in the gloomy darkness, I could see Matt's expression. I've gotten to know it so well lately. It's that How-Am-I-Going-to-Tell-Her-This-One look.

"You know we're in pretty good shape," he said. "Compared to a lot of other people we're doing fine."

That's how he does it. He kind of slides into it. Breaks it to me gently. Points out how fabulous our life is before he sticks the knife in.

"Just say it," I demanded.

"It's possible Horton's been killed," Matt said. "For food."

I thought I was going to be sick. I don't know why that

hadn't occurred to me. Maybe because until a couple of months ago, I didn't live in a world where pets were regarded as food.

"Look," Matt said. "We've all let Horton out. If someone wanted to catch him for whatever reason, they'd have plenty of chances. All you did was let him out at night. You're not at fault. No one is."

But I am, and he knows it, and Mom knows it, and Jonny'll know it, and most of all I know it. If Horton's dead, if he's been killed, I'm the one responsible.

I really don't deserve to live. Not because of Horton, but if there is only so much food left, I haven't done anything to earn it. What do I do? Gather kindling? What kind of contribution is that?

I hate Sundays. Everything is worse on Sundays.

July 18

Monday.

I stayed out all day, searching, and gathering kindling.

I fell asleep in the woods this afternoon, just collapsed into sleep. The mosquitoes must have loved me. I have half a dozen bites I don't remember from this morning.

I got in around 4 and Mom was waiting for me in the kitchen.

"Did you eat today?" she asked. "I didn't see you come in and eat."

"I skipped brunch," I said. "I forgot about it."

"You don't forget about food," she said. "You fasted yesterday. Today you eat. Those are the rules."

"You sure do like making up rules," I said.

"You think I like this?" Mom yelled. "You think I like seeing my children go hungry? You think I'm getting any pleasure from all this?"

Of course I don't. And I should have apologized on the spot and hugged Mom and told her how much I love her and how brave she's being and how I wish I could be just like her.

Instead I ran to my room and slammed the door behind me. Just like I was 12 again. It's going to be suppertime soon and I know if I don't go out, Matt's going to drag me out. Even if he doesn't use actual force, he'll drag me out with guilt.

The funny thing is I'd just as soon not eat. It turns out if you don't eat for long enough, the idea of food becomes nauseating. That's probably how Megan's been doing it. Only she thinks going hungry is good and I know it sucks.

Suppertime's going to be so much fun.

July 19

No Horton.
No word from Jonny.
Mom and I didn't talk.
Matt isn't talking much, either.

July 20

Today's the anniversary of the day men first walked on the moon. I learned that when I was doing all those papers about the moon.

I hate the moon. I hate tides and earthquakes and volcanoes. I hate a world where things that have absolutely nothing to do with me can destroy my life and the lives of people I love.

I wish the astronauts had just blown up the damn moon when they had the chance.

July 21

I have now gathered almost enough kindling to build a house, but Matt keeps telling me there's no such thing as enough and I should bring in more. It's not like I have anything else to do, so I keep going out and gathering.

In a week I'll be going to Springfield. I know, I just know, everything'll be better there, and that when I get home, this whole nightmare will be over.

I was out doing my gathering thing when Mom found me. "Sammi's here," she said. "Go on in."

This is the most Mom's said to me in days. I figured a visit from Sammi must have really cheered her up. Maybe she brought us a can of spinach.

Sammi actually looked pretty good. She's always been obsessive about her weight, but she didn't look like she'd lost very much since I saw her in June.

We went out onto the porch and stared out at nothing. "I've come to say good-bye," she said. "I'm leaving tomorrow morning."

"Where are you going?" I asked, remembering the laundry on the clothesline. Sammi has a kid brother a year younger than Jonny but she hates him. She fights with her parents all the time, too. I was just as glad I wasn't going to be in that car.

"I met a guy," Sammi said, and I burst out laughing for the first time in a week. I don't know why that struck me as funny, except it was so obvious and I hadn't even thought of it.

"Miranda," Sammi said.

"Sorry," I said, swallowing a few more giggles. "You met a guy."

"I'm going with him," she said. "He's heard things are better down south. Lots of people are saying that. We're going to Nashville and if that doesn't work out, we'll try Dallas."

"Do your parents know?" I asked.

Sammi nodded. "They say it's fine. He's been giving us food so they think he's great. And he is. He's forty and he knows lots of people. He's been bringing us food for a couple of weeks now, and he even got gas for Dad's car, and lots of bottled water. Mom and Dad would love it if he stayed, but he's been planning on moving out for a while now. He says he's been waiting until I was ready."

"How long have you known him?" I asked. "You never mentioned him at school."

"I met him about four weeks ago," she said. "Love at first sight. At least for him, which is a good thing. He can have any girl he wants. I'm lucky he wants me."

"You don't sound all that happy," I said.

"Well, I'm not," Sammi said. "Don't be an idiot, Miranda. I may like older guys, but not that much older. Twenty-one, twenty-two, twenty-three was my absolute limit and that was after this whole moon thing and I was drunk. But he's given my folks cartons of canned goods and gas and Mom says maybe things really are better in Nashville and I'll have a chance. She says the best thing a parent can do for a child now is to send them someplace where they have a chance. Only you need protection, which he'll provide me."

"Does he have a name?" I asked.

"George," Sammi muttered and we both burst out laughing. "Okay, I never thought I'd end up with a forty-year-old named George," she said. "And maybe we won't stick together. Maybe when we're in Nashville I'll find myself a nice twenty-two-year-old who can feed me and then I'll dump George. Or maybe he'll dump me. Enough guys have. Either way I'll be out of here, which is all I ever wanted."

"I tried to visit you," I said. "A couple of weeks ago. No one was home."

"I've been thinking about visiting you, but George takes up

a lot of time," Sammi said. "I stopped in on Megan on my way here. She seems pissed that she's still alive."

"I hope you come back," I said. "I hope we get to see each other again."

"You were the only good thing about this place once Becky died," Sammi said. "You know, when she died, I figured out that life is short and you have to make the best of what time you have. Of course I didn't expect it to be quite this short, and I didn't think the best would be a forty-year-old guy named George. But that's how it goes. Anyway, I'm really going to miss you and I wanted to say good-bye."

She got up and we hugged. She never once asked how I was doing or how Mom and Matt and Jonny were. She came, she told me her news, and she left.

I know I'll never see her again. I hate her for leaving and I feel sorry for her for leaving the way she is and for a change the ache in my stomach isn't from hunger. Or at least not from hunger alone.

July 22

The best day in ages.

It started with finding Horton at the kitchen door. He was scratching and yowling and demanding to be let in immediately.

We all heard him. It was just after sunrise, or what passes for sunrise these days, and we raced out of our bedrooms and ran downstairs. Matt got there first, but I was right behind him, and Mom was less than a foot away.

Matt opened the door, and Horton strolled in like the past week hadn't happened. He rubbed his head against our ankles and then walked over to his food bowl. Fortunately there was still some dry food in it, which he ate in two gulps.

Mom opened up a can of food for him and poured him some fresh water. We all watched as he ate. Then, just because he's a cat, and cats love to drive people crazy, he used the litter.

"He couldn't do that outside?" Mom asked, but she was laughing when she said it. We were all laughing. I think Horton was laughing right along with us.

He curled up on Jonny's bed and slept for the next six hours. When I came back in from my kindling hunt, he was still asleep on the bed. I petted him and scratched his ears and told him how much we loved him. I guess he agreed because I could hear him purring.

Then Mom went to the post office to pick up our mail and there were five letters from Jonny waiting for her. The last one was dated Monday. He's fine, camp is fine, he's eating okay, playing baseball is fun, etc. I don't think any of the letters was more than a paragraph long and they all said pretty much the same thing, but it didn't matter. We heard from Jonny. Mom could stop worrying.

We celebrated at supper tonight. Mom declared this National Good News Day. She brought Mrs. Nesbitt over and we feasted. Mom warmed up a can of chicken and served it with noodles and mixed vegetables. We even had dessert: canned peaches. Mrs. Nesbitt donated a jar of apple juice.

It's been getting chillier and chillier and after supper we went into the sunroom and built a fire in the woodstove. Not a big roaring fire, but enough to take the chill off. Mom lit a couple of candles and we had the oil lamp going and the wood-stove cast off a glow.

We spent the evening sipping our apple juice (I think Mom was pretending it was wine) and telling stories. Mrs. Nesbitt told us about what things were like during the Depression and World War Two and what was different now and what was the same. Mr. Nesbitt was on a submarine during the war and she told us things he had told her about what life was like there.

Horton sat on all our laps. He hopped from one lap to another until he finally settled on Matt's. I guess Matt is as close to Jonny as Horton could find.

I feel so much better about things. After a day like today, I feel like we will make it through, that if we love each other and work hard enough, we'll survive whatever might happen next.

July 25

I dreamed that Becky was working in a candy store. I saw her and she told me to come in and take as much candy as I wanted. There were counters filled with different kinds of chocolates, and after the most wonderful, agonizing indecision, I asked for a piece of rocky road fudge. I even ate a bite or two before I woke up, and I swear my mouth tasted of chocolate until I realized it was a dream.

I couldn't hear anyone moving around, so I stayed in bed and fantasized about chocolate. I thought about chocolate cake and Oreo cookies and chocolate chocolate-chip ice cream and hot-fudge sundaes and hot chocolate. Hershey bars and Nestlé Crunch and Peppermint Patties. German chocolate cake (which I don't even like). Black Forest cake. Reese's Peanut Butter Cups. Chocolate milk. Chocolate shakes. Soft vanilla ice cream cones chocolate dipped.

Now the closest I get to chocolate is in my dreams.

July 27

"Could we have a moment?" Mom asked me, which I figured meant something was happening that I wouldn't like. Mom and I have been getting along great all week and I didn't see how I could have done anything too awful without knowing it. So I guessed it was just more end-of-the-world stuff.

We went into the sunroom, which probably should be renamed the gray room.

"There's been a change in plans," Mom said. "I got a letter from your father, and it affects you."

"Is he okay?" I asked. "Is it Grandma?"

"Your father is fine," Mom said. "And Lisa is well. He doesn't know how Grandma is; he hasn't heard from her in a while. Miranda, I know you've been looking forward to your month in Springfield, but that's not going to happen this year."

"Why not?" I asked, trying to sound mature and civilized about it. What I wanted to do was scream and pout and throw a temper tantrum.

Mom sighed. "You know how things are," she said. "Anyway, Lisa is desperate to see her parents, to be with them when the baby is born. And your father is equally worried about Grandma. So they're planning to close the place in Springfield, pick up Jonny at camp, and visit for a couple of days before they take off. You'll get to see your father, but you won't have an extended visit. Sweetie, I'm really sorry."

I know she is. I know she loves me and she's worked really hard to make sure Matt and Jonny and I all see Dad and talk to him and feel like he's still our father.

But I also know that if Jonny and I were in Springfield for August, that would stretch our food supplies out a lot longer, like 60 suppers' worth, not to mention breakfasts and lunches. Sometimes I wonder if when Mom looks at me, she sees me or she sees a can of carrots.

I know I've been crazy thinking about Springfield as some kind of pre-moon heaven. Conditions there must be about the same as they are here. Dad has some sense of how things are going here, and if there was plenty of everything in Springfield, at the very least he'd tell Matt and Jonny and me to move in with him. Lisa might not like it, but I bet he'd tell Mom to come, also.

I understand how scared Lisa must be, being pregnant with the world in the condition it's in. I'd want to be near Mom if I were pregnant.

Of course if I were pregnant Mom would kill me.

Speaking of not being pregnant. I haven't seen Dan in weeks, not since I stopped going to Miller's Pond. I know it's impossible to call since the phones aren't working anymore and it's tricky to drop in for a visit, but he does know where I live, and I don't see why he's ignoring me. Even Peter shows up occasionally, if only to tell us a dozen new ways people are dying.

I wonder how far Sammi's gotten and how Dad and Lisa plan to get gas along the way. Maybe things really are better down south or west. Maybe we should be leaving, too. I don't see what good staying here is doing.

Matt came in this evening from his day of tree chopping and he showed off his biceps. It was sad, really. His biceps were impressive, but he's gotten so thin. It looked like all his muscle tone was in his upper arms. He said that actually his legs got a good workout with all the chopping as well, and except for being hungry, he's never felt stronger in his life.

I'm glad one of us is feeling strong, because it sure isn't me.

Maybe Dad'll bring us food from Springfield.

Maybe there really is a Santa Claus.

July 29

Jonny, Dad, and Lisa are due sometime tomorrow. Mom says she wrote to Jonny's camp to let them know Dad would be picking him up. She can only hope the camp got the letter.

Life was easier when you could count on the telephone working.

At supper tonight, Mom said she didn't know how long Dad and Lisa would be staying here, but she thought a week, maybe less.

"I don't want him driving all the way to Las Vegas worrying about us," she declared. "So for as long as he and Lisa are here, we're going to be eating three meals a day."

"Mom," Matt said. "Is that realistic?"

"We'll manage," Mom said. "We've managed so far."

Half of me, okay more like ¾, loves the idea of 3 meals a day. Even with what passes for meals around here, that's pretty exciting. I'm used to being hungry now, and it really isn't that bad, but still. Not being hungry sounds fabulous.

But there's that mean little part of me that's wondering if Mom's changing the rules because she doesn't know what to do about Jonny. We (except for Mom) were on 3 meals a day, at least officially, when he left.

Sometimes at night when I have trouble falling asleep, I think about the future (which only makes it harder for me to fall asleep, but I do it anyway, like probing a cavity with your tongue). Not the immediate future, which is bad enough, but the 6-months-from-now future, or the year-from-now future, if we're still alive.

Mom must be trying to work out the future as well. Maybe she thinks we'd be better off if Matt moved on, like lots of people are doing, or if I found some guy to protect me, the way Sammi did. Then whatever food she has would be for Jonny until he's old enough to take care of himself. But I know Mom loves Matt and me too much to sacrifice us. And Jonny needs food now to keep growing and stay strong.

Which is a real problem for Mom. One that I think she's decided not to deal with until after Dad and Lisa are gone.

July 30

Jonny and Dad and Lisa are here.

They got here this evening, and it's been wonderful.

Jonny looks good. He says they fed them pretty well, even though the farm was hard work and cut into baseball time.

Dad's lost a few pounds, but he's always been thin and it's not like he looks gaunt. Just thinner. Definitely older, though, than when I saw him in April. His hair is a lot grayer and his face is way more lined.

Lisa looks okay. You can tell she's pregnant, but she isn't big yet. I don't know if she should be looking more pregnant than she is. But her face is still round and her skin tone is great. My guess is Dad's seeing to it that she's eating properly, even if that means he's eating less than normal.

I could see Dad checking all of us out, just like we were checking out him and Lisa. I wish I weighed more (never thought I'd say that!), because I could see he was worried. And he has enough to worry about. I guess he had seen that Jonny looked pretty much the same and hoped Mom and Matt and I would, too.

Not that Dad said anything except how great we all looked and how wonderful it was to see us and how much fun they'd had driving Jonny home and hearing all about baseball camp.

But even though it was wonderful seeing that Dad really is okay, because you have to worry when you don't see someone for a long time, the best part was all the stuff he brought us.

He and Lisa came in a minivan and it was loaded top to bottom. Dad had labeled all the boxes, and he left at least half of them in the van (which we hid in the garage—you don't leave stuff out anymore). Even so it took us 10 or 15 minutes to unload the boxes just for us.

It really was like Christmas. Dad brought us cases of canned food: chicken noodle soup and vegetables and fruit and tuna fish. I actually lost count of how many cases, but I'd guess at least 30, with each case holding two dozen cans. Boxes of pasta and powdered milk and mashed potatoes. Jars of meat sauce and applesauce. Cases of bottled water and a half dozen jugs of distilled water.

"Where did it all come from?" Matt asked. Mom was crying too hard to talk.

"The college," Dad said. "It's not opening in the fall and the dorm kitchens had all this food. Lots of the staff had already gone, so those of us who were still there divvied up what was there. I'm taking a lot with us, for the road, and for Lisa's parents and Mom, just in case they need it."

But that wasn't all, although it certainly could have been. They gave us four blankets and batteries and a box of matches and sheets and towels and washcloths and toothpaste. Perfumed soap for me. Kerosene. Insect repellent and sunscreen (we all laughed at that). Tracksuits for all of us, which of course were baggy but still wearable. And two working power saws and a two-handled saw.

"I figured while I was here, I'd help with the firewood," Dad said.

Oh, and a battery-run lamp, which we agreed made the sunroom look bright and cheerful.

Mom calmed down enough to go into her room and pull out the boxes of stuff we'd bought for Lisa's baby. All those cheap clothes she'd been so excited to find.

So help me, Lisa burst into tears when she saw what Mom had gotten. She kept hugging Mom and me, thanking us for thinking of her and the baby. Dad started crying, too, and the only things that kept me from crying right along with them was my thinking how totally weird this all was and Jonny rolling his eyes and Matt looking so embarrassed, which made me want to laugh instead of cry.

Lisa unfolded every single piece of clothing, and we ooohed and aaahed like it was a baby shower. Well, Matt and Jonny skipped the ooohing and aaahing and unpacked some of the food instead.

I have to admit the little overalls really were cute.

We stayed up until past 10, and then Mom, who's sleeping in the sunroom so Dad and Lisa can have her bedroom, shooed us out.

I'm staying up late because I feel rich with batteries. It's fun to be extravagant. I know it won't last, that even those mountains of food Dad brought us aren't going to last forever.

But for tonight, I can make believe.

July 31

Dad says however much wood we think we're going to need, we're actually going to need a whole lot more, and the most important thing he can do while he's here is chop. He also said we can't store the wood outside, even right by the side of the house.

"It'll be gone by October," he said. "Nothing's going to be safe."

Mom thought about it, and decided the best place to store the firewood was the dining room, since we never eat in there anymore (not that we ate there all that often before).

So after breakfast this morning, which we all ate, we moved the furniture out of the dining room and into the living room. All the breakables had to be moved first, and it was tricky because we couldn't wrap things up in newspaper like we would have if there still were newspapers. But we didn't break anything. Then came the furniture: the breakfront and the sideboard and the table and chairs. Even Lisa carried chairs out, although Dad watched over her like she was one of the breakables.

"The living room looks like a used-furniture store," Jonny said.

"Like an antiques shop," Mom corrected him.

Either way, the living room is pretty much unusable now, but we haven't been spending much time in there anyway.

Once the furniture was moved, Dad and Matt went out to cut down trees.

Jonny and I carried the logs we already had into the dining room. Mom covered the dining room floor with sheets so it wouldn't get permanently scarred. After we finished bringing the firewood in, Jonny went out to help Dad and Matt. I went into the woods and collected more kindling. I think I crossed onto Mrs. Nesbitt's property, but I know she won't mind if I take some of her kindling. She really ought to move in with us. I don't know how she's going to make it through the winter otherwise.

I'm so used to skipping brunch that I did without thinking about it, which is pretty funny. The first time in ages when we don't have to worry about food, and I skipped a meal anyway.

Supper was a disappointment, just tuna fish and canned string beans. Somehow I'd imagined a feast.

Mom and Lisa actually giggled when they saw my reaction. "We're going to have a real dinner party on Tuesday," Mom said. "Just hold on."

A real dinner party. I wish we'd saved the dining room until then.

But even if the food wasn't so exciting, supper tonight was actually fun. It was great having Jonny back, and it was his first chance to tell us about what camp had been like. A lot of the kids hadn't shown, which meant more food for the ones who were there, but fewer guys to play ball with. And the farm work was hard, especially in the beginning, but after the sky had been gray for a while, the animals began feeling the difference and the chickens didn't lay as many eggs and milk production went down.

Only we didn't want to talk about that, so we switched topics real fast. Dad told jokes, and it was so funny watching Mom and Lisa's eyes roll.

But I think the best thing that happened today was that Horton finally forgave Jonny for leaving him. Horton's been ignoring Jonny since he got home. He's been sitting on Matt's lap, on my lap, on Mom's lap, once even on Dad's lap. And since Lisa doesn't want to have a thing to do with him, Horton's been flinging himself at her.

We've all been laughing about it, except maybe Lisa, and maybe Jonny, and maybe me, since I keep remembering how hysterical I was at the thought of having to tell Jonny his precious Horton was gone forever.

But tonight after supper, we sat around in the sunroom, with our lovely battery light shining, and Mom crocheting while Lisa watched, and Dad, Matt, Jonny, and me playing Monopoly, which was irresistible to Horton, who had to knock pieces around. Once he'd established the floor was his turf and he was allowing us to use it out of his great benevolence, he checked us all out, and then curled up right next to Jonny and demanded to get his head scratched.

Which Jonny did. Horton purred like a kitten, and for a glorious moment, all felt right with the world.

It turns out Mom's definition of a dinner party is us, Dad and Lisa, Mrs. Nesbitt and Peter. I think it's a little weird for Mom to invite Peter, but then again it's weird having Lisa staying here, so why not.

Mom asked me to bike over to Mrs. Nesbitt's to let her know, and then to Peter's office to invite him. Jonny's been chopping wood from the trees Dad and Matt have been cutting down, so I was the one most available.

Mrs. Nesbitt's been huffy about Dad ever since the divorce, but when I invited her, she practically glowed with excitement. "I'm not getting out very much these days," she confided, which struck both of us as so funny, we laughed until we cried.

I biked into town, inhaling dank ashy air, and went first to Peter's office, only there was a sign on his door saying he'd closed his office and could be found from now on at the hospital.

It wasn't surprising that Peter's closed his office, but it was another one of those things that make me realize how different the world's become. The past couple of days have been so great, I'd been forgetting what's really going on. Even the gray, which I thought I'd never get used to, is just part of life now.

Things are different when you know where your next meal is coming from.

I went to the hospital, which was incredibly busy. I was stopped in the lobby and asked who I wanted to see. I said Peter and it was personal.

The hospital still has electricity and it was weird seeing a building all lit up. It was like a fairyland, or at least like a theme park. HospitalLand! It made me think of the amusement park dream I had a while ago.

Of course things were different at the hospital. The gift shop was closed and so was the coffee shop. I guess it's a no-frills hospital, but even so, it seemed magical.

The security guard (armed, I noticed) paged Peter and finally I was told to go to the third floor east wing. "Elevators are only for the sick, the elderly, and the handicapped," the guard said. I took the hint and used the stairs.

Peter looked exhausted, but otherwise okay. I told him Dad and Lisa were with us, and that Jonny had gotten home safely, and that we were having a dinner party tomorrow night and Mom wanted him to come.

If Peter felt weird about it, it sure didn't show. He grinned almost as big as Mrs. Nesbitt and said he'd be delighted. "I haven't left here in almost a week," he said. "I'm due an evening out."

It's funny. I sort of dread Peter's visits. He always brings us something, even if it's just a can of spinach. But it feels like all he knows how to talk about are illness and death.

But he looked so happy at the invitation that it made me feel good to know he'd be coming tomorrow for a real meal and a nice night out, even if it was with his kind-of girlfriend, her kids, her ex-husband and his pregnant wife, and, of course, Mrs. Nesbitt.

As I was walking down the hallway to the staircase, I ran into Dan. I was so startled to see him, I gasped. He looked just as shocked.

"What are you doing here?" I asked him before he had the chance to ask me the same thing.

"My mother's here," he said. "West Nile. She's going to be okay. But it's been a rough couple of weeks."

I felt awful when I thought about how angry I'd been at him.

Dan took my arm. "There's something I want to tell you," he said. "Where are you going?"

"Just to the stairs," I said. "I mean, back home."

"I'll walk you outside," he said, and he removed his arm, which made me sad. Somehow I thought that his arm would slide down to my hand and we'd walk together like we used to. But instead we walked like two different people, each with important stuff on our minds.

We went outside to the bike rack, where my bike chain was double locked. "Miranda," Dan said, and then he stopped.

"It's okay," I said. "Just tell me."

"I'm going to be leaving soon," he said. "Next Monday probably. I would have gone sooner, but I wanted to make sure Mom was going to be okay before I did."

I thought of Sammi and Dad and Lisa and wondered how many more people would be leaving my life. "Do you know where?" I asked.

Dan shook his head. "First we thought we'd all be going," he said. "Mom and Dad and me. To California, because that's where my sister lives. Only we saw her name on one of the lists. That's how you find out. Nobody notifies you. You just see the name. Dad took it okay. He didn't go crazy or anything. But Mom was hysterical and she kept not believing it, so I said if I could figure out a way I would go."

I wanted to tell him how sorry I was. I wanted to kiss him and hold him and comfort him. Instead I just stood there and listened.

"Dad said that was a mistake and we had to keep on living, and Mom was so beside herself it didn't really matter," he continued. "You don't know what it's like. I'm glad you don't, Miranda. I'm glad this hasn't really touched you yet. I hope it never does. And then it was summer and I couldn't really figure out what I was supposed to be doing. So I swam. And I thought about loving you, but it didn't seem fair to you or me. Because Dad decided I should leave. It was his idea, and he told me first, before he told Mom, because he knew she'd get hysterical. He swapped his car for a motorcycle and he taught me how to ride it.

"I didn't want to go. I didn't want to leave my folks, or you. But Dad insisted and I would have gone weeks ago except Mom got sick. Dad and I both worried if I left while she was sick she might not make it. But now she's recovering, and I need to get going while the weather is still okay. Dad says the first frost should be in a couple of weeks."

"In August?" I said.

Dan nodded. "Dad says we'll be lucky if we go without a heavy frost before September. Has your family thought about leaving?"

"My father and stepmother are," I said. "They're staying with us for a few days and then they're going west."

"Maybe I'll see them on the road," Dan said. "Miranda, I wish things could have been different. I want you to know I liked you a lot before all this. I was getting up my nerve to invite you to the prom."

I thought about how much that invitation would have meant to me. "I would have said yes," I said. "Maybe we'll still get to go to a prom someday."

"If I'm here, it's a date," he said. "I'll try to write, but I don't know if letters are going to get through. Miranda, I'll never forget you. No matter what happens, I'll remember you and Miller's Pond. That was the only good thing that's happened."

We kissed. It's funny how much that kiss meant. I may never kiss another boy again, not the same way I kissed Dan.

"I have to get back in," Dan said. "Mom'll be wondering."

"Good luck," I said. "I hope wherever you end up, things are better."

We kissed again, but it was a quick good-bye kiss. Dan walked back into the hospital while I stood there and watched.

I know Dan thinks I'm lucky, that I've been "untouched" by everything that's happened. And I know I'm self-pitying to think otherwise. But sometimes I wonder if the big cannonball horror of knowing someone you love has died is all that much worse than the everyday attrition of life.

Except I know it is. Because Dan lost his sister and I've lost no one, not to death at least, not that I know. And Dan has the same attrition that I have, only his mother's been close to dying, also.

Honestly, I know how lucky I am.

But my heart feels like breaking because he didn't ask me to the prom in May. I could always have had that. And now I never will and I don't think I'll ever have anything nearly as wonderful to dream about.

August 2

What a feast!

Mom and Lisa baked bread (using the last of the yeast). Of course we couldn't have a regular mixed salad (It's amazing the things one misses. Who would have thought I'd be nostalgic for iceberg lettuce?), but Mom took a can of string beans and a can of kidney beans and tossed them with olive oil and vinegar and declared it a two-bean salad. Our main course was spaghetti with meat sauce. Sure, the meat came out of a jar but I don't remember the last time I had any kind of beef, except in my dreams. For a vegetable, we had mushrooms.

Peter brought two bottles of wine, one white and one red,

since he didn't know what we'd be having for dinner. Mom let Jonny and me have a glass of wine, because, hey, the world is coming to an end so why not.

Mrs. Nesbitt made dessert. She baked meringue shells from powdered egg whites and filled them with chocolate pudding.

We ate in the sunroom. We set up the metal folding table and covered it with a pretty tablecloth and carried in the dining room chairs from the living room. Mom lit candles and we had a fire going in the woodstove.

Mom used to pride herself on her cooking. She was always trying out recipes. The way the world used to be, Mom would never have served jarred meat sauce or canned mushrooms. But she was so proud and excited by dinner tonight. And we made an equal fuss over Mrs. Nesbitt's dessert.

Maybe it was the smell of fresh baked bread or maybe it was the wine, or maybe it was something as basic as having enough food, but we all had a great time. I'd wondered what it would be like having Peter and Dad together, but they handled things the way Mom and Lisa do, like they were old friends and having dinner together was the most normal thing in the world.

We all talked. We all joked. We all enjoyed ourselves.

After dinner, Matt and I cleared off the table. Nobody wanted the evening to end, so we kept sitting around the table.

I don't remember what we were talking about, but it couldn't have been anything too serious because we didn't talk seriously all evening long (even Peter kept his dead stuff to himself), when Jonny asked, "Are we all going to die?"

"Come on," Mom said. "My cooking isn't that bad."

"No, I mean it," Jonny said. "Are we going to die?"

Mom and Dad exchanged looks.

"Not in the immediate future," Matt said. "We have food and fuel. We'll be okay."

"But what happens when the food runs out?" Jonny asked.

"Excuse me," Lisa said. "I don't like to discuss this." She got up and left the room.

Dad looked torn. Finally he got up and went after her.

So we were back to us, the us I've gotten used to the past couple of months.

"Jon, you're entitled to an honest answer," Peter said. "But we don't know what's going to happen. Maybe the government will get more food to us. There have to be supplies somewhere. All we can do is go day to day and hope for the best."

"I won't survive all this, I know," Mrs. Nesbitt said. "But I'm an old woman, Jonny. You're a young boy, and a strong healthy one."

"But what if things get worse?" I asked. I still don't know why, but maybe it was because Jonny'd just been told he'd live and nobody was bothering to tell me that. "What if the volcanoes aren't the last bad thing to happen? What if the earth survives but humans don't? That could happen, couldn't it? And not a million years from now, either. That could happen now or next year or five years from now. What happens then?"

"When I was a kid, I was fascinated by dinosaurs," Peter said. "The way kids are. I read everything I could about them, learned all the Latin names, could recognize one just from a skeleton. I couldn't get over how those amazing animals could just disappear. But of course they didn't disappear. They evolved into birds. Life may not continue the way we know it today, but it will continue. Life endures. I'll always believe that."

"Insects survive everything," Matt said. "They'll survive this, too."

"Great," I said. "Cockroaches are going to evolve? Mosquitoes are going to be the size of eagles?"

"Maybe butterflies will grow," Matt said. "Picture butterflies with foot-long wingspans, Miranda. Picture the world blazing with the color of butterflies."

"My money is on the mosquitoes," Mrs. Nesbitt said, and we were so startled by her cynicism that we burst into laughter. We laughed so loud Horton woke up with a start and leaped off Jonny's lap, which made us laugh even louder.

Dad came back down then, but Lisa never did.

August 3

Dad and Matt worked all day. When Dad came in for supper, he told us he and Lisa would be leaving first thing tomorrow morning.

I knew I shouldn't be surprised, but it still hurt to hear it.

Lisa pretty much stuck to bed today. Mom went in there a couple of times to make sure she was okay but it didn't seem to make a difference.

"She's worried about her parents," Mom said to me. "And of course she's worried about the baby. She wants to be settled in as soon as possible, and the longer they wait, the harder it may be to travel."

I wonder if Lisa would be in such a hurry to go if Jonny hadn't asked about the world ending.

Dad made tuna fish sandwiches for himself and Lisa and took hers up to their room. For a long time I thought he might stay there and then leave early tomorrow morning and I wouldn't have a chance to see him again.

But after an hour or so, he joined us in the sunroom. "How about sitting on the porch with me, Miranda?" he said.

"Sure," I said, and the two of us walked out together.

"I haven't had much of a chance to talk with you," Dad said after we sat down on the porch swing. "I've spent a lot of time with Matt and Jonny, but not much with you."

"That's okay," I said. "Cutting the wood was the important thing."

"You and your brothers are the important thing," Dad said. "Miranda, I want you to know how proud of you I am."

"Proud of me?" I asked. "Why?"

"For a million reasons," Dad said. "For being smart and funny and beautiful. For finding swimming when skating didn't work out. For all the things you're doing to make your mother's life easier. For not complaining when you have so much to complain about. For being a daughter any father would be proud of. I knew asking you to be the baby's god-mother was the right thing, and the past few days I've realized just how right it is. I'm so glad I'm your father. I love you so much."

"I love you, too," I said. "And the baby is going to be all right. Everything will be; I just know it."

"I know it, too," Dad said, and we hugged. We sat there quietly for a while, because we both knew anything we said would spoil the mood.

Then Dad got up and went back to Lisa. I sat on the porch a little while longer, and thought about babies and butterflies and what the rest of my life was going to be like. When I thought every thought I possibly could think, I went back inside and listened for a while to the silence.

August 4

Dad and Lisa left at 6 this morning.

We all got up when they did and we had breakfast together. Mom found a jar of strawberry jam and used the last of the bread. We had canned peaches and powdered orange drink mix. Dad and Mom had coffee. Lisa had tea.

Dad hugged all of us and kissed us all good-bye. It took all my willpower not to cling to him. We all know we may never see each other again.

Dad promised he'd write every chance he got, and he'd make sure to let us know how Grandma is.

When they got in the car, Lisa did the driving. I think that's because Dad was crying so hard, he knew he couldn't drive.

NINE

August 6

I woke up this morning thinking, I'll never see Sammi again. I'll never see Dan again.

I am so scared I'll never see Dad again.

I don't know how I'll survive if I never see sunlight again.

August 7

I went into Matt's room before supper to see if he had any library books to return tomorrow.

Matt walked in as I was looking. "What the hell are you doing in my room?" he shouted.

I was so startled I just stood there.

"I've been chopping wood all day," he said. "I'm tired and I'm filthy and hungry and I have to be with Jonny every damn minute and I swear I could kill Dad for not staying here to take care of us."

"I'm sorry," I stammered.

"Well, so am I," he said. "Fat lot of good that does."

August 9

We're all in a funk. You would think knowing we actually have food in the house would cheer us up, but nothing seems to.

I've noticed that Mom's skipping breakfast again, and for the past couple of days I haven't seen her eat lunch, either. Matt's been chopping wood all day long, so I guess he's not eating any lunch. He hasn't been real chatty lately.

Nobody's telling me what to do, but I guess I'd better go back to brunch, also.

It scares me that Mom is eating less when we do have food in the house. It must mean she doesn't think the stuff Dad brought (and what we still had before he came) is going to last long enough.

You've got to think something in this world would get back to normal. I don't remember the last time we had electricity, not even for a few minutes in the middle of the night. Mom makes sure at least one of us goes into town every day, to see if there's any news at the post office (it's become the community bulletin board) or if there's a food giveaway, but we all come home empty handed.

It's getting colder, too. The temperature today never even hit 60.

August 11

First frost. Just a light one, but nonetheless.

"Why are we staying here?" Jonny asked me this morning. "Everybody else is moving down south."

"Everybody else isn't moving," I said, mostly because I was flustered by the question. Jonny's never been much of a talker, but since he came home from camp, he's been even quieter than usual. It's like this whole business has made him old before he ever had a chance to be a teenager.

"Half the kids at camp said their families were planning to

move," Jonny said. "And camp was less than half full. I ran into Aaron in town yesterday, and he said so many kids from school had already left they're talking about closing down some of the schools."

"Aaron isn't exactly a reliable witness," I said.

"His father is on the school board," Jonny said.

"Okay," I said. "So he is a reliable witness. But we're not going anywhere, and you'd better not talk to Mom about it."

"Do you think we should go?" Jonny asked. It felt so strange, because he sounded like I do when I ask Matt stuff like that.

"We can't leave Mrs. Nesbitt," I said. "And to get in our car and drive someplace, without knowing where we'd end up, or if there'd be food there and a place to live? Some people can do that. I don't think Mom can."

"Maybe one of us should go," Jonny said. "Matt or me. You could stay here with Mom and Mrs. Nesbitt."

"You're not old enough," I said. "So stop thinking about it. We'll be okay. We have food, we have wood, we even have some oil for the furnace. Things are bound to get better. They can't get worse."

Jonny grinned. "That's what they all say," he pointed out. "And they've all been wrong."

August 14

At supper tonight (canned chicken and mixed vegetables), Jonny said, "I know my birthday is coming but I don't expect any presents so don't worry about it."

I had totally forgotten about Jonny's birthday.

When I list all the things I miss, I need to include shopping.

Mom said that was very mature of Jonny, and she had to admit she didn't have anything for his birthday, but that didn't mean it wasn't going to be a special day. Which I guess means an extra vegetable at supper, or maybe some canned fruit salad for dessert.

Or maybe we'll drink that other bottle of wine Peter brought and all get drunk.

It kind of annoys me that Jonny's making these big grownup gestures and I'm not. I can't exactly say don't worry about my birthday, since it's in March, and I think we'll have lots of other stuff to worry about between now and then.

I'm back to two meals a day, but that's not exactly a big grown-up gesture around here.

Also, even though none of us is saying it, we're all worried because there's been no word from Dad. The mail is so weird, letters can take weeks to arrive, and probably a lot of mail doesn't make it through at all. There's no reason to think we'd have heard anything by now, but it's scary to think of him and Lisa driving into the void.

Mom listens to the radio every morning, and I'm pretty sure if the rest of the United States had evaporated or something, she'd mention it. So Dad and Lisa are probably safe wherever they are.

Still, we'd all like to hear.

August 15

I asked Mom if things were better than they had been. Had all the bad stuff, the floods and the earthquakes and the volcanoes, stopped?

She said no, that once the moon's gravitational pull had changed, things could never go back to where they'd been.

But things aren't any worse, I said.

Mom obviously didn't feel like answering that.

How much worse can they get? I asked.

Mom explained that there were volcanoes erupting in all

kinds of unexpected places like Montreal. It seems there's a volcano there that never erupted because the earth's crust had been too thick, but now that the moon's pull is so much stronger, the lava was able to break through the crust. The volcanoes cause fires and the earthquakes cause fires and the tsunamis get bigger and bigger so there's less and less coastline and people are fleeing places with volcanoes and earthquakes and floods so things are getting worse even in the stable places.

And, of course, there are epidemics.

Once Mom got started, there was no stopping her. We've already had three nights with frost, but New England and the upper Midwest have already had weeks of killing frost. All the crops there have died.

Oh, and there was an earthquake right by a nuclear power plant, and it exploded or something. I think that was California.

"Now do you see how lucky we are?" she demanded.

"I never said we weren't!" I yelled, because I hadn't. Or at least I hadn't today. All I did was ask if things were getting better, which isn't exactly the same as saying I wish we had electricity and hot chocolate and television and a prom with an actual date to look forward to.

All of which I think about every morning when I wake up and every night before I fall asleep.

"Don't use that tone with me!" Mom shouted.

"What tone?" I shouted right back. "You're the one who's using a tone! How come you can yell at me and I have to just take it?"

We really went at it. Which we haven't done in weeks, not since that whole horrible business with Horton. How ungrateful I am. How I just sit around and do nothing. How self-pitying I am.

"You're damn right I'm self-pitying," I shouted right back at her. "Why shouldn't I be? It's bad enough my life is like this and I have no idea if I'm going to survive. I'm stuck with a mother who doesn't love me. I should have gone with Dad and Lisa. He loves me even if you don't!"

"Go," Mom said. "Just get out. I don't want to look at you."

I was so stunned it took me a moment to run out of the house. But once I did, I had no idea where to go or what to do. I got on my bike and let my legs tell me where to go. And much to my surprise (although I guess not to my legs' surprise), I ended up at Megan's.

Megan's mom looked about ten years older than she had when I saw her last month. But she smiled when she saw me, like it was the most normal thing for me to be popping in for a visit. At least she didn't remind me of Becky's mom anymore.

"Megan's in her room," she said. "She'll be glad to see you."

I went up to Megan's room. For a moment I wondered what the hell I was doing there. But I knocked on her door and told her it was me and went on in.

Megan was lying on her bed reading the Bible. It was scary seeing how thin she'd gotten. But she didn't look crazy or anything and these days you take what you can get.

"Miranda!" she squealed, and for a moment she was my Megan. "I'm so happy you're here. Sit down. Tell me everything."

So I did. Every single thing. Mom and the fights and Jonny and Matt and Dad and Lisa and Horton. And how Dan was going to ask me to the prom only now he's gone. I must have talked nonstop for half an hour, with Megan interrupting me only to ask a question or make some kind of sympathetic noise.

"Boy," she said when I finally finished. "Your life is terrible."

I didn't know whether to burst into tears or laughter. Laughter won.

"I'm having one of those 'Except for that, Mrs. Lincoln, how did you like the play?' moments," I said.

"Everyone is," Megan said.

"Even you?" I asked.

Megan nodded. "I know what I need to do," she said. "And I'm doing it as best I can. But even though I know it's God's will and I can't question, I want to know Mom's soul is saved and Dad's and yours and everyone else's I've ever loved. I pray and I pray but I don't think it's making any difference. We're all in hell, Miranda. God knows what's best for us, but it's still hell."

"Does Reverend Marshall think that way?" I asked. I was pretty shocked to hear Megan talk like that.

"He says God is punishing us for our sins," she said. "We're all sinners. I know how sinful I am. I covet things, Miranda. Food. I covet food so much sometimes. And I have lustful thoughts. Don't look so shocked. I'm sixteen. You think I never had a lustful thought?"

"Who for?" I asked.

Megan laughed. "Tim Jenkins," she said. "And James Belle. And Mr. Martin."

"We all had crushes on Mr. Martin," I said. "Half the girls at Howell High are going to hell if having a crush on Mr. Martin is a sin. But Tim Jenkins? I didn't think he was your type. He's kind of wild, Megan."

"I know," she said. "I used to think if he loved me, I could get him to reform. But that wasn't how I lusted after him, if you know what I mean. I didn't lust after him just so I could save his soul."

"And Reverend Marshall thinks all the horrible stuff has happened because you lusted after Tim Jenkins?" I asked.

"That's kind of simplistic," Megan said. "My point was that I'm as much a sinner as anybody else and I've hardly had a chance to do anything. I might have lustful thoughts, but Sammi's actually done something with hers, and if God is angry with me, then He's angry at her, too, and pretty much everybody else on earth. We really have made a giant mess of things."

"Speak for yourself," I grumbled, and we both laughed.

"I can't believe the moon came crashing in because I want to go to the prom with Dan," I said. "What's the point of God making us human if He doesn't want us to act like we're human?"

"To see if we can rise above our natures," Megan said. "Eve got Adam to eat the apple, and that was the end of the Garden of Eden."

"It all comes back to food, doesn't it," I said, and we laughed again.

I can't tell you how it felt to be laughing with Megan. I know she's crazy to be flinging herself into death, when so many people are dying you practically have to take a number and wait your turn. And she looked like a talking skeleton. But she was still Megan. For the first time since all this happened, I felt like I'd gotten something back.

"I think I'll go home," I said. "I don't have anyplace else to go."

Megan nodded. "Miranda," she said, and she took one of those long pauses I've come to expect from people. "Miranda, I don't know if we're ever going to see each other again."

"Of course we will," I said. "Or are you and your mother planning on leaving?"

"I think she'll go after I die," Megan said. "But we're staying until then."

"In that case, I'm sure I'll see you again," I said.

Megan shook her head. "Don't come back," she said. "I have to show God I'm truly repentant and I can't do that if you make me think about Tim Jenkins and food and how awful things are now. I don't want to be angry at God and seeing you makes me feel that way, just a little bit. So I can't see you again. I have to sacrifice our friendship, because I don't have much left I can sacrifice to prove to God how much I love Him."

"I hate your God," I said.

"Find your own then," she said. "Go, Miranda, please. And if you ever hear from Sammi, tell her I prayed for every day, just like I pray for you."

"I will," I said. "Good-bye, Megan."

And then the worst thing happened. She'd been propped up on her bed for the whole time I'd been there. But when I got ready to go, she struggled to get off the bed, and I could see she barely had the strength to stand. She had to support herself as we hugged and kissed, and then she fell back onto the bed.

"I'm fine," she said. "Go, Miranda. I love you."

"I love you, too," I said and I ran away from her, away from her house, without even saying good-bye to her mother. I got back on my bike and rode straight home. I probably burned off three days' worth of calories, I rode so fast.

I put the bike in the garage and raced into the house. Mom was sitting in the kitchen sobbing.

"Mom!" I cried, and I flung myself into her arms.

She hugged me so hard I could barely breathe. "Oh, Miranda, Miranda," she kept crying. "I'm sorry. I'm so sorry."

"I'm sorry, too," I said and I was. Not for anything I'd said earlier. I was sorry because I make Mom worry and there's nothing I can do to keep her from worrying.

I love her so much. In a world where there's so little good, she's good. Sometimes I forget that or resent it. But she is good and she loves me and every thought she has is to protect Matt and Jonny and me.

If God's looking for sacrifices, all He has to do is look at Mom.

August 18

Jonny's birthday.

Matt took the afternoon off and we played baseball. We took turns, catching, pitching, fielding, and hitting.

Mom hit a ball so long it took Matt five minutes to find it.

Then we went to Mrs. Nesbitt's for dinner. I have to admit that was a nice change, eating around someone else's kitchen table.

She made quite the meal for us. We started with fruit salad and then we had tuna noodle casserole and peas. For dessert she'd made oatmeal raisin cookies that Jonny's always loved. I could tell Mom was concerned because all that good oatmeal was going to cookies, but she had two anyway. The rest of us pigged out—I know I ate at least four cookies, which probably guarantees me a first-class ticket to hell for gluttony.

But Mrs. Nesbitt beamed while we were eating. She must have been planning those cookies for weeks now, and she pulled off the surprise.

Jonny said he wanted to make a speech. So we cheered him on. He actually stood up, and I guess he'd been working on what he wanted to say, because it was pretty close to perfect.

He said he knew times were tough now and we didn't know if the future was going to get any better, but the important thing was we had each other and as long as we stuck together, we could make it through. He even said he loved us.

Mom was crying, but they were happy tears. I know, because I shed a few myself.

It's funny. I remember my birthday so vividly, the fights Mom and I had because I wanted a big boy/girl party and Mom wanted something simpler and easier. I yelled, "Trust!" at her and she yelled, "Temptation!" right back at me. We started fighting over it the day after her birthday and I don't think we stopped until the day before mine. Four weeks of fighting over what kind of party I could have.

In the end it was perfectly fine, boys and girls, pizza, cake, no beer, and a certain amount of unsupervised making out.

It's hard to believe I was ever that young.

I guess Jonny never will be.

TEN

August 22

Mom went to the post office today (still no word from Dad), and at supper she told us that there was a notice for a big meeting for all concerned at the high school on Friday. Announcements about the school year.

Usually by this point in August there's a shift in weather to remind you that the good times are about to end. A little chill in the evening. The days aren't quite as long. Just a sense that in a couple of weeks it's going to be schooltime again.

But lately all the days have been the same: cool and gray and dry. Sometimes it's muggy, but it never rains. And the sun doesn't shine, so it's hard to tell if the days are getting any shorter.

I hadn't been thinking about school. But now that I am, I realized I'm looking forward to it. It won't be school like I remember. It'll probably be worse than it was in June, and that was pretty bad. But at least it'll be something to do. People to see. And I may not like tests and homework (Who does?), but at least you can pretend it's for a purpose. School is all about what's going to happen: a test on Friday, report cards at the end of the month, graduation in two years.

We don't talk about the future anymore. Not even what's going to happen tomorrow. It's like we'll jinx tomorrow if we even mention it.

No matter how bad school might be, it's still good. I'll go to the meeting with Mom on Friday to see what's being planned.

August 26

I write stuff down in here and I don't read it. Things are bad enough without having to remind myself of just how bad things are.

But I just read what I wrote a couple of days ago. All about how wonderful school is and all that crap. Tests. Whoo-whoo. Report cards. Whoo-whoo. The future. Biggest whoo-whoo of them all.

Mom and Jonny and I all went to the meeting this evening. Matt liked the idea of a little quiet time, so he stayed home.

The high school auditorium was full, which I would have thought was a good sign, but it was full of parents and kids, and the kids were all ages. It could have been full with every parent and kid left in the school district, for all I know.

The president of the school board (who turned out to be Aaron's father — Jonny was pretty excited about that) and the other members of the board who were still in town and a couple of principals stood on the stage. Aaron's father did the talking.

"The unconfirmed numbers indicate that half the school-age children in the district won't be returning to school here," he said. "And a somewhat higher percentage of teachers, principals, and staff have indicated they won't be returning."

It's funny. I go into town at least twice a week, and while I've certainly noticed fewer people on the streets, I haven't given it much thought. All the stores are closed. One gas station is open on Tuesdays. But I've been assuming the reason I'm not seeing people is because there's nothing to do if they do come into town. I hadn't realized it was because people were moving out. Or too sick to get to town. Or dying.

"Our resources are limited," Aaron's father said. "The governor contacted all the heads of school boards in Pennsylvania last week and told us to expect no help from the state. Every district is on its own. We're certainly in no worse shape than other districts, but that's not saying very much."

It was quiet then. Even the little kids who were crying shushed.

"The board, what remains of the board, has been trying to figure out how to handle our circumstances," Aaron's father said. "These decisions haven't been made quickly or easily. We have children here, too."

I thought he was going to say that there wasn't going to be school, but he didn't. At least not exactly.

"We think the best use of our resources at least for the time being is to keep two schools open," he said. "The high school and Maple Hill Elementary. Parents should send their children to whichever school is closer to their home. We'll start school on August thirty-first."

"What about buses?" one parent called out.

"No bus service," Aaron's father said. "Not for the foreseeable future."

"I live six miles away from the high school," another parent said. "And Maple Hill's got to be ten miles away. I have two elementary school kids. How are they supposed to get to school?"

"You'll have to make your own arrangements," Aaron's father said. "Perhaps you could carpool with neighbors."

A lot of people laughed at that.

"What about food?" another parent yelled. "My kids are hungry. I've been counting on school lunches."

"We can't supply lunches," Aaron's father said. "Give your children a large, nourishing breakfast, and feed them again when they get home from school."

"You want to tell us where that large nourishing breakfast is going to come from?" a woman yelled.

Aaron's father ignored her and all the other people who were starting to make noise. "Naturally, the schools don't have electricity," he said. "We ask every parent to give their child a flashlight to take to school. We'll try to make the best use of natural light, but as we all know, lately that's been hard to come by. We're going to start with a nine AM to two PM school day, but we'll probably change that as the days get shorter."

"What about heat?" someone yelled.

I have to give Aaron's father credit. I'd have been running out of there by then, but he just took it.

"The schools are heated by natural gas," he said. "I spoke to a vice president of the company last week. He was unable to assure me that there'd be any natural gas going through the pipelines much past September."

"Wait a second," a man yelled. "Is that just for the schools or for everybody?"

"Everybody," Aaron's father said. "Believe me, I questioned him carefully about that. The man I spoke to said the best-case estimate right now is for the gas supplies to end by early October."

"Even for the hospital?" someone asked. "They have electricity. Will they have heat, too?"

"I can't speak for the hospital," Aaron's father said. "Perhaps they have some electrical heating system. The schools don't. We're dependent on natural gas, and we need to assume that we won't have any by October."

"So you want my kids to walk ten miles to starve and freeze at school!" a woman yelled. "Is that what you're telling us?"

Aaron's father just plowed on. "In case there's any uncertainty about this, there'll be no after-school activities," he said. "And many of the high school classes can no longer be offered. We're going to try to divide the teachers as evenly as possible between the two schools, and we think there'll be enough teachers, but no one should assume that a certain teacher or subject will be available. No more science labs or gym. We're fortunate that Mrs. Underhill, the school nurse, is still working with us. She'll divide her days between the two schools. She's requested that if a child complains of any discomfort, that child not be sent to school. We have no way of contacting parents if a child needs to be sent home. And naturally, we're concerned that an infected child could make classmates sick as well."

"How do we know Mrs. Underhill is going to stay on?" a man shouted. "Or any of the teachers? What if they decide to get the hell out of here?"

"That might happen," Aaron's father said. "None of us can be certain what next month is going to be like, or the month after that or after that. We're trying to do the best we can, and it's our opinion that even a little bit of school is better than none. If you think your children would be better off being homeschooled, simply go to one of the two schools and sign up for the grade-appropriate textbooks." He stood there for a long brave moment and then said, "Any other questions?"

It turned out there were, lots of them, but they mostly had to do with natural gas. I guess this was the first people had heard that the supply was going to run out.

It wasn't until I got home that I realized we use natural gas for the stove and the water heater.

I asked Mom about that and she said we'd cook our food and heat our water on the woodstove, so we'd be okay. She says she doesn't know what people who don't have woodstoves are going to do, but she guesses they'll move out, try down south or something. Although she heard on the radio this morning that North Carolina has already had a frost, so she isn't sure things are going to be much better anyplace else.

No one's crops are doing well because there's been no sunlight anywhere for over a month. Or rain, for that matter. So we're all going to freeze and starve no matter where we live.

She didn't exactly put it that way. Actually she said we'd be fine because we had heat and food and each other.

She also told Jonny and me to think about school. If we want to give it a try, that's fine by her. If we want to stay home, she and Matt would teach us and that would also be fine. We shouldn't worry if one of us wanted school and the other wanted to stay home. We should each decide what we wanted for ourselves, and she would go along with the decision.

I think I'm going to give school a try. It's going to be so weird, school without Megan and Sammi and Dan and most of the other kids I know. But if I'm not used to weird by now, I don't know when I will be.

August 27

Mom says we're about equidistant from Maple Hill and the high school, and she doesn't think anyone will care which school we pick. But if we do decide to go to school, she'd prefer it if Jonny and I went to the same one.

I talked to Jonny about it this afternoon. He said he wasn't that crazy about going to school, but if he did, he'd rather go to Maple Hill. I guess it's because it's familiar to him.

Of course I'd rather go to the high school. Maple Hill is a real baby school: K through 3. I don't even know if I'd fit in the desks.

Which is pretty funny because Jonny's taller than I am.

August 28

An all-bad day.

First of all, my watch stopped. I guess it needs a new battery, only it isn't like I can get a lift to the mall and have a new one put in. The clock in my bedroom is electric, so that hasn't run for weeks now.

It used to be I could look out the window and get some sense of what time it was. Oh, not if it was 2 AM rather than 3 AM, but dawn looked different than midnight.

Only with the sky gray all the time, dawn's harder to recognize. You can sort of see the sky is lighter, but there's nothing like a sunrise anymore. So now when I'm in bed, I have no idea what time it is. I don't know why that should be important to me, but it is.

When I finally did get out of bed this morning, Mom looked super grim. We had a choice of bad news.

First of all, there was a killing frost last night. Leaves are already starting to fall off the trees and now any plants that were outside have died. It feels like late October and we all know if it's like this in August, it's going to be hell this winter.

Mom had brought in what she could of the vegetables she planted last spring, but of course nothing had done very well. Tiny tomatoes. Tinier zucchini. We were glad for them, and, sautéed in olive oil, they were a real treat. But her dreams of canning pints and pints of vegetables vanished, and I know she's worried about our food supply in a couple of months' time.

We spent today digging out all the root vegetables, the potatoes and carrots and turnips she'd planted. They all looked smaller than normal, too, but at least they're something and we can eat them for a few days and save on the canned food.

Then when Mom was through telling us about killer frosts, she said the past two days when she'd turned on the radio, she hadn't gotten any signal.

We have three radios with batteries, and she tried all of them. We all tried all of them, because nobody wanted to believe her. But of course she was telling the truth. All any of us got was static.

I haven't been listening to the news for months now. I haven't wanted to know any more than I have to. But I know Mom listens every morning for a few minutes and she tells us what we need to know.

Now we won't know what we need to know.

I guess the radio stations ran out of electricity. Matt says even if the most powerful stations had their own generators, those generators have limited capacity.

But without hearing what's going on in the real world, it's easy to think there is no real world anymore, that Howell, PA, is the only place left on earth.

What if there is no more New York or Washington or LA? I can't even imagine a London or Paris or Moscow anymore.

How will we know? I don't even know what time it is anymore.

August 29

Something scary happened today, and I don't know if I should tell Mom or Matt.

I volunteered to do the bike run into town today. I wanted to get the feel of biking to the high school, in case Jonny and I end up there. Maple Hill we'd do back routes, but it makes more sense to bike through town to get to the high school.

Also I had some library books to return. I don't know what we'll do when the library closes. It's open two days a week, Monday and Friday, same as the post office.

I bundled up (temperature was 42 degrees, and the way the air tastes and how dark it is all the time makes you feel even colder), loaded the bike, and started toward town. I was pedaling downhill on Main Street when I felt like something was different. It took me a moment to figure out what it was and then I realized I could hear people laughing.

Nowadays, because nobody is driving anymore, sound really carries. Only there isn't much sound to hear. There's always a crowd at the post office and sometimes there are people at the library but that's pretty much it for town. I guess the hospital is busy and noisy, but I haven't been there in a while. So even though you could hear noise, there usually isn't any noise to hear.

I didn't like the way the laughter sounded. It was scary hearing it, and I slowed my bike down and kind of hid in a place where I could look down the couple of blocks and see what was going on.

There were five guys on Main Street. I recognized two of them: Evan Smothers, who's a year ahead of me in school, and Ryan Miller — he was on Matt's hockey team. The other guys looked to be about the same age, maybe a little older.

Ryan and one other guy were holding guns. Not that there was anyone there for them to shoot. The street was empty except for the five of them.

Two of the guys were removing the plywood off storefronts.

Then one of them would break the pane glass and go into the store.

All the stores in town are empty. There isn't much to take out of any of them, so I don't know why they even bothered. It was the plywood they seemed most interested in. They'd remove sheets of it, and put it into a pickup truck.

I stood there watching for 5 minutes or so (now that I don't have a watch, time is a guess on my part). No one tried to stop them. No one even showed up on the street. For all I know, I was the only person who saw what they were doing.

Then I remembered if I backed up a block or two I could take the back route to the police station.

I don't think I've ever been so scared in my life. The gang didn't seem to realize I was there, but if they did, they could have shot me. Maybe they wouldn't have. Maybe they just would have laughed at me. There was no way of knowing.

But it made me so mad to see them destroying the stores and stealing the plywood and having a truck that must have had gas. I thought about Sammi and the guy she went off with and how gangs like this must be all over the place, taking things from people who need them and selling the things to people who could pay. However they pay.

So I got more angry than scared and backed up the hill very quietly and biked around to the police station. I had no way of knowing if the cops could get to Main Street in time, but at least I could identify two of the guys.

Only when I got to the police station, it was closed. The doors were locked.

I banged hard against them. I didn't want to yell because I was only a couple of blocks away from where the gang had been taking down the plywood and I was scared they'd realize I was there. I peeked into the window. Of course things were dark, but I couldn't see anybody.

It isn't like Howell has a big police department. We never needed one. But I figured someone was there all the time.

I guess I was wrong.

I tried to figure out where else I could go. My first thought was the firehouse. But then I remembered that the last time Peter came over he said that people were setting fires in their houses to keep warm and then the houses caught fire, and the firehouse had been closed and they were seeing a lot of burn cases in the hospital. We should be careful with fire.

It was a very Peter speech. At least he's stopped saying we should be careful with mosquitoes because they vanished when the frosts started.

Thinking about Peter made me think about the hospital. At least there'd be people there. I biked around an extra half mile or so to avoid going straight through town and went to the hospital.

Things really were different there from the last time. There were two armed guards standing in front of the main entrance and another two by the emergency door. There must have been 20 people standing by the emergency door.

I went to the main door.

"No visitors allowed," one of the guards said. "If you have a medical emergency go to the emergency door and wait for a nurse to admit you."

"I need to talk to a police officer," I said. "I went to the police station and there was nobody there."

"We can't help you," the guard said. "We're privately hired. We have nothing to do with the police department."

"Why are you here?" I asked. "Where are the police?"

"We're here to make sure no one enters the hospital who isn't in need of medical care," the guard said. "We keep out people who want to steal food and supplies and drugs. I can't tell you where the police are."

"They've probably moved out," the second guard said. "I know a couple of them took their families and started south about a month ago. Why do you need the police? Has anyone attacked you?"

I shook my head.

"Well, it's not wise for a girl your age to be out by herself," the guard said. "I won't let my daughters or my wife go outside anymore unless I'm with them."

The other guard nodded. "Times like these, you can't be too careful," he said. "No place is safe for a woman anymore."

"Thank you," I said, although I have no idea what I was thanking them for. "I guess I'll go home now."

"Do that," the guard said. "And stay home. Tell your parents they need to be more careful with their children. One day a girl like you might go out for a bike ride and never come home."

I shivered the entire ride home. Every shadow, every unexpected noise, made me jump.

I won't go to the high school. The only way of getting there is through town. But the only way of getting to Maple Hill is by back routes. And anyone could be there as well. It isn't like I can count on Jonny to protect me.

When I got in, Mom didn't notice that the library books were the same ones I'd taken with me. She asked if there were any letters from Dad, and I lied and said there weren't.

It probably isn't a lie, but I felt bad saying it just the same. I don't know what to do.

August 30

At supper tonight, Mom asked Jonny and me what we'd decided to do.

"I don't think I'll go to school," Jonny said. "It isn't like anybody else is going to."

"You do realize you'll have to study here," Mom said. "You can't just sit around and do nothing."

"I know," Jonny said. "I'll work hard."

"What about you, Miranda?" Mom asked.

I immediately burst out sobbing.

"Oh, Miranda," Mom said in her Not Again voice.

I ran out of the kitchen and flew upstairs to my room. Even I knew I was acting like a 12-year-old.

After a few minutes, Matt knocked on my door and I told him to come in.

"You okay?" he asked.

I blew my nose and nodded.

"Anything bothering you in particular?" he asked and the question was so ridiculous I began to laugh hysterically.

I thought Matt was going to slap me, but then he started laughing right along with me. It took both of us a few minutes to calm down, but finally we did, and I told him about what had happened in town. Everything. I told him who the guys were and how the police station was closed and what the guards had said at the hospital.

"You didn't tell Mom any of this?" he asked. "Why not?"

"She has enough to worry about," I said.

Matt was silent. "The guards are probably right," he said after a little bit. "You and Mom shouldn't go out alone anymore. I guess it's safe going to Mrs. Nesbitt's, but no farther."

"So we're prisoners," I said.

"Miranda, we're all prisoners," Matt said. "You think I want to be living like this? I can't go back to Cornell. I don't know if there is a Cornell anymore, but even if there is, I can't drive there and I can't bike there and I can't hitch a ride there. I'm stuck, too. I don't like it any more than you do."

I never know what to say when Matt admits he's unhappy. So I kept quiet.

"You're right about high school," he said. "It's not a good idea to go to town anymore. I'll go to the post office and library from now on. But if you want to go to Maple Hill, I'll go with you in the morning and pick you up in the afternoon."

I thought about it. It isn't like I was all that excited about going to school. On the other hand, it makes me mad to think of being forced to stay home. I may never leave Howell again. I'd like to at least be able to leave my house.

"Okay," I said. "I'll try Maple Hill. But don't tell Mom what happened. I don't want her to worry any more than she has to."

Matt nodded.

I guess tomorrow is my first day of school. Whoo-whoo.

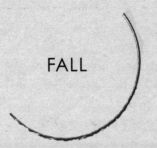

FALL

ELEVEN

August 31

When Matt and I got to school this morning, I saw kids divided into three groups waiting to get in. K through 5 were in one group (by far the biggest), 6 through 8 were in a second, and 9 through 12 in a third.

I said good-bye to Matt and went into the third group.

The high school group counted itself and there were 31 of us. I recognized a few faces, but there was no one there I remembered taking any classes with, let alone being friendly with. Our informal survey showed 16 freshman, 7 sophomores, 4 juniors, and 6 seniors.

"I guess we won't have to worry about class size," one of the seniors said, which of course turned out to be completely wrong.

Eventually they opened the doors and we went in. The younger kids were told to go to the cafeteria, the middle school kids to the gym, and the high school kids to the music room.

When we got there, there weren't enough chairs for us, and what chairs there were, were mostly meant for 7-year-olds. So we sat on the floor and waited. And waited. And waited.

Of course I have no idea how long we waited but it felt like forever.

Eventually Mrs. Sanchez walked in. I nearly wept, I was so happy to see a familiar face.

Mrs. Sanchez smiled at us. "Welcome to Maple Hill High School," she said. "I'm pleased to see each and every one of you."

A few kids laughed.

"I know how difficult this is for you," Mrs. Sanchez said. "And I'd like to tell you things are going to get better, but of course I can't be sure that's true. All I can do is be honest with you, and trust you to make whatever decisions are right for you."

"There isn't going to be high school?" one of the younger kids asked. I couldn't tell whether that made him happy or sad.

"As you can see, not many of the high school age students have come here," Mrs. Sanchez said. "We've heard that forty-four ninth through twelfth graders are at the high school now. Obviously many families have moved away, and I suppose quite a number have decided to homeschool this year."

What we all knew but nobody was saying was that quite a number just didn't care about school anymore. And I guess some may have died. We certainly didn't say that.

"So we're it?" a kid asked.

"We don't know that for sure," Mrs. Sanchez said. "Not every parent attended the meeting. We certainly hope more students will show up."

"You should have offered free food," a girl said, and we all laughed.

"How many high school teachers are here?" the senior girl asked. "How are we going to be divided up?"

Mrs. Sanchez had that uncomfortable look I've come to associate with grown-ups. "That is a problem," she said. "There are four high school teachers at the high school. There's a chemistry teacher, a Spanish teacher, a math teacher, and a biology teacher. Here we have an English teacher and me. I'm certified to teach history, although I haven't since I became principal."

"Wow," the girl said. "Put all of you together and you practically have a faculty."

Mrs. Sanchez ignored her sarcasm. "Of course it won't be school as any of us remember it, but we should be able to cobble some kind of curriculum together," she said. "But that will only work if we're all in the same building."

"So we're not going to go to school here after all?" one of the younger kids asked.

"We think it makes more sense to put all the high school students in the high school," Mrs. Sanchez said. "Of course we'll be sharing the building with other students, but we'll have our own space. The idea is to teach two groups of ninth graders, and have the sophomores, juniors, and seniors take classes together. We'll know better after we've done it for a while."

I thought of the gang, of the two guys with guns. My stomach clenched.

"What if it isn't safe to get to the high school?" I asked. "I'd have to bike through town to get there and I was told by an armed guard that girls shouldn't go anyplace without protection."

I like Mrs. Sanchez and I know it wasn't fair to put her on the spot like that. It wasn't even sensible. Not everybody has to go through town to get to the high school. And I had Matt to protect me. But I couldn't shake the image of those two guys with the guns.

"We all have to decide for ourselves what's best," Mrs. Sanchez said. "There are no good answers to this situation. You do have the option of homeschooling. All you have to do is go to the office, tell someone there what courses you'd be taking, and your textbooks will be provided. That's the best we can do, I'm afraid."

"This is crazy," one of the older boys said. "I've been working my butt off so I can go to a good college. That's all I've ever heard. Get into a good college. And now you're telling me there are maybe a half dozen teachers, and I don't even know what level they teach. Are any of them AP math? AP history? AP physics?"

"What difference does it make?" another boy asked. "It isn't like there are any colleges left."

"I know how unfair this all is," Mrs. Sanchez said. "But we'll try to do our best for you. And we'll support any decision you make. If you do decide to go to the high school, please stay here. Anyone else, please go to the office and get your textbooks. I'll leave you now so you can discuss things freely among yourselves."

Most of the kids continued sitting. A few left with Mrs. Sanchez.

"How dangerous is town?" a girl asked me.

"I don't know," I said. "I heard there were guys with guns."

"I heard there are girls missing," one of the younger girls said.

"They could have just left town," I said. "Lots of people are leaving."

"Michelle Schmidt is missing," one of the girls said.

"You're kidding," I said. Michelle was in my French class.

"She was walking home from church with her little sister and some guy grabbed her," the girl said. "That's what I heard."

Three more kids got up and left the room.

I don't know why I didn't go with them. I knew I wasn't going to go to high school. But it felt good to be sitting there with kids my own age, at least pretending to go to school. I was with people and not just Mom and Matt and Jonny and Mrs. Nesbitt.

I wanted that feeling to last as long as it could. Because high school had turned into Springfield, just another stupid dream.

"You'd think somebody would do something," one of the older girls said. "Call the police or the FBI or something."

"There aren't any more police," I said.

"I don't think there's any FBI, either," another girl said. "My mother knows someone who knows someone in Washington and he said the government isn't there anymore. The president and everybody went to Texas. Texas is supposed to have gas and electricity and plenty of food."

"Maybe we should all move to Texas," I said.

Another two or three kids got up and left.

"So this is it?" the senior boy asked. "Are we all planning to go to the high school?"

"I guess so," one of the other boys said.

"I have to ask my parents," a girl said. "They didn't want me to go to the high school, but I don't think they're going to want me at home, either."

"Does anybody else ever wonder what the point is?" a girl asked. "Why are we pretending there's a future? We all know there isn't."

"We don't know that," another girl said. "We don't know anything."

"I really think if we pray hard enough, God will protect us," one of the younger girls said.

"Tell that to Michelle Schmidt," a boy said.

Suddenly I felt like I was surrounded by death, the way I feel when Peter gives us a new thing to worry about. I really didn't need to know kids were missing.

So I got up. I felt if I was going to die anyway, I'd rather do it with my family around.

I walked to the office, where I saw a woman looking very frazzled and not at all happy.

"You going to be homeschooled?" she asked. "High school textbooks are over there."

I went to where she pointed. There were piles of textbooks scattered around in no order.

I realized I should take textbooks for Jonny as well as myself. I started with his, because it made me feel like I was doing something positive and not just running away.

Of course I didn't know exactly what Jonny was planning to study. At first I thought if I was stuck with French, he should be stuck with French. But then I decided he'd probably prefer Spanish. There are more Spanish-speaking baseball players.

I took both. I took earth science and biology textbooks and two years' worth of math textbooks and world and American history and four different English textbooks, just for Jonny. I wouldn't have taken any textbooks home for myself except I knew I'd never get away with that. So I selected a French III book and math and chemistry and an English textbook. I threw in an economics textbook and a psychology textbook because at some point I'd thought maybe I'd take them.

I piled the books up neatly and went back to the main office to see if I was supposed to sign for them or something. The frazzled-looking woman was gone.

Then I did the strangest thing. I saw boxes of school supplies, pens and pencils and blue books and notepads, all just sitting there.

I walked over making sure nobody could see me. I emptied my book bag and filled it with blue books and pads and pens and pencils.

For all I know, I'm the only person in the world keeping a journal of what's been going on. The journal books I've been given over the years are all full, and I've been using Mom's typing paper. I haven't asked her permission and I'm not sure she'd give it to me if I did. At some point, she might want to start writing again.

I can't remember the last time I was so excited. It felt like Christmas filling my book bag with supplies. Better than Christmas, though, because I knew I was stealing and that made it even more exciting. For all I know, taking a blue book is a hanging offense. Assuming there are any cops around to hang you.

I kept wanting to take more. I ended up with another half dozen blue books tucked in under my belt. My clothes are too big for me anyway, so I figured the blue books would help me keep my pants on. I filled my pocketbook with pens and pencils.

Then the frazzled woman came back in. I scurried away from the supply room and went back to my pile of textbooks.

"I'm going to need help carrying these books out," I said. "I took for my brother and me."

"What do you expect me to do about it?" the woman snapped.

Actually I didn't expect her to do anything. I carried the books in four trips to the front door and waited until Matt showed up. We divvied the books between us and biked home.

When we got there, I told Mom what had happened. She asked why I didn't want to go to the high school.

"I think I'll do better at home," I said.

If Mom disagreed, she didn't have the energy to put up a fight. "I expect you to work hard," she said. "School is school no matter where you go."

I told her I knew that, and went up to my room. Sometimes I feel like my room is the only safe place left. I wonder if Megan feels that way, if that's why she doesn't leave hers.

Life sucks.

I wish I had some fudge.

September 1

I picked up my textbooks. Either textbooks are a lot heavier than they used to be, or I don't have as much strength as I did 3 months ago.

September 2

There didn't seem to be much point starting schoolwork on a Friday.

September 5

Labor Day. I'll look over my textbooks tomorrow.

TWELVE

September 6

I told Mom I was doing history (she never would have believed me if I said math) and stayed in bed all morning.

I finally got out around 11 and went downstairs to get something to eat. It was 23 degrees outside, but there was no heat on in the house and the woodstove wasn't going. I heated a can of soup and ate that. Then I went back to bed.

That afternoon I heard Mom go up to her bedroom. She's been taking naps lately, which is something she never did. You'd think she'd be teaching Jonny or something, but I don't think she cares about his schoolwork any more than she cares about mine. Not that I blame her.

So I'm in bed, wearing my flannel pajamas and my robe and two pairs of socks and there are three blankets and a quilt over me, and I'm trying to decide which is worse, being cold or being hungry. Part of me says the worst thing is being bored and if I did some schoolwork I'd be distracted, but I tell that part of me to shut up.

I got out of bed and something made me go to the pantry. I've been choosing not to see how our supplies are holding out, because I don't want to know. I want to believe everything is just going to work out and food will magically appear. In some ways it already has, and I want to think it always will.

Mom's let us know she'd prefer us not to go to the pantry. Whatever food is available for us to eat, she leaves in the kitchen cabinets. I guess she doesn't want us to worry.

Matt and Jonny were outside, working on our wood supply. I told myself I should join them, I should go out to gather more kindling, but the truth is even the woods scare me these days.

The pantry actually kind of reassured me. It looked to me like there were lots of cans of food and boxes of pasta and rice. Horton's supplies were in one corner, and there seemed to be plenty of canned and boxed food for him and bags of kitty litter. Mom's a stockpiler under the best of circumstances, so the pantry is always pretty full. She probably had a near-full pantry back in May.

Seeing all those cans and boxes and bags of food made me mad, like why are we starving ourselves when we still have food? When the food runs out, we'll probably die, so what difference does it make if that's November or January or March? Why not eat while we can?

That's when I saw the bag of chocolate chips. I'd forgotten all about them, how I'd thrown them into my shopping cart on Crazy Shopping Day.

I went a little crazy. There was food in the pantry that Mom wasn't letting us eat and there was chocolate, real chocolate, in the house and Mom was hoarding it because it has no nutritional value and if we're only eating a little bit every day, we're better off with spinach.

And they were MY damn chocolate chips.

I ripped open the bag and I poured chocolate chips down my throat. I could hardly taste them, I was swallowing them so fast. I must have devoured a third of the bag before I could calm down enough to savor the taste. Chocolate. It tasted just the way I'd remembered only better. I couldn't stop eating them. I knew I was making myself sick. My stomach was already protesting but I kept flinging chocolate chips into my mouth. I didn't want to share the chocolate with anybody. It was mine.

"Miranda!"

It's funny. Somehow I knew I'd get caught. Maybe because I was prepared, I made the moment as dramatic as possible. I swallowed another mouthful of chips and wiped my mouth with the back of my hand. I must have seen that in a movie somewhere.

It worked. Mom started screaming. I'm not even sure she was coherent.

I was, though. I screamed right back at her. She was hoarding food. We didn't have to starve. Why wasn't she letting us eat three meals a day? What difference did any of it make? I still had the bag of chocolate chips in my hand, and I made some kind of wild gesture because the chips went flying all over the pantry floor.

Mom froze. That was a lot scarier than her hysterics.

I froze too for a moment. Then I started picking the chocolate chips off the floor. I got a handful of them and didn't know whether I should put them back in the bag. I stood there like an idiot waiting for Mom to become human again.

"Eat them," she said.

"What?"

"Eat them. You wanted them. Eat them. Pick them up and eat them. They're yours. Eat them all. I don't want to see a single chocolate chip on the floor."

I bent down and started picking up all the chocolate chips from the floor. As I gathered them, I put them in my mouth. Whenever I missed one, Mom pointed it out to me. She actually kicked a couple of them toward me and told me to eat them.

I really felt sick by then.

Finally I got all the chocolate chips off the floor. There was still about a quarter of a bag left.

"Eat them," Mom said.

"Mom, I don't think I can," I said.

"Eat them," she said.

I thought I'd throw up. But Mom terrified me. I don't know why. She wasn't even yelling at that point. It was like talking to an icicle. She stood there absolutely still and watched me eat each and every last chocolate chip. I thought, This isn't my mom. This is some strange creature that's taken over her body.

Then I thought it would serve her right if I threw up all over her, but I managed not to.

"Give me the bag," she said when I'd finally gotten the last chocolate chip down.

I did as she told me.

"Fine," she said. "That was your food for today and tomorrow. You can join us for supper on Thursday."

"Mom!" I yelled. "It was just some chocolate chips."

"I was saving them for Matt's birthday," she said. "I'm not going to tell him why he isn't getting any dessert on his birthday. I don't expect you to tell him, either. But you've eaten enough for four people, so you're going to skip your next four meals. Maybe then you'll understand how important food really is."

"I'm sorry," I said. I hadn't been thinking about Matt. His birthday is in a couple of weeks, but what are birthdays nowadays? "Can't you make him something else for his birthday?"

"What you did was wrong," Mom said. She sounded more Momlike by then, or at least the Mom I've gotten to know over the past few months. "I can't have you or your brothers walking in here and eating whatever you feel like. This food has to last all of us for as long a time as possible. Why can't you understand that? What if you stroll in here and help yourself to a can of peaches? Or string beans? I know you're hungry. I'm hungry, too. But the only chance we have is if we're very, very careful. Maybe things will get better in a couple of months. Maybe it'll take longer. If we don't look toward the future, we have nothing to live for and I won't have that."

"I'm sorry," I said. "I'll never do it again. I promise."

Mom nodded. "I know you're not a bad girl, Miranda," she said. "I know it was just thoughtlessness on your part. And punishing you doesn't make me feel any better. But I meant it about the meals. You can eat again Thursday night. It won't kill you to go without food that long. You have enough calories in you right now to last for a week. Now just go to your room. I really don't want to deal with you anymore."

My stomach aches like it used to when I'd pig out on Halloween candy. Only worse, because then I'd have a full stomach. And I wouldn't hate myself so much.

I hurt Mom. Without even knowing it, I hurt Matt. Jonny, too, since he would have loved a dessert. Mrs. Nesbitt. Maybe even Peter.

I'm a selfish, selfish pig. I don't deserve to live.

September 7

Jonny came into my room this morning.

"Mom said you ate something from the pantry yesterday," he told me. "And you're not allowed to eat again until tomorrow night. And if she ever finds out that Matt or I did that we'll get the exact same punishment."

For some reason that made me feel better. I get it into my head sometimes that Mom loves me less than Matt or Jonny.

"That's pretty much what happened," I said.

Jonny looked kind of excited. "What did you eat?" he asked.

"A can of string beans," I said.

"Is that all?" he asked. "You can't eat today because of a can of string beans?"

I told him to get the hell out of my room and stay out.

And that was the only conversation I had all day.

September 8

Mom fried two potatoes from the garden. She also heated up a can of string beans. For dessert we had a can of fruit salad.

The prodigal son would have been jealous.

September 12

Monday.

I should be doing schoolwork.

September 14

Matt's birthday. He's 19.

For supper we had artichoke hearts, almost like a salad, and then linguini with white clam sauce. Mrs. Nesbitt brought her home-baked oatmeal raisin cookies, which Matt likes but not nearly as much as he likes chocolate. Thinking about that made me feel sick all over again. I ate one cookie (I knew Mom would be furious if I didn't), but it tasted like dust.

Megan's right about my being a sinner. But she's wrong about hell. You don't have to wait until you're dead to get there.

September 16

Matt went to the post office today and brought home two letters from Dad.

The first was from a day or two after he left. It said how

wonderful it was to see all of us and how he was so proud of us and he knew we'd be okay and we'd see each other again soon.

The second letter was dated August 16. He and Lisa had made it to the Kansas border, but Kansas wasn't letting anyone in unless they could prove they had parents or children who owned property there. Which of course he and Lisa don't. The border guards didn't care that all they wanted to do was drive through Kansas to get to Colorado. He said that they had some options. There were rumors of officials who could be persuaded to look the other way.

"What does that mean?" Jonny asked.

"Bribed," Matt explained. "Give them what they want and they let you in."

The problem with that was first you had to find the official, Dad went on, and then you had to have something he wanted. In addition, there were restrictions against letting pregnant women in, and Lisa's pregnancy was showing.

They could try to get in by a back road, but there were reports of vigilantes keeping strangers out.

They could drive down to Oklahoma and get to Colorado that way. They didn't have enough gas, and rumors were things were as bad or worse in Oklahoma, but they were still thinking about it. Lisa was determined to get to her parents.

The temperature was about 40 and he and Lisa were staying at a refugee camp. No heat, no food, limited plumbing. They were only allowed one more day there and then they had to get back on the road. If they had to, they could go back to Missouri. Because of the earthquakes there, the state was pretty much unpoliced.

That was pretty much how the letter ended and it scared all of us. Dad never wants us to worry. Three years ago when he lost his job, he made it sound like it was his life's dream to be out of work. Life is full of unexpected opportunities. When a window closes a door opens.

And of course for him the door did open. He got the job in Springfield, met Lisa, and the next thing we all knew he was married with a baby on the way.

Only now Dad wasn't talking about windows and doors and unexpected opportunities.

It was the first report we've had in a long time about what's going on outside of Pennsylvania. Travel restrictions. Vigilantes. Refugee camps. And that's in the part of the country where things are supposed to be better.

"I'm sure we'll get another letter from him soon," Mom said. "Saying he and Lisa have made it to her parents and that everything is all right."

We all knew she was saying that because she had to.

If we never hear from Dad again, we'll never know what became of him. It's possible he and Lisa will make it to Colorado, and things there aren't horrible, and they'll be okay and the baby will be okay and we'll never know.

At least that's what I'm telling myself. Because I don't want to tell myself anything else.

September 17

I went out to get kindling (I've been such a baby afraid of the big bad forest) and when I came back, I found Mom sobbing at the kitchen table.

I dropped the bags of kindling and went over and hugged her. Then I asked what had happened.

"Nothing," she said. "I was thinking about that man. The one the day we bought the groceries, with the baby on the way. The baby should be born by now, and I started thinking about if it is okay, if he and his wife and their other child are okay, and I don't know. It just got to me."

"I know," I said, because I did know. Sometimes it's safer to cry about people you don't know than to think about people you really love.

THIRTEEN

Matt and Jonny were at Mrs. Nesbitt's this morning getting her house ready for winter (she refuses to move in with us) when I came in for brunch. I'd just taken out the can of peas and carrots when I heard a thud and Mom cry out.

I ran to the living room and there was Mom sprawled out on the floor.

"I tripped," she said. "I am such an idiot. I tripped."

"Are you okay?" I asked.

She shook her head. "My ankle," she said. "I don't think I can stand on it."

"Stay where you are," I said, like she had a choice. "I'll get Peter."

I ran to the garage and got my bike. I've never biked as fast as I did to the hospital.

But when I got there, they wouldn't let me in, even when I explained there'd been an accident and we were friends with Peter. All the guard would do was take my message.

I stood outside waiting. The house is so cold we all wear extra layers and jackets, but I'd been in such a hurry I hadn't thought to put on my winter coat or gloves or a scarf. I'd worked up a sweat biking so fast and that didn't help any.

The guard didn't seem to be in any hurry to take my message to Peter. First he made me write it out, and then he read it, and then he demanded I show him some ID. Which, of course, I didn't have on me. I begged him to take the message to Peter. He grinned. I could tell he was used to people begging him for things and he liked it.

I felt the same kind of nauseous sick I'd felt from the chocolate chips.

I stood there begging and crying and wanting to kill him. So help me, if I could have gotten my hands on his gun I would have shot him and anybody else who tried to keep me from getting help for Mom. The guard stood there and laughed.

Then a second guard came by and asked what was going on. I told him. He didn't laugh, but he did say there was nothing they could do to help.

"This is a hospital," he said. "The doctors don't make house calls."

The first guard thought that was a riot.

"Just let me get the message to Dr. Elliott," I said. "That's all I'm asking."

"We can't leave our post to bring someone a message," the second guard said. "Your best bet is to wait here and if someone you know comes out, maybe you can get him to take the message in."

"Please," I begged. "Please. My mother is lying alone hurt. Please don't make me wait here any longer."

"Sorry, Miss," the second guard said. "We have our rules, too."

The first guard just kept grinning.

So I stood there. People left the hospital but none of them

was willing to go back and bring Peter my note. They all pretended not to see me, like I was a beggar on the street and they didn't want to have to give me money or feel guilty because they hadn't.

I stood for as long as I could, and then I sat down on the frozen ground. The first guard walked over to me and gave me a little nudge with his shoe.

"No loitering," he said. "Stand or go."

"Sorry, Miss," the second guard said. "Rules."

I kept thinking of Mom, wondering if I should go back home. It was so hard to tell how much time had elapsed. It felt like hours, but I had no way of knowing. Jonny had probably gone back to the house. Mom had given him orders not to eat any of Mrs. Nesbitt's food, so he probably came home for lunch. At least that's what I told myself. I couldn't bear the thought of going home without Peter and I couldn't bear the thought of Mom all alone on the living room floor. I told myself Jonny had gone home and brought Mom some blankets and helped her off the floor and everything was okay.

I hadn't eaten since supper the night before and I started feeling woozy. I felt myself kind of floating onto the ground. I don't think I really lost consciousness because I remember the second guard coming over and lifting me up.

"Don't do that, Miss," he said. "It won't do you any good."

I think I thanked him. I went back to standing and willed myself not to faint, not to cry. I asked more people who came out to help me. No one paid any attention.

The first guard said something about getting something to eat. He sauntered off, like going for a meal was the most normal thing in the world to do. I thought maybe the second guard would take pity on me then and let me in, but he just stood there and refused to look at me.

Then Matt showed up. "Mom's worried sick," he said. "What's going on here?"

"Matt?" the second guard said.

"Mr. James?" Matt said.

"I didn't realize this was your sister," the guard said. "Go in. Hurry. I could get in a lot of trouble if Dwayne finds out what I did."

Matt raced into the hospital.

Dwayne came back while Matt was still in the hospital. "You still here?" he said, but I ignored him.

After a few minutes, Matt and Peter came outside. "We'll take my car," Peter said. "I have a bike rack."

It was all I could do not to burst into tears. At that moment I realized I no longer had the strength to bike home.

The drive took maybe 10 minutes. I was too exhausted and sick and worried to enjoy the sensation of being in a car.

Matt explained that Jonny had gone home around 1, and when he found Mom on the floor, she was more worried about me than about herself. She was pretty sure nothing was broken, but she couldn't stand and Jonny wasn't strong enough to help her get up. She sent Jonny to Mrs. Nesbitt's to get Matt, and he came home and carried Mom to the sunroom and started a fire. Then he biked over to the hospital to find me.

I'd been standing outside for about three hours.

Peter didn't even try to apologize for the guards. He said there had been incidents and conditions at the hospital were bad enough without people breaking in. I know he might be right, but I didn't want to hear it. And even though it was crazy of me, it made me mad that Matt could get in because the guard knew him, and I couldn't because the guard didn't know me. I told myself to be grateful the guard knew Matt, but the last thing I was feeling was gratitude.

Peter pulled into the driveway and went right into the sun-room. Matt and I unloaded our bikes from the rack.

"You okay?" Matt asked me. "Did the guards give you a hard time?"

"I'm fine," I said.

But the truth was I longed to take a hot shower and wash the whole experience away. All I could think of was how much pleasure Dwayne had gotten out of my misery. I still would have killed him if I had the chance.

But I didn't tell Matt any of that. He didn't need to hear it. We went inside and found Peter examining Mom's ankle.

"A bad sprain," he said. "But nothing's broken. She won't need a cast."

He pulled an Ace bandage out of his doctor's bag and wrapped up her ankle tightly. "Don't even think about stairs for a week," he said. "Stay in here. Matt, you and I will bring your mother's mattress down here. Laura, you can get up to eat and go to the bathroom, but nothing more. Keep your foot propped up when you're sitting. Put as little weight on it as possible. I don't suppose you have a cane?"

"There's one in the attic," Mom said.

"I'll get it," Jonny said. He grabbed a flashlight and flew up the stairs.

While he was gone, Peter pulled out some surgical masks and handed them to us. "Air quality," he said almost apologetically. "We're seeing a lot of asthma cases these days. You might want to wear one of these whenever you do anything outside."

"Thank you," Mom said. "Matt, wear one when you chop wood. Do you understand?"

"Yes, Mom," Matt said. He quickly put one on. "Mom always wanted me to be a doctor," he said, and we all pretended to laugh.

Jonny came down with the cane. Peter inspected it and declared it acceptable. Mom wasn't to walk anywhere without it for the next 10 days. She wasn't even to think about leaving the house for 2 weeks. He'd try to get over once or twice to check on her in the meantime.

Then he and Matt went upstairs and lugged Mom's mattress down. I brought her sheets and blankets and pillows. Jonny shoved the furniture around so there'd be room for the mattress. With the woodstove giving off heat and light, the sunroom looked almost cheerful.

"I feel like such a fool," Mom said. "I'm putting everyone to so much bother. And Peter. I know how busy you are. I can't thank you enough for coming over."

"Oh, Laura," Peter said, and he took her hand. I realized if things had been normal, if none of this insanity had happened, he and Mom would have been going out for the past 4 months, regular, normal going-out. And Mom would have been happy.

Mom asked Peter if he could stay for supper, but Peter said he had to go back to the hospital. They were all on crazy schedules, 16 hours on, 8 hours off, because the staff was no longer at full strength. He really couldn't take any more time off.

"But I'll be back," he said. "I promise. And I want you to promise you'll stay off that foot and let the ankle heal on its own. There's no reason for you to limp any longer than necessary."

"I promise," Mom said.

Peter bent down and kissed her. Then he left and we could hear the sound of his car. Such a funny sound.

"I'm so sorry," Mom said to us. "I know this is going to be a terrible bother for all of you."

"Don't worry about it," Matt said. "We just want you to follow Peter's instructions and get better."

"I'll take care of suppers," I said. "Don't worry about that, Mom."

"I'm not worrying about anything," Mom said. "I know you'll all do whatever has to be done. I just wish I could help you."

I know I'm going to have to be strong for the next couple of weeks. No more whining. No more picking fights. I'll have to do whatever Mom asks me and not protest and not complain. I know I can do it.

But for that one moment I felt so weak, so helpless. I felt nothing but fear and despair and the most awful need to be anyplace else. I told myself it was hunger, but I knew that was a lie.

As long as Mom was all right, I could fool myself into thinking we'd all be all right. But even though I knew Mom could have fallen anytime and sprained her ankle anytime, this felt as though it was the beginning of the end.

So while Matt and Jonny were busying themselves getting Mom set up, I slipped upstairs to my bedroom and wrote all this down. All the things I could never tell any of them.

I thought of Dad and how I may never see him again. I thought of Lisa and wondered if she and the baby would be all right, if I'd ever get to know if I had a new sister or brother. I thought of Grandma and wondered if she was still alive.

I cried and I pounded my pillow, pretending it was Dwayne, and when I calmed down I wrote.

And now I'll go downstairs and make supper and pretend everything is just fine.

September 19

Mom was looking lonely in the sunroom this afternoon, so I decided to keep her company. She was sitting on the couch with her foot propped up, and I sat down next to her.

"I want to thank you," she said. "And tell you how proud I am of you."

"Of me?" I said.

"The way you raced out of here when I fell," she said. "I know you've been reluctant to go anyplace on your own, but you didn't hesitate for a moment. And standing there all that time. I'm very grateful and I'm very proud."

"I wish I could have done more," I said. "I felt awful leaving you that way. It never occurred to me they wouldn't let me in."

Mom reached over and began stroking my hair. "You are so beautiful," she said. "The past few months have been so awful and you've been very brave. I've been at fault not telling you that. I'm so proud to be your mother."

I didn't know what to say. I thought about all the fights I'd provoked over the past few months.

"We'll get through," Mom said. "We have each other and we'll survive."

"I know we will," I said.

Mom sighed. "You know what I miss most?" she asked, and then she laughed. "At least today. It changes every day."

"No, what?" I asked.

"Clean hair," she said. "Daily showers and clean hair. My hair is such a mess. I really hate it."

"It's okay," I said. "It's no worse than mine."

"Let's cut it," she said. "Miranda, get a pair of scissors and cut my hair. Come on, do it right now."

"You sure?" I asked.

"Positive," she said. "Hurry."

I found a pair of scissors and brought it back to her. "I've never cut hair before," I said.

"What do I have to lose?" she asked. "It's not like I'm going to any fancy parties. Cut it real short. It'll be easier to keep clean that way."

I didn't have the slightest idea what I was doing, but Mom cheered me on and reminded me to cut from the top as well as the sides and back.

When I finished, Mom looked like a plucked chicken. No, worse. She looked like a plucked chicken that hadn't eaten in months. The cut emphasized her cheekbones and you could see how much weight she'd lost.

"Do me a favor," I said. "Don't look in a mirror."

"That bad?" she asked. "Oh, well. It'll grow out. That's the great thing about hair. Do you want me to cut yours?"

"No," I said. "I've been thinking of letting my hair grow real long."

"Cornrows," she said. "Those little braids. They don't need shampooing too often. Do you want me to braid your hair like that?"

"I don't think so," I said, picturing me with cornrows and Mom with her new punk hairstyle.

Mom stared at me and then she burst out laughing. It was real laughter, too, and before I knew it I was laughing as hard as I had in months.

I think I'd forgotten how much I love Mom. It was good to be reminded.

September 20

I went to visit Mrs. Nesbitt this afternoon. Mom used to go almost every day, but she can't now, so I volunteered.

She had her furnace going and her house was actually warm.

"I don't know how long the oil is going to last," she said.

"But then again, I don't know how long I'm going to last. I figure as long as I don't know which of us is going to go first, I might as well stay warm."

"You can move in with us," I said. "Mom really wants you to."

"I know she does," Mrs. Nesbitt said. "And it's selfish of me to stay here. But I was born in this house and I would prefer to die in it."

"Maybe you won't die," I said. "Mom says we'll make it through."

"I believe you will," Mrs. Nesbitt said. "You're young and strong and healthy. But I'm an old woman. I've lived a lot longer than I ever thought, and now it's my time for dying."

Mrs. Nesbitt hasn't heard from her son and his family since the first tsunamis. There's no way of knowing if any of them are still alive. I guess Mrs. Nesbitt feels she would have heard from one of them by now if they still were.

We talked about all kinds of stuff. Mrs. Nesbitt always has stories about Mom when she was growing up. She used to babysit Mom's mother and I think I like those stories the best. I know Mom loves to hear them, since she was so young when her parents died.

I'll go back tomorrow. There's so little I can do, but visiting with her and making sure she's okay and then reassuring Mom about it is something.

One good thing about Mom's sprained ankle. She's forgotten that I should be doing schoolwork. I don't think she's been pestering Jonny, either.

What a strange, strange life this is. I wonder what it'll be like when things get back to normal, if they ever do. Food and showers and sunlight and school. Dates.

Okay. I never had dates. But if I'm going to dream, I might as well dream big!

September 23

Peter managed to drop by. He checked Mom's ankle and agreed it was definitely getting better, but she still shouldn't put any weight on it.

We left Mom and Peter alone for a while. He probably told her about diseases and accidents and plagues.

He's entitled. I noticed how much older he's looking. I should have noticed it last week, but I was so crazed by the time I saw him, I didn't really see anything. It's not just that he's thinner. There's a sadness in his eyes. He seems weary.

I mentioned that to Matt when we had a chance to be by ourselves.

"Well, he's dealing with illness all the time," Matt pointed out. "Most of his patients are probably dying. And he's alone. He's divorced and he had two daughters, but they both died."

"I didn't know that," I said.

"Mom told me," he said.

I guess all the worrying Peter would do for his own family, he's doing for us.

How am I going to feel when people I love start dying?

September 26

Matt and I went to the library today. It's only open on Mondays now. They don't know how much longer they'll stay open.

As we were leaving, I saw Michelle Schmidt. I guess she hasn't vanished after all.

I wonder how much I hear is true and how much is just made up. Maybe everything is fine with the world and we just don't know it.

The joke would sure be on us if that's the case.

September 29

It's funny how much I'm enjoying things these days. I think we all are. We're so used to worrying we hardly even notice it.

Actually, life is pretty cozy. We have the woodstove going full-time because of Mom, so there's always a warm spot in the house. We spend our daytimes doing whatever needs to be done. Matt and Jonny are still bringing in firewood ("Better too much than too little" is Matt's mantra and I can't argue with him). I'm doing whatever housework there is to be done (the worst is the clothes washing, which has to be done with as little water as possible, all by hand, and very yucky) and visiting Mrs. Nesbitt every afternoon. I go after lunchtime so she won't try to feed me (although she does, but I always say no, thanks) and I stay for an hour or so. A lot of times we hardly even talk; we just sit at the table and stare out the kitchen window together. Mom says she and Mrs. Nesbitt do the same thing so I shouldn't worry.

Mom now trusts me to go to the pantry and I get to select our suppers. A can of this and a can of that. There's less food there than there was when I had my great chocolate chip feast, but as long as we don't eat too much, we'll be okay for a while.

Ever since I saw Michelle Schmidt and realized she had never disappeared the way the kids at school thought she had, I feel like things really are better than we've been letting ourselves believe. So what if I'm deluding myself? Better to delude myself that things are okay than to delude myself that things are doomed. At least this way I smile.

After supper when we're all feeling good because we're not too hungry, we've taken to playing poker. I like 7-card stud the best. Jonny and Matt like Texas Hold 'Em, and Mom prefers 5-card draw. So dealer decides.

Matt went into the attic and dug out a box of poker chips. Jonny is the best player, and as of tonight I owe him $328,000 and a utility infielder (we're high-stakes gamblers).

I think even Peter is feeling better about things. He came over this evening, proclaimed Mom able to walk around again as long as she is careful and avoids stairs, and he didn't mention a single new way people are dying. We convinced him to stay for supper and I put out an extra can of tuna. This is the first time I can remember when Peter came over and didn't bring us anything, so either he's run out of supplies or he's now officially family. I hope it's family. Because I owe him $33,000 from a single hand of Omaha Hi.

Horton is on a diet (not of his choosing). Maybe it's the warmth of the woodstove, or maybe he just hopes we'll feed him, but he's very affectionate lately. He keeps Mom company all day and in the evenings he sits on the most available lap or else by the woodstove.

Matt brought down an old portable typewriter because Mom is thinking about writing down some of the stories she knows about her great-grandmother and her family. What life was like in this house before there was electricity and indoor plumbing.

I like thinking about that. It makes me feel connected, like I'm a part of some bigger thing, like family is more important than electricity. The sunroom was just a porch back then, but

I can imagine my great-great-grandmother's family sitting around in the parlor, with the oil lamps glowing, and the men tired out from chopping wood and the women tired out from doing the laundry.

Actually, Mom says the family had two servants and one of them did all the laundry, but the women were probably tired out anyway.

I wonder if they imagined the future. I bet they never could have guessed what things would be like today.

FOURTEEN

October 2

I turned on the stove to boil water and no flame came out. I ran the hot water in the kitchen and the water stayed cold.

I guess Aaron's father knew what he was talking about when he said the natural gas would be turned off by October.

Mom says it's okay. We can heat our food and boil our water on the woodstove. She's refusing to let us use up the last of our oil for the furnace, but at least we're not dependent on gas for our heat. A lot of families are worse off than we are.

We've all been taking just one shower a week for a while now, but with no hot water I guess no more showers at all. And no hot water is going to make washing clothes that much harder.

I know it shouldn't bother me but it does. I can see Mom's upset, too, even though she's acting like she isn't. I guess it's because things have been kind of level for a while, and now they're worse again. Not big bad worse (at least not for us or Mrs. Nesbitt, who also has a woodstove and oil heat), but worse anyway.

We played poker tonight, but none of us were really into it. Which is probably why for the first time I was the big winner.

Matt, Jonny, and I all went to the library. Mom's ankle still isn't strong enough for her to bike.

The library was open, but Mrs. Hotchkiss was the only person working there. She said that this was the last day the library would be open; they just couldn't keep it open with no heat. There was no limit on how many books we could take. Mrs. Hotchkiss told us to take as many as we possibly could. If the library reopens in the spring, we can always bring them back.

So we loaded up. We had our backpacks and the bikes all have baskets, so we managed a dozen or more books each. We looked for ourselves and for Mom, too. Since we've been playing poker, we've been reading less, and of course there are plenty of books in the house (including lots of old ones in the attic). But it's still upsetting to think the library won't be there.

Mrs. Hotchkiss said she and her husband were going to Georgia. Her husband has a sister there. Jonny asked her how they were going to get there, and she said walk if they had to.

"The temperature's been below freezing for the past two weeks," she said. "If it's this bad in October, none of us will make it through the winter."

"I think we should go, too," Jonny said as we were getting on our bikes to go home. "We should go to Kansas and see if we can find Dad."

"We don't know where Dad is," Matt said. "He could be in Colorado. He could be back in Springfield."

"No," I said. "He would have stopped off here if they came back east."

"We still don't know where he is," Matt said. "Jon, Mom and I have talked about it a lot, about what we should do. There's no point in going. We have shelter. We have firewood, so we won't freeze. It's not like we're going to be able to find food anyplace else."

"We don't know that," Jonny said. "Maybe there's food in Kansas."

"Dad couldn't even get into Kansas," I said.

"Missouri, then," Jonny said. "Or Oklahoma. I don't see why we're staying here just to die."

"We're not going to die," Matt said.

"You don't know that," Jonny said. "What if the moon crashes in?"

"Then it won't matter where we are, we'll die anyway," Matt said. "Our chances of survival are best here. This isn't just happening to Pennsylvania, Jon. It's all over the world. We have a roof over our heads. We have heat. We have water. We have food. How long do you think we'd survive biking our way across country?"

"Dad got gas," Jonny said. "We could get gas."

"Dad bought black market gas," Matt said. "He had connections. And at that, his gas ran out."

"Black market?" I said.

Matt looked at me like I was an infant. "How do you think he got all that food?" he said. "You didn't really think it was just waiting to be taken, did you?"

"Does Mom know?" I asked.

Matt shrugged. "Dad and I talked about it while we were cutting down trees," he said. "I don't know what he talked to Mom about. He probably didn't tell her. Mom's happier not knowing things. You know that."

I do, but I didn't realize Matt knew it also.

"So we're stuck here?" Jonny asked.

"I'm afraid so," Matt said. "But things will get better. Maybe not right away but we'll make it."

That's Mom's answer for everything. Hold on and wait until things get better. It didn't sound any more believable coming from Matt.

But I know he's right about our not going. It's like the world before Columbus. People leave and you never hear from them again. They might as well have fallen off the face of the earth.

We have each other. As long as we have each other, we'll be all right.

October 6

Mom's writing again. Or at least she's typing.

"I'd forgotten how hard it is," she said. "The letter A in particular. My left pinky isn't really up to it on a manual typewriter."

It's been so long since it rained I don't remember what it sounds like. It's getting harder to remember sunlight, also. The days are getting shorter, but it doesn't matter.

The air's getting worse, too. The longer you stay out the dirtier you are when you come in. Mom's worried about what all the ash is doing to Matt's and Jonny's lungs, even with the face masks, but they still keep chopping firewood for as long as they can every day.

Mom and I scrub the clothes as hard as we can, but even though we're hanging them indoors, they're still gray. We wash ourselves every night, and the washcloths are filthy and we can never get them really clean. The towels aren't much better.

Matt says if the air is getting dirtier it probably means more volcanoes are erupting, but we have no way of knowing. The post office is still open, but less and less mail is coming and it's all weeks or months old when it finally arrives. Anything could have happened in September and we'd have no way of knowing.

One good thing about the extra ash. It's completely blocked out the moon. Before, especially on windy nights, you could make it out. But now it's totally gone. I'm glad I don't have to see it anymore. I can pretend it's not there and if it isn't, maybe things will get back to normal.

Okay. I know that's crazy. But I'm still glad I don't have to see the moon anymore.

October 10

Columbus Day.

In honor of the holiday, I asked Mom to cut my hair really short, the way I'd cut hers. Her hair hasn't grown out yet but I've gotten used to it, and I hate washing my hair now. It never gets clean and it's so lank and disgusting. I figured short would be better.

So Mom chopped my hair off. When she finished, I looked at myself in the mirror. It was all I could do to keep from crying.

But I didn't. And Mom kissed me and hugged me and told me I was beautiful with short hair.

"It's a good thing the bars are closed," she said. "You could pass for twenty-one."

I really do love her. At least we're not fighting anymore.

Matt and Jonny came in and I could see how shocked they were. But Matt said I looked great and asked Mom to cut his hair as well. Mom ended up cutting all our hair.

We threw the hair in the woodstove and watched it sizzle.

October 13

It was 2 degrees below zero this morning.

Mom and Matt had a big fight. Matt said we had to start using whatever oil we had. Mom said we should wait until November at least. Matt won the argument. He said our pipes were going to freeze and we might as well use up the well water while we still could.

He and Jonny moved Mom's mattress out of the sunroom and into the kitchen. Then they went upstairs and got all the mattresses and one by one carried them downstairs.

I went upstairs, closed off the heat registers, and closed the doors.

"We can go back to using our bedrooms in the spring," Mom said. "This isn't forever."

For the time being, Mom and I are sleeping in the kitchen and Matt and Jonny are in the living room. Mom and I are actually better off, since the kitchen gets a little bit of warmth from the woodstove in the sunroom. We also have more space. Matt, Jonny, and I piled the dining room furniture and living room furniture together so there's room for the two mattresses in there, but they barely have space to move around. When the fuel oil runs out, we'll all move into the sunroom.

I keep telling myself it isn't like I've been comfortable in my bedroom. It's freezing in there, so cold sometimes I lie in bed shivering, unable to fall asleep. But it's been the only space I could call my own. I have my candles, my flashlight, and no one tells me not to use them. I can write or read or just pretend I'm someplace else.

I guess it's better to be warm.

I want to weep. And I feel like I have no place left where I can.

October 14

Matt still goes to the post office every Friday to find out if there's any news. He came in while Mom and I were washing clothes at the kitchen sink. He gestured to me and I followed him into the pantry.

"I have bad news," he said. "Megan's on the dead list."

That's what they have now, the dead list. If you find out someone is dead, you write their name on the list. Just the local people, of course, since there's no way of knowing if anybody in the rest of the world has died.

I guess I didn't say anything because Matt kept talking. "Her mother is on the list, too."

"What?" I said. "Why?"

"I'm just telling you what I know," he said. "They were both on the list. I didn't see their names last week, but that doesn't mean anything. You know how the list is."

"Megan's dead," I said. It's funny how weird that sounded. Megan's dead. The world is dying. Megan is dead.

"I asked at the post office, but there were only a couple of guys there and neither one knew anything," Matt said. "Lots of people are dying. It's getting harder to keep track."

"Megan wanted to die," I said. "But I don't think her mother did."

"People aren't necessarily choosing anymore," Matt said. "Anyway, I thought you should know."

I wonder if I cry whether my tears would be gray.

October 15

I got up this morning and realized Reverend Marshall would know what happened to Megan and her mother. I told Mom where I was going and she asked if I wanted Matt to come along. I said no, I'd be fine. Actually I didn't care if I was going to be fine or not. What difference does it make?

It took me a half hour to get to Reverend Marshall's church, and by the time I got there, I was wheezing. I don't know how Matt and Jon are managing outdoors. I felt like ice and I was glad to find the church had heat.

There were a few people praying in the church. I haven't seen anyone other than family since the library closed. It felt strange seeing people, hardly more than skeletons, really. I had to remind myself how to speak, how to ask questions, how to say thank you. But I managed and someone told me Reverend Marshall was in his office. I knocked on his office door and went in.

"I'm here about Megan Wayne," I said. "I was her best friend."

"Her best friend on earth," Reverend Marshall said.

I didn't have the energy to argue theology with him so I just nodded. "She's dead," I said, like he wouldn't know it. "And her mother, too. I thought maybe you could tell me what happened."

"God took them," he said. "I pray for their souls."

"Megan's soul is just fine," I said. "Her mother's, too. How exactly did God take them?"

Reverend Marshall looked at me like I was a mosquito he wanted to swat. "It's not our place to question God's decisions," he said.

"I'm not questioning anyone except you," I said. "What happened?"

"God chose the moment of Megan's death," he said. "What the earthly cause was we'll never know. Her mother summoned me one morning and we prayed over Megan's remains. She asked me to bury Megan in their backyard, but the ground was frozen and I knew I couldn't do it alone. I went back to the church to ask for help and when we returned to the house we found Mrs. Wayne had hung herself."

"Oh God," I said.

"I suppose she felt we'd bury the two of them together that way," Reverend Marshall said. "But of course we couldn't touch her impure remains. We took Megan to the churchyard, and buried her here, if you want to say good-bye to her."

I'd said good-bye to Megan a long time ago. And I couldn't bear to be in that man's company a moment longer. I said no and turned around to leave. But as soon as I did I realized there was something that was bothering me. I turned back and stared at him.

Reverend Marshall had never been overweight and he wasn't now. But he hadn't lost any weight.

"You're eating," I said. "Your congregation is starving and you're eating. Do you make them give you their food?"

"My congregation chooses to bring me food," he said. "I merely accept what they offer."

"You're despicable," I said, and I don't know which one of us was more surprised that I even knew the word. "I don't believe in hell so I'm not going to say I hope you end up there. I hope you're the last person living on earth. I hope the whole world dies before you and you're left here healthy and well fed and alone. Then you'll know what Mrs. Wayne felt. Then you'll know what impure really is."

"I'll pray for you," he said. "As Megan would have wished me to."

"Don't bother," I said. "I don't want any favors from your God."

I guess people heard me because a couple of men came in and escorted me out. I didn't put up any resistance. Frankly, I couldn't get out of there fast enough.

I biked over to Megan's house. The front door was wide open. The house was so cold I could see my breath.

I was scared I'd find Megan's mom but her body was gone. The house had been ransacked, but that's to be expected. Whenever a house is deserted, people come in and take everything that can possibly be used.

I went up to Megan's bedroom. Her bed was still there so I sat down and thought about what she'd been like when we first became friends. I remembered fights with her and going to the movies and that stupid science project we worked on together in 7th grade. I thought about Becky—how Megan, Sammi, and I would visit her and how we'd laugh, even though Becky was so ill and we were so frightened. I sat on Megan's bed until I couldn't bear it anymore.

When I got home, I went straight to the pantry and closed the door. I guess Mom wasn't worried I'd eat anything because she left me alone in there until she needed to get food out for supper.

It made me sick to eat. But I ate anyway. Starvation was Megan's way out, not mine.

I'll live. We'll live. I will never make Mom face what Mrs. Wayne faced. My existence is the only gift I have left to give her, but it will have to do.

October 18

I dreamed about Megan last night.

I was walking into homeroom and I realized it was my 7th-grade homeroom. And there was Megan and she was talking with Becky.

I got very confused. "Is this Heaven?" I asked. I hated 7th grade and the very idea that it was Heaven was upsetting.

Megan laughed. "This is hell," she said. "Can't you tell them apart yet?"

I woke up then. It's funny sharing the kitchen with Mom. I feel like she knows what I'm dreaming, like even my thoughts aren't private anymore.

But she slept through my dream. I guess she has dreams of her own.

October 21

Matt came home from the post office today and said unless they had volunteers they were going to have to close. So he's volunteered to work there on Fridays.

"Why bother?" Jon asked. "We're not going to hear from Dad."

"We don't know that," Mom said. "I think working at the post office is a good idea. We all should be doing more than we are. It isn't good for us to sit around and do nothing. We need to be out, doing things for other people. We need to have a reason to be alive."

I rolled my eyes. I bring in kindling and visit Mrs. Nesbitt and wash our clothes and clean Horton's litter. I mean, that's my life. Sitting in the kitchen with Mrs. Nesbitt with neither of us saying a word is the high point of my day.

"All right," Mom said. "You don't have to say anything."

"Who, me?" Jon and I said simultaneously, which really was pretty funny.

"This isn't fun for any of us," Mom said. "Matt, I'm glad you'll be working at the post office. Jonny, Miranda, do whatever you want. I'm past caring."

There's a part of me that almost wishes she meant it. But most of me is scared that maybe she really did mean it.

October 24

The temperature was 17 this morning, which practically constitutes a heat wave nowadays. If you looked up at the sky hard enough you could almost make out the sun.

"Indian summer," Mom said when the thermometer reached 29. "No, I mean it. I bet if the ash weren't so thick this would be Indian summer."

We keep the thermostat at 50 degrees, so it's always cold. I figured I might never see 29 degrees again.

"I'm going skating," I said. "The pond's been frozen for a month by now. Mom, are your skates still in your closet?"

"I suppose so," she said. "Be careful, Miranda. Don't take any chances with the ice breaking."

"I won't," I said, but I was so excited I hardly cared what she said. Mom's shoe size and mine are close enough that I knew her skates would fit me fairly well. I went upstairs and found her skates in no time. I'd forgotten how beautiful ice skates are.

I haven't been to Miller's Pond since I stopped swimming. I spend a lot of time in the woods around our house, but this was the longest I'd walked in them in months. The path was covered with dead leaves, but I didn't have any trouble following it.

The strangest thing about the walk was how quiet things were. I'm really used to quiet by now. No TV, no computer, no cars, no noise. But this was the first time I noticed how the woods were quiet, too. No birds. No insects. No squirrels rustling around. No animals scurrying away at the sound of me crunching the leaves. I guess all the animals have left town. I hope Kansas lets them in.

I could see from a distance that there was someone already skating. I had a rush of excitement. For one totally ridiculous moment I thought it was Dan.

But as I got closer, I could see, whoever he was, he actually knew how to skate. I stood still for a few moments, and watched as the skater landed double axels.

For a second I thought I should just go away. But I was too excited. I practically ran the rest of the way to the pond to see if I could be right, if it really could be Brandon Erlich.

It was. "You're alive," I said as he bowed to my applause.

"I may be, but my quad sure isn't," he said.

"We thought you were dead," I said. "I mean your fans did. You were training in California. We didn't hear anything about you."

"I was touring," he said. "We were safe and sound in Indianapolis. It took a long time to get word to my parents and it took even longer to get back here. But I've been here for a few months now. Do you skate, too?"

I looked down self-consciously at Mom's skates. "I used to," I said. "I used to take lessons with Mrs. Daley."

"Really?" he said. "She was my first coach."

"I know," I said. "Sometimes she'd tell us how you were doing. We all rooted so hard for you. I bet you'd have medaled at the Olympics."

Brandon grinned. "My mom still thinks that's going to happen," he said. "Like suddenly everything's going to be okay by February. Were you any good? Did you compete?"

"A little bit," I said. "On the intermediate level. I had most of my doubles and I was working on a triple toe when I broke my ankle. Not even from skating. Just one of those dumb accidents. I took up swimming after that."

"Swimming," Brandon said. "That's a lost art form. Put on your skates. Let's see how you do."

"They're my mother's," I said. "I haven't been on the ice in a long time." It felt funny lacing up the skates while Brandon was watching.

"Don't try any jumps," he said. "Just do some stroking. Let me see how your edges are."

So I skated and he skated alongside me. I was wobbly at first, but then I got my feet under me and it felt almost natural being there.

"Not bad," he said. "I bet Mrs. Daley was sorry when you stopped skating."

I'd forgotten how glorious it felt to be skating, to glide across the ice. I never wanted to stop. But in just a few minutes it was hard to breathe.

"The air," Brandon said. "I've been at it for a couple of weeks now and I've been building up resistance. Don't push too hard today. Give your lungs a chance to adjust."

"Are your parents okay?" I asked after I caught my breath. "My mother knows your mother. You have enough food?"

"Does anybody?" Brandon asked. "We haven't starved yet, so I guess we're okay." He stroked around the pond to build up speed and did a camel spin. Brandon used to have the most beautiful camel in the world. "Come on," he said. "How was your spiral? Up to Mrs. Daley's standards?"

"No," I admitted. "My free leg was never high enough for her."

"Then it's a good thing she isn't watching," he said. "Show me your spiral."

It was an embarrassment. "Don't ask for my layback," I said. "I'm totally out of shape."

"Well, you're certainly not overweight," he said. "If you practice enough, you should be fine. We'll hold our own Olympics. You can win the gold and the silver and the bronze."

He reached out for my hand and we skated together, no sound but the sound of our blades (well, mine mostly) against the ice. I knew he was skating slowly to keep pace with me. I knew I was keeping him from practicing his jumps, his spins, his footwork. I knew the world really must have ended because I was skating with Brandon Erlich, the way I had so often in my fantasies.

It really was heaven until I started coughing.

"That's enough for one day," he said. "How about watching me? I miss an audience."

So I stood by the side of the pond and watched Brandon do footwork and spins.

After a few minutes, he started coughing, and skated to the edge of the pond. "It's cold standing here," he said. "Colder than the rinks."

"And darker," I said.

He nodded. "So you were a fan?" he asked. "Because I was local or did you really like my skating?"

"Both," I said. "Mrs. Daley was always telling us about you. I love how you skate. Your line. Your extension. You were more than jumps. I really believed you could win at the Olympics."

"I was a long shot," he said. "But I was aiming for gold."

"Is Mrs. Daley all right?" I asked. "I haven't seen her since all this happened."

"She and her husband left here in August," Brandon said. "They have a daughter in Texas."

"How about all the other skaters?" I asked. "Do you know how they are?"

He shook his head. "The ones on tour with me were okay when we split up," he said. "They were desperate to get home. I wasn't quite so desperate, but after a while I couldn't figure out any other place to go, so I made it back here. My father cried when he saw me. My mother always cries, but it was the first time I'd ever seen my father cry. I guess that means something."

"I've stopped crying," I said. "My best friend died and I just got mad."

"Come on," Brandon said. "Skate."

So I did. It was a nothing skate, just stroking and a two-footed waltz jump and a ridiculous Ina Bauer. When I finished I didn't feel mad anymore.

"Come back tomorrow?" he asked. "I'd forgotten how much fun it is to skate with somebody."

"I'll try," I said, unlacing my skates and putting my shoes back on. "Thank you."

"Thank you," he said. He went back on the ice and when I left him he was stroking around the pond, beautiful and alone.

FIFTEEN

October 26

Mom tripped over her shoes yesterday morning, by the side of her mattress. She fell at a funny angle and hurt her ankle again.

She wrapped it back up with the Ace bandage and said she wasn't going to baby herself this time; if she limped for the rest of her life, so be it. But she couldn't even manage to stand.

She told Matt that she'd be fine in the kitchen, that there was no reason to move her back into the sunroom and have the woodstove going just for her, but he insisted. But since the pipes would freeze if we didn't keep the heat on (it was 12 degrees this afternoon; I guess Indian summer was pretty short this year), he and Mom decided the rest of us would keep sleeping where we had been.

Some of this I'm okay with. I wouldn't have been crazy about doing the laundry with Mom lying on the mattress in the kitchen. It's hard enough to maneuver around when she's in the other room. But at least this way if I step on a mattress, I don't have to worry that I'm stepping on her.

And I won't have any more housework to do. Mom gave up dusting and sweeping when we moved downstairs. The dining room is a lost cause, and it was too hard for her to get around the mattresses on the living room floor.

So the only real problem is that it's up to me to make sure the fire doesn't go out in the woodstove. It's the only source of heat in the sunroom so it has to keep burning all night.

I wake up a lot anyway. I just have to put a log or two on the fire every time I do. I made Mom promise if she woke up cold she'd yell to me to get up, but I don't know if she really will.

Matt says he wakes up, too, and he'll check on it, which means he'll walk through the kitchen to get there and probably wake me up anyway.

It would make sense for me to sleep in the sunroom, but the idea of even a little bit of privacy is so thrilling to me, I can't bear to give it up.

Mom and I have been alternating visiting Mrs. Nesbitt, so I'll just take over her shift. If nothing else, that'll give me an excuse to leave the house. But no more skating. There's no way I could leave Mom to go to the pond and skate. It doesn't matter. I spent a lot of yesterday trying to decide if it all really happened or if I just made it up. Me skating with Brandon Erlich. Us actually talking. Him being so nice.

I've made up stranger stuff than that.

He was probably just being nice when he asked me to come back. He probably prefers skating by himself rather than being stuck with some dumb fan-girl klutz.

Mom was upset that I wouldn't be able to go skating. She told me she'd be fine, but of course I couldn't leave her like that.

"When you're better, I'll go skating again," I told her. "The pond isn't going to thaw out anytime soon."

"I'm afraid not," she said. "But I feel so bad for you. You were finally doing something you enjoyed and now I've screwed things up again."

I thought she was going to cry, but she didn't.
I guess none of us is crying anymore.

Peter came by unexpectedly (well, all visits are unexpected these days, so what I mean is he wasn't summoned) and checked out Mom's ankle. He agreed it wasn't broken, but he said this sprain is worse than the last one and Mom needs to stay off her feet for at least two weeks, maybe more.

He also thought Mom might have broken one of her toes, but he said there's nothing that can be done about it, so why even worry. Which is pretty funny, coming from Peter.

There doesn't seem much point to sleeping all night, since I have to check the fire regularly, so I'm grabbing naps day and night. I sleep for two to three hours, then wake up and do whatever needs to be done, and then go back to sleep. Actually the smartest time for me to sleep would be in the early evening, when Matt and Jon are home and can tend the fire, but that's the time I most want to be awake. Sometimes I nod off anyway.

It's driving Mom crazy that she can't do anything, but there's not much any of us can do about that.

Oh, and I have an exciting new job as well. Mom can't make it to the bathroom and Matt located a bedpan in the attic, and I get to clean it. I keep threatening to put kitty litter in it.

It's funny. Mom sprained her ankle a few weeks ago, and things were okay. It was a good time. Not that much has changed since then, but it certainly isn't a good time.

I told Mrs. Nesbitt about Peter's visit and what he'd said about Mom. I didn't leave any of it out, including the part where Peter said that even after Mom could walk around the house she wasn't to think about walking outside.

"I guess you're stuck with me for a while," I said.

Mrs. Nesbitt surprised me. "Good," she said. "It's better that way."

I thought it had taken courage to tell Mrs. Nesbitt about Mom's ankle. It took a lot more courage to ask her why it was better that way.

"I didn't want your mother to find me dead," Mrs. Nesbitt said. "It won't be fun for you, either, but you're younger and I mean less to you."

"Mrs. Nesbitt!" I said.

She gave me one of those looks that used to terrify me when I was very little. "This is no time for make-believe," she said. "I could be dead tomorrow. We need to talk honestly. No point beating around the bush."

"I don't want you to die," I said.

"I appreciate that," she said. "Now when I do die and you find me, here are the important things. First of all, do whatever you want with my body. Whatever is easiest. Peter dropped by to visit me after he left your house and he told me that a dozen or more people are dying every day around here. I'm no better than any of them, and probably a fair amount worse than some. Peter says the hospital is still taking bodies so if that's what works for you, it'll be fine for me. Never liked the idea of burial anyway, always preferred cremation. My husband's ashes are scattered in the Atlantic somewhere so it's not like our graves would be side by side."

"All right," I said. "If I find your body, I'll tell Matt and he'll get you to the hospital."

"Good," she said. "Now after I'm gone, go through the

house and take everything you can possibly use. Don't worry about leaving things for my heirs. I haven't heard from my son or his family since May so I have to assume they won't be needing my things. If any of them show up at your doorstep and you still have something of mine, give it to them. But don't worry about it. Go through the whole house, attic to cellar. My car has some gas in it, so you can put all my things in it and drive back to your place. Don't be bashful. I won't be needing anything and the more you have, the better your chances. This is going to be a long and terrible winter and I'd be very angry if I thought you left something behind that could have helped you get through it."

"Thank you," I said.

"After I die, wrap me up in a sheet," she said. "Don't waste a blanket on it. And even if someone in my family comes back, I want your mother to have my diamond pendant and you to have my ruby brooch. Those are my gifts for the two of you and don't you forget it. Matt's to have the painting of the sailboats, because he always liked that when he was little, and Jonny should have the landscape in the dining room. I don't know if he likes it or not, but he's entitled to something and that's a good piece. You probably can't use any of my furniture, but you might want to take it for firewood."

"You have antiques," I said. "We couldn't burn them."

"Speaking of burning things, I burned all my letters and diaries," she said. "Not that there was a single interesting word in any of them. But I didn't want you to be tempted so they're all gone. I kept the albums, though. Your mother might get a kick going through them, seeing the old pictures of her family. You have all that?"

I nodded.

"Good," she said. "Don't tell your mother any of this until after I'm gone. She has enough to worry about. But when I've died, you be sure to tell your mother I loved her like a daughter and all of you like grandchildren. Tell her I'm just as glad she didn't see me at the end and she should never feel guilty that she couldn't come by for one last visit."

"We love you," I said. "We all love you so much."

"I should think so," she said. "Now tell me. Have you started your schoolwork yet?"

Of course I haven't, but I recognized a change of subject and went along with it.

When I got home I put wood in the stove and curled up for a nap. It was easier sleeping (or pretending to sleep) than trying to make small talk with Mom about Mrs. Nesbitt. I've never really thought about what it would be like to be an old woman. Of course nowadays I'm not sure I'll live long enough to be any kind of a woman.

But I hope when I get closer to death, however old I might be, that I can face it with courage and good sense the way Mrs. Nesbitt does. I hope that's a lesson I've truly learned.

November 1

Matt hovered around the house all morning, which was unusual. He's been even more obsessive about chopping wood ever since Mom moved back into the sunroom. I know it's because we're using up firewood earlier than planned, but it still annoys me just a little. I'd like him to stay indoors occasionally and clean the bedpan.

Sometime this afternoon I could hear the sound of a car in our driveway. Matt bolted outside and the next thing I knew he, Jon, and a couple of guys I didn't recognize were moving sheets of plywood out of a pickup truck and into the sunroom.

Mom watched but she didn't say anything, so I guess she knew about it.

After the guys left, Matt and Jon spent the rest of the day covering the windows in the sunroom with the plywood. When the house was first built, the sunroom didn't exist—it was just a back porch, and windows in the kitchen and dining room looked out on it. But when the porch was enclosed, the spaces stayed where the kitchen and dining room windows were even though the actual windows were removed. That's where a lot of the light in both rooms comes from, since the sunroom has skylights and three walls of windows (plus the outside door, of course). Matt blocked off the kitchen/sunroom window with the plywood, and put a sheet of plywood in front of the dining room/sunroom window so it can be pushed aside for easier access to the firewood.

Now the only natural light in the sunroom comes from the skylights. Not that there's been much sunlight lately, but the room is a lot darker.

Then, just in case I wasn't miserable enough, they blocked off the window over the kitchen sink. So now the only natural light in the kitchen is what comes from the skylights in the sunroom through the kitchen/sunroom door. In other words, just about none.

"Are you blocking off the living room windows, too?" I asked.

"No reason to," Matt said. "Once we stop using heat, we'll close off the living room. But we still might use the kitchen."

I'm so angry I could scream. For starters, I'm sure Matt got the plywood from the gang I saw in town, and I hate that he didn't tell me he was going to. No discussion. He knew what was best and he just went ahead and did it. (Okay, he talked to Mom about it. But I wasn't consulted.) And he doesn't understand what it's like to be cooped up in this house all day long. The only time I get out is when I visit Mrs. Nesbitt and that's just a short walk there and back.

I know Matt and Jon have it harder than me. Matt eats so little and he's doing physical work. When he comes in, he's exhausted. The other day he fell asleep during supper.

But he didn't have to cover the kitchen window. Not yet anyway. He could have waited until we ran out of oil. He didn't care what it would mean to me. He never even asked.

I'd move into Mrs. Nesbitt's but I can't leave Mom.

Sometimes I think about how things used to be. I'd never been anyplace, not really. Florida once and Boston and New York City and Washington and Montreal and that was it. I'd dream of Paris, of London, of Tokyo. I wanted to go to South America, to Africa. I always assumed I could someday.

But my world keeps getting smaller and smaller. No school. No pond. No town. No bedroom. Now I don't even have the view out the windows.

I feel myself shriveling along with my world, getting smaller and harder. I'm turning into a rock, and in some ways that's good, because rocks last forever.

But if this is how I'm going to last forever, then I don't want to.

November 5

I was in the kitchen washing out Mom's bedpan when the water stopped running.

I turned on the faucets in the downstairs bathroom and nothing came out. I went upstairs and checked that bathroom. Nothing.

I waited until Matt came in before telling him. For a moment he got mad at me.

"You should have told me right away!" he yelled. "If the pipes are frozen I might have been able to do something."

But I know it's not because the pipes have frozen. It's because the well's run dry. We haven't had any rain since July. No matter how careful we've been with water, it was bound to run out eventually.

Matt and I walked over to the well to check it out. Of course I was right.

When we came in, Jon was sitting with Mom in the sunroom, so we joined them. "How long can we survive without water?" he asked.

"It's not that bad," Matt said. "We still have bottled water and soda to drink. No more laundry, I guess. And Miranda'll just have to share a bedpan with Mom." He grinned like that was some kind of joke.

"We don't have that much bottled water," Jon said. "What if it never rains again?"

"We'll get some snow before too long," Matt said. "But in the meantime we can cut some chunks of ice from Miller's Pond. We'll boil it and hope for the best."

"Isn't there someplace else we could get ice?" I asked. "How about your little friends in the black market?"

"They're not my little friends and they don't have any water or ice," Matt said. "Or if they do, they're not selling it. If you can think of someplace closer than the pond, great. But that's the best I can come up with."

I thought about Brandon skating on the pond. I told myself it had never really happened so it didn't matter.

"Since there's no water left, there's no reason to keep the heat on," Matt continued. "We might as well conserve the oil and move into the sunroom."

"No!" I shouted. "I won't!"

"Why not?" Jon asked, and I could tell he was genuinely surprised. "It's warm in here. Even with the furnace on, it's cold in the house. Why not move?"

"I spend a lot of time in the kitchen," I said. "Not just sleeping. And it's bad enough now. I'll freeze to death if we turn the heat off. Is that what you want? You want me to freeze to death?"

"You won't be spending any more time in the kitchen," Matt said. "Except to get stuff out of the pantry. We don't cook in there anymore or eat in there and now you won't be doing any washing in there. If something happens to the firewood and we don't have any heating oil left, we'll freeze to death. It's better to keep some in reserve."

"What difference does it make?" I said. "We're never going to make it through the winter. It's November and already we're out of water and the temperature is below zero and there's no way of getting more food. We're dying in increments, Matt. You know that. We all know that."

"Maybe we are," Mom said, and I was almost startled to hear her speak. She's been talking a lot less since she hurt her ankle again, and she's really cut down on her rah-rah speeches. "But as long as we don't know what the future is going to bring us, we owe it to ourselves to keep living. Things could get better. Somewhere people are working on solutions to all this. They have to be. It's what people do. And our solution is to stay alive one day at a time. Everyone dies in increments, Miranda. Every day we're one day closer to death. But there's no reason to rush into it. I intend to stay alive as long as I possibly can and I expect the same from you. The only sensible thing to do is for all of us to stay in the sunroom."

"Not tonight," I said. "Please, not tonight."

"Tomorrow morning," Mom said. "We'll bring the mattresses in then."

"It'll be okay," Matt said to me. "In some ways, it'll be better. You won't be the only one responsible for the fire. We can take turns stoking it. You'll sleep better."

"Yeah," Jon said. "You'll have it easy, Miranda. You won't even have any housework to do."

So tonight is my last night alone. And my world has gotten even smaller.

SIXTEEN

November 7

Mrs. Nesbitt died.

I don't know when, but she was in bed and I like to think she died in her sleep. Her eyes were closed and she looked peaceful.

I kissed her cheek and covered her face with her top sheet. I sat silently by her side for a while, mostly to see if I was going to cry, but I didn't and I knew I couldn't sit there forever, no matter how peaceful it was.

I knew she wanted us to have everything, but I made a point of taking out her diamond pendant and ruby brooch first. Then I went downstairs and took the two paintings off the wall she wanted Matt and Jonny to have. I piled all the things on the kitchen table and tried to decide what to look at next.

What I really wanted to do was go through her kitchen cabinets and see what food she had left, but the very thought of it made me excited and that didn't seem like the proper way to feel. It made me feel like a cannibal.

So I found a flashlight and started with the attic. I didn't know what I was going to find there but Mrs. Nesbitt had told me to go from the attic to the cellar and I had no desire to go to the cellar.

The attic was filled with boxes and trunks. It was ice cold in there and I knew I didn't have the energy to go through every single one of them. So I hopped from box to box.

There were lots of old clothes, which I didn't think would be any help to us. There were also boxes of papers, accounts from Mr. Nesbitt's business.

I opened a box called Bobby's Things and found something great in there. Most of the stuff was from school, papers he'd written and the letters he'd gotten from being on the school basketball team. But toward the bottom I found a shoebox filled with old baseball cards.

I thought about how Jon hadn't gotten a birthday present and I clutched that shoebox. I'd surprise him with it at Christmas. Or before Christmas if I don't think we'll make it that long.

I went downstairs then and walked through the bedrooms and looked in the closets. There were clean towels and washcloths that Mrs. Nesbitt must not have used. Clean sheets and blankets and quilts. No matter how warm we might be in the sunroom, extra blankets seemed like a good idea. There were boxes of tissues I knew we could use, and rolls of toilet paper. Aspirin and painkillers. Cold remedies.

I took a clean pillowcase and started putting stuff in there, starting with the baseball cards. I didn't put any of the blankets in there, but I did throw in some of the towels and washcloths. There really wasn't any logic to what I put in and what I left out. I'd be sending Matt over to fill the car and he could pick up anything I forgot to take.

Then I allowed myself to go to the kitchen. I opened the

cabinets and I saw cans of soup and vegetables and tuna and chicken. All the stuff we'd been eating for months now. There wasn't enough for us to eat three meals a day. But every can would keep us alive a little bit longer.

I knew, without her ever telling me, that Mrs. Nesbitt had been going hungry so we could have the food. I thanked her silently and kept looking.

In the back of one of the cabinets I found a box of chocolates, unopened, with a Happy Mother's Day card attached. Mrs. Nesbitt never was one for chocolate. You would have thought her son knew that.

I took the chocolate and put it in the bottom of the pillowcase along with the baseball cards. I couldn't decide whether to give it to Mom at Christmas or on her birthday.

Then I realized there was a funny noise in back of me. I turned around and saw the kitchen faucet was dripping.

I grabbed a pot and put it under the faucet and turned it on. Actual water poured out.

Mrs. Nesbitt's well hadn't run dry. There was only one of her and she hadn't used up all her water. Her insistence on keeping the heat on had prevented the pipes from freezing.

I grabbed a lot of the cans and an unopened box of raisins and rammed them into the pillowcase. Then I went through the entire house, top to bottom, looking for containers for the water. Everything I found that could possibly hold water, bottles and jugs and canisters and barrels, I dragged into the kitchen. I filled them all just for the joy of hearing running water.

I was tempted to pour myself a glass of water and drink it, but even though the water was probably clean, I knew it should be boiled first. But then I thought to look in Mrs. Nesbitt's refrigerator. Sure enough, she'd been using it for storage space, and there was an untouched six-pack of bottled water.

I let myself drink one. It was all I could do to keep from gulping it down in three giant swallows. But I sipped it instead, like a fine wine.

It's funny. All the food there and I wasn't tempted by any of it. But I couldn't resist the water.

Then just because I could, I took a washcloth, dampened it with sink water, and washed my face and hands. Soon I took off all my clothes and gave myself a sponge bath. The water was cold and the kitchen wasn't much warmer, but it was glorious feeling clean again.

I got back into my dirty clothes and slipped the five bottles of drinking water into what I was starting to think of as my Santa bag and realized I couldn't carry much more. There was no way I could manage to take the paintings, but I did put the two pieces of jewelry in my pants pocket. I heaved the bag over my shoulder and went out the kitchen door.

I've been alternating between walking on the road and through the back woods to get to Mrs. Nesbitt's so I knew no one would think it suspicious if they didn't see me on the road. I only hoped no one would see me in the woods, since if they saw the Santa bag they'd know right away that I'd been taking things from Mrs. Nesbitt's house. If anyone got there before Matt, we'd lose the food, the water, everything.

I walked as fast as I could, cursing myself for having filled the pillowcase with so much stuff. It was one of my non-brunch days and I was hungry. The water gurgled in my stomach.

I spotted Matt and Jon chopping away. They'd cut firewood for Mrs. Nesbitt, I remembered. More stuff for them to take from her house.

For a moment I was torn between speaking to them while I was still holding on to the bag or going to the house to drop the bag off and then going to talk to them. But I'd have to tell

Mom if she saw me carrying stuff in, and I was just as happy to postpone that. So I positioned myself with the bag behind a tree just in case someone could see me talking to Matt and Jon.

"Mrs. Nesbitt died," I whispered. "She told me a few days ago to take everything we could use. She still has running water. Her car has a little gas in it."

"Where is she?" Jonny asked.

"She's in her bed," I said. "Peter told her the hospital was taking bodies and she said we should bring her there if that was easiest for us. We had a long talk about things a few days ago."

"Do I have to do that?" Jonny asked. "Do I have to go in?"

"No," Matt said. "But you have to help us bring stuff over. There's a wheelbarrow in her garage. We can fill it with firewood for you to take back here. Miranda, would you mind going back in?"

"No, of course not," I said.

"Okay, then," he said. "We'll strip the house. Do you have any idea how to drive?"

"The gas pedal makes it go and the brake makes it stop," I said.

Matt grinned. "You'll be fine," he said. "We'll drive the van there and we'll bring all our empty bottles and jugs so we can fill them with water. We'll load things up and I'll drive the van back and you'll drive Mrs. Nesbitt's car. Then I'll go back and get Mrs. Nesbitt and take her to the hospital. By the time I get back, the house will be ransacked, but we'll have gotten everything we can out of there."

"When you go back for Mrs. Nesbitt, fill the car up again," I said. "Honestly, she wouldn't mind."

"Okay," Matt said. "Take the bag in and tell Mom. Jon, come with me. Let's get water containers."

So we all went back to the house. Mom was sitting on her mattress, staring at the fire. She heard me come in and then she saw the pillowcase.

"Where did you get that?" she asked.

"It's Mrs. Nesbitt's," I said. "Mom, I'm sorry."

It took her a moment to realize what I was saying. Then she did and took a deep breath. "Was it peaceful?" she asked. "Could you tell?"

"She died in her sleep," I said. "Just the way she wanted."

"Well, that's the best we can hope for," Mom said.

When we got to Mrs. Nesbitt's, Jonny stayed outside and loaded the wheelbarrow with wood. Matt and I went inside. Matt filled all the containers we'd brought with water, and I packed up the blankets and towels and sheets and food and the photo albums and the two paintings.

While we were in the kitchen, Jon raced in. He'd found two barrels in the garage and a couple of plastic recycling bins and a heavy garbage pail.

The garbage pail weighed so much when we filled it with water that it took all three of us to lift it into the van. Jonny and I managed the recycling bins together.

We did everything as quietly as we could, but of course if anyone heard the car motor, they'd know something was up. The rule is family first and Matt said everyone thought of us as Mrs. Nesbitt's family, so we should be okay, but it was still scary until we got both cars loaded and both engines running.

Then of course I had to drive down the driveway, onto the road, and up our driveway to the sunroom door.

The important thing, I kept telling myself, was not to panic. There were no cars on the road, so I wasn't going to hit anybody. It was more a question of whether I'd hit a tree. I kept my hands locked on the steering wheel and drove about five miles an hour. The whole trip couldn't have taken more than five minutes, but it felt like an eternity.

If I was that nervous driving, I knew I wasn't ready to die.

Jon arrived with the wheelbarrow, which he left in our garage. Then he and Matt and I unloaded the cars. We put everything in the kitchen to be gone through later. I thought Mom was going to cry when she saw all the water.

Matt asked me if I wanted to go back with him and bring Mrs. Nesbitt to the hospital. Before I had a chance to agree, Mom said no.

"Miranda's done enough," she said. "Jonny, go with your brother."

"Mom," Jonny said.

"You heard me," Mom said. "You say you want to be treated like an adult. Then behave like one. Miranda's said her good-byes to Mrs. Nesbitt. Mine, too, I'm sure. It's your turn to do so and I expect that you will."

"Okay," Jonny said. He sounded so young, I wanted to hug him.

"This is going to take a while," Matt said. "Don't open the door while we're gone. You should be fine, but don't take any chances."

"We'll be safe," Mom said. "Be careful. I love you both."

After they left, I made Mom drink one of the bottles of water. Then I sat with her and told her about the conversation I'd had with Mrs. Nesbitt. I pulled the pendant out of the Santa bag and handed it to her.

"It was her fiftieth-birthday present," Mom said. "Her husband gave it to her. There was a big surprise party and I think she was genuinely surprised. Bobby brought Sally home for the party so we all knew it was serious. They got married later that year."

"She told me to give you her photo albums," I said. "I bet there are pictures from the party."

"Oh, I'm sure there are," Mom said. "Here. Help me with the clasp. I think she'd like to know I'm wearing the pendant."

I helped Mom on with it. She's gotten so thin I could see her shoulder blades.

"She gave me this brooch," I said, showing it to Mom.

"She loved that brooch," Mom said. "It was her grand-mother's. Cherish it, Miranda. That's a very special gift."

Then I went back to work. The bottles and jugs got moved to the kitchen. I put the food in the pantry and then I changed Mom's sheets. I took a pot, filled it with water, and after it had heated up, I helped Mom shampoo her hair. I hid the baseball cards and the chocolate, and put everything else away.

Matt and Jon got home around suppertime. They had seen Peter and there was no problem with the hospital taking Mrs. Nesbitt. Then we ate tuna and red beans and pineapple chunks. And we toasted the best friend we'll ever have.

November 8

Mom hobbled her way (which she probably shouldn't have done) into the pantry this afternoon. Matt and Jonny were doing their wood-chopping things.

I left Mom alone in the pantry for a while (I'm losing all sense of time), but then I figured I'd better make sure she hadn't fallen. So I went into the pantry and found her sitting on the floor weeping. I put my arm around her shoulder and let her cry. After a while she calmed down and then she embraced me.

I helped her up and she leaned on me as we went back to the sunroom.

I have never loved Mom as much as I love her now. I almost feel like some of Mrs. Nesbitt's love for Mom has seeped into me.

November 10

Peter came over this afternoon. Each time I see him, he looks five years older.

He didn't talk much to us. He just lifted Mom off her mattress, blankets and all, and carried her into the living room.

They stayed there a long time. Matt and Jon came in while they were there, and we all whispered, so Mom wouldn't be disturbed by the sound of our voices.

When they came back into the sunroom, Peter put Mom down so gently on her mattress, I almost wept. There was so much love and kindness in that gesture. Peter told us to take care of Mom and make sure she doesn't try to do too much. We promised we would.

I wonder if Dad was ever that gentle with Mom. I wonder if he's that gentle now with Lisa.

November 11

Veterans Day. A national holiday.

Matt stayed home from the post office.

I think this is the funniest thing ever.

November 15

I went to my bedroom to look for clean(er) socks, and while I was up there, I decided to weigh myself.

I had on a fair number of layers of clothes. Even though we have the woodstove going day and night, the sides of the sunroom don't get too warm. And of course leaving the sunroom to go to the pantry or the kitchen or upstairs is like hiking to the North Pole. You don't just stroll there in a bikini.

I had on my underwear and my long johns (sometimes I remember how upset I was when Mom bought them last spring, and now I thank her over and over, at least in my mind) and jeans and sweatpants and two shirts and a sweatshirt and a winter coat and two pairs of socks and shoes. I didn't bother with a scarf and I kept my gloves in my pocket because I knew I wasn't going to be upstairs too long.

For the great weighing-in, I took off my shoes and my coat. According to the scale, my clothes and I weigh 96 pounds.

I don't think that's too bad. Nobody starves to death at 96 pounds.

I weighed 118 last spring. My real concern is how much muscle I've lost. I was in good shape from all the swimming and now I don't do anything except carry firewood and shiver.

I'd like to go back to the pond and do some more skating, but I feel guilty leaving Mom alone. When I left her alone to visit Mrs. Nesbitt, I was doing something for someone else. But skating would just be for me, and I can't justify that.

Matt and Jon are both thin, but they look like they're pure muscle. Mom looks skinny and sickly. She's been eating less than the rest of us for a while now, but she also started out weighing more so I don't think she's at starvation level, either.

We have food but we're so careful with it. Who knows when we'll get any more. Even Peter doesn't bring us any when he visits.

Thanksgiving is next week. I wonder if we'll have anything to be thankful for.

November 18

Matt came flying home from the post office today. There was a letter from Dad.

The only problem was the letter was sent before the other one. I guess he wrote a letter between the two we'd already gotten.

This one was from Ohio. It didn't say much, just that he and Lisa were doing well and so far they had enough gas and food and camping out was fun. They met lots of other families who were also going south or west and he'd even run into someone he'd known in college. Lisa threw in a PS to say she could feel the baby move. She was sure it was a boy but Dad was equally sure it was a girl.

It was so strange getting that letter. I couldn't understand why Matt was so happy. It wasn't like there was any new news in it, since we know Dad and Lisa made it farther west than that. But Matt said it means mail is still traveling and is totally unpredictable, so a newer letter from Dad could arrive at any time.

Sometimes I feel like I miss Dad and Sammi and Dan more than I miss Megan and Mrs. Nesbitt. They all deserted me but I can't blame Megan or Mrs. Nesbitt for not writing. I know I can't blame Dad or Sammi or Dan, either. Or I shouldn't blame them, which is more accurate.

I have no privacy. But I feel so alone.

November 20

It was minus 10 when I went out with the bedpan. I'm pretty sure that was early afternoon.

Matt keeps chopping wood. There's already too much for the dining room, so he's started a pile in the living room.

I wonder if we'll have any trees left by the time winter ends. If it ends.

We still have water but we ration it.

Thanksgiving.

Even Mom didn't pretend we had anything to be thankful for.

Matt came home today from the post office with two special treats.

One was Peter.

The other was a chicken.

It wasn't all that much of a chicken, maybe a little bigger than a Cornish hen. But it was dead and plucked and ready for cooking.

I guess Matt knew he'd be getting it, and had arranged for Peter to join us in our Day After Thanksgiving Feast.

There was a moment when I thought about where the chicken had come from and what Matt must have given up for us to have it. But then I decided the hell with it. It was chicken, a real honest-to-goodness-not-from-a-can chicken. And I'd be a fool to look a gift chicken in the mouth.

No matter what Matt might have given up for the chicken, it would have been worth it for the look in Mom's eyes when she saw it. She looked happier than she has in weeks.

Since the only way we can cook is on top of the woodstove, we were kind of limited. But we put the chicken in a pot with a can of chicken broth and salt and pepper and rosemary and tarragon. Just the smell of it was heaven. We made rice and string beans, too.

It was wonderful beyond description. I'd forgotten what actual chicken tastes like. I think we each could have eaten the entire chicken, but we shared it very civilly. I had a leg and two bites of thigh.

Peter and Jon broke the wishbone. Jon won, but it didn't matter since we all have the same wish.

November 26

I guess the chicken really revitalized Mom, because today she decided we were all wasting our lives and that had to stop. Of course it's true, but it's still pretty funny that Mom felt the need to make a big deal out of it.

"Have any of you done a bit of schoolwork all fall?" she asked. "You too, Matt. Have you?"

Well, of course not. We tried to look shamefaced. Bad us for not doing algebra when the world is coming to an end.

"I don't care what you study," Mom said. "But you have to study something. Pick one subject and work on that. I want to see open schoolbooks. I want to see some learning going on here."

"I absolutely refuse to study French," I said. "I'll never go to France. I'll never meet anyone from France. For all we know, there isn't a France anymore."

"So don't study French," Mom said. "Study history. We may not have a future, but you can't deny we have a past."

That was the first time I ever heard Mom say that about the future. It shocked any possible fight out of me.

So I picked history as my subject. Jon picked algebra and Matt said he'd help him with it. Matt admitted he'd been wanting to read some philosophy. And Mom said if I wasn't going to use my French textbook, she would.

I don't know how long this burst of studying is going to last, but I understand Mom's point. The other night I dreamed that I found myself in school for a final and not only hadn't I been to class and didn't know anything, but the school was just the way it had been and everybody there was normal looking and I was dressed in layers of clothes and hadn't washed in days and everyone stared at me like I was a drop-in from hell.

At least now if it's a history test, I'll have a fighting chance of knowing some of the answers.

November 30

There's nothing like schoolwork to make a person want to play hooky.

I told Mom I wanted to go for a walk and she said, "Well, why don't you? You've been spending entirely too much time indoors."

I love her but I could throttle her.

So I layered up and walked over to Mrs. Nesbitt's house. I don't know what I was looking for or what I was expecting to find. But the house had been ransacked since the day she'd died. That was to be expected. We'd taken everything we could use, but there was stuff like furniture that we didn't need and other people had taken for themselves.

It felt funny walking around the empty house. It reminded me of Megan's house when I'd gone there, like the house itself was dead.

After I'd walked around awhile, I realized what I wanted to do was explore the attic. Maybe that hadn't been gone through, or at least not as thoroughly.

And sure enough, even though all the boxes had been opened and contents pulled out, there was plenty of stuff left in there. And that's when I knew I was there looking for a Christmas present for Matt. Jon had the baseball cards. Mom had the box of chocolates. But I wanted Matt to have something, too.

Most of what was lying around on the floor was old linens, tablecloths, and stuff like that. There were piles of old clothes, too, nothing anyone could have found usable.

When I'd gone through the attic the first time, it had been crowded with boxes, but everything was neatly packed away. Now it was chaos. Not that it mattered. I looked through piles of things, through boxes that had been gone through but nothing taken out. And finally I found something I could give Matt.

It was a dozen or so different colored pencils from an old color-by-number picture set. The pictures had all been carefully colored in, but their backs were blank, so I decided to take them, too.

Back in high school, Matt had done some drawing. I wasn't sure he'd even remember it, but I did, because he did a sketch of me in a much better layback position than I'd ever really managed. Mom had loved it and wanted to hang it up, but it embarrassed me because I knew it wasn't really me and I threw a tantrum until she gave up on the idea. I guess she kept the picture, but I don't know where she hid it.

At some point Matt's going to stop chopping firewood and when he does he can take up art again, to go along with his philosophy studies.

I went through the other stuff in the attic, but the pencils were definitely the high point. So I thanked Mrs. Nesbitt and went home. Just to be sneaky, I went in through the front door and took the color-by-number set up to my bedroom before returning to the sunroom.

We may not have a chicken for Christmas dinner, but at least there'll be presents.

December 1

For the third straight day the temperature was above zero this afternoon, so I took Mom's skates and went to the pond.

There was no one there. (I'm really starting to think that

whole Brandon thing was a hallucination.) In a funny way, it was better that I was alone, since I never am at home. Mom can definitely hobble around now, so I don't have to hover around her all the time, but it's way too cold in the house to spend much time anyplace but the sunroom.

I skated around the pond, nothing fancy and incredibly slow. I had to be careful, since there were chunks of ice missing. I guess people have been hacking away at it for water, the way we will once Mrs. Nesbitt's water runs out.

The air is so bad I don't know how Matt and Jonny manage. I'd skate for a few minutes and then start coughing. I probably didn't skate for more than 15 minutes total, but I was exhausted by the time I finished, and it took most of my strength to get back home.

Matt, Mom, and I are down to one meal a day, but at least we're eating 7 days a week. And maybe the temperature really is warming up, and that'll make things better.

SEVENTEEN

Fridays Matt goes to the post office first thing in the morning. Lately he's been coming home in the early afternoon. Even
though the days are all gray, there's still a difference between
daytime and night and it gets dark very early now.

Mom, Jon, and I were in the sunroom and it must have
been before noon because Jon hadn't gotten anything to eat.
We had two oil lamps going because, even in daytime with the
fire in the woodstove, we still need two lamps to have enough
light to read by.

Jon was the first one to notice. "Does it seem darker to
you?" he asked.

He was right. It was darker. First we looked at the oil lamps
to see if one of them had gone out. Then we looked at the
woodstove.

Mom tilted her head up. "It's snowing," she said. "The skylights are covered with snow."

With the windows covered by plywood, we can't see what's
going on outside. But since the only change in the weather for
months has been the temperature, there hasn't been much
need to see what's happening.

The kitchen window is covered with plywood, too, and we can't get to the windows in the dining room, so we all went to the living room to see what was happening.

It must have been snowing for an hour or more. It was coming down at a furious pace.

As soon as we realized it was snowing, we also realized the wind was blowing. "It's a blizzard," Jon said.

"We don't know that," Mom said. "The snow could stop in a minute."

I couldn't wait. I grabbed my coat and ran outside. I would have done the same for rain or sunlight. It was something different and I had to experience it.

Jon and Mom followed me. "The snow looks weird," Jon said.

"It's not quite white," Mom said.

That was it. It wasn't dark gray, like the piles of plowed snow in March. But it wasn't pure white, either. Like everything else these days, it was dingy.

"I wish Matt were home," Mom said, and for a moment I thought she meant that she wished she could share the moment with him, the excitement of snow. But then I realized she was worried about him getting home. The post office is about 4 miles from here, which isn't that far if you're biking, but could take a long time to walk, especially in blizzard conditions.

"You want me to go get him?" Jon asked.

"No," Mom said. "He's probably on his way home now. And it's not like he'll get lost. I'd just feel better if he were home."

"One good thing," I said. "If there's any kind of accumulation we'll have a water supply."

Mom nodded. "Jonny, get the barrels and the garbage cans, and put them outside," she said. "We can collect snow in them."

Jon and I took everything that could hold snow and put them by the side of the house. By the time we had the last recycling bin out there, the garbage can already had an inch of snow in it.

Jon was right. It was a blizzard.

We went back in but none of us could concentrate on our books. We kept our coats on and sat in the living room, watching the snow fall and waiting for Matt's return.

At some point Jon made himself some lunch. While he was in the sunroom I asked Mom if I should go get Matt.

"No!" she said sharply. "I can't risk losing two of you."

I felt like she'd punched me. Matt couldn't possibly be lost. We couldn't survive without him.

Mom didn't say anything after that and I knew to keep my mouth shut. Finally she went back to the sunroom and when she did, I went outside and walked toward the road just to see what conditions were like. The wind was so fierce it came close to knocking me over. The snow was falling almost sideways and I couldn't see more than a few feet ahead.

I barely made it to the road, but when I got there I couldn't see anything anyway. Matt could have been 20 feet down the road and I wouldn't have known. Mom was right. I couldn't possibly have made it to town. I could only hope Matt could make the long walk and that he'd known enough to leave once the snow had begun falling.

I went back in and made up some nonsense about going outside to check on the snow collection system. If Mom suspected differently she didn't say anything.

We went back and forth between the sunroom and the living room. Mom went out just past the front door and stood there for a few minutes until I made her come in.

I could see how excited Jon was, the way a kid is when it snows. It was killing him to suppress his excitement. It was killing Mom to suppress her fear. And it was killing me to see both of them trying to hide their feelings.

As the day progressed the sky grew darker and the wind stronger.

"I really think I should go find Matt," Jon said. "I could take one of the oil lamps."

"Maybe he should, Mom," I said. At this point Jon is stronger than me and a lot stronger than Mom. He might even be stronger than Matt, just because he's been eating more. If Matt needed help, Jon was the only one of us who could give it to him.

"No," Mom said. "For all we know Matt is staying in town with a friend to wait the storm out."

But I knew Matt wouldn't do that. He'd come home. Or at least he'd try to. He'd be as worried about us as we were about him.

"Mom, I really think Jon should go out," I said. "Just a little way down the road but with a lamp. It's getting so dark Matt could go right past our drive and not realize it."

I could see how much Mom hated the idea. I decided to try a different approach.

"How about if I go out first?" I said. "And then in a few minutes Jon could take over for me and then I could take over for him. We'd rotate, and that way neither one of us could get into any trouble."

"Yeah, Mom," Jon said. "I'll go first. Send Miranda out in a few minutes."

"All right, all right," Mom said. "Fifteen minutes and then I'll send Miranda out."

Jon looked really excited and in a funny way I didn't blame him. Mom made sure he was thoroughly bundled up: coat and gloves and scarves and boots. She told him not to go too far and to hold the lamp as high as he could to give Matt a beacon.

I waited alongside Mom. We didn't say anything. I didn't dare and Mom was way too wound up to make small talk. Finally she gestured to me to get ready.

"I hope this isn't a mistake," she said.

"We'll be fine," I said. "I bet I'll bring Matt home with me."

But by the time I reached the driveway I wasn't even sure I'd make it to where Jon was. It didn't seem to matter how many layers of clothes I had on, the wind was so fierce it cut right through everything. I especially felt it on my face. I put the scarf over my mouth and nose, but even so my face burned with the cold. The snow and the darkness made it impossible for me to see anything except what the lamp illuminated. I stumbled several times and the wind blew me over twice. The snow seeped through my pants and even my long johns grew cold and wet.

At one point I pulled the scarf away from my mouth so I could gulp air. But I fell into the snow and swallowed a mouthful, which got me coughing. I wanted to give up and go back to the sunroom, to the woodstove. But Jon was out there waiting for me to relieve him. My idea. My big bright idea.

I have no idea how long it took me to get to Jon. He was jumping up and down, the light swinging wildly.

"You stay warmer that way," he told me.

I nodded and told him to go back to the house. I gestured toward where I remembered the house to be. "Tell Mom I'm fine," I said, even though we both knew it was a lie.

"I'll be back in a few minutes," he said.

I watched as he began trudging back. But in a minute or two I couldn't see him anymore, even though I knew he wasn't very far away.

As I stood out there I began laughing at myself, at how desperate I'd been to be alone. Now I was as alone as any human being could be, and all I wanted was to be back in the sunroom with Matt and Jonny and Mom and Horton all taking up space.

I knew I'd be okay as long as I stayed put. I wasn't going to get lost and Mom would see to it I wasn't out long enough to freeze to death or even to get frostbite. The only one of us in danger was Matt.

But with the wind whipping around and the snow blinding me and my entire body freezing from the cold and the damp, it was hard to feel safe and secure. In addition to everything else, I was hungry. I'm always hungry except right after supper, but I was hungry the way I get right before supper, so I figured it must be around 5.

I realized Jon was right about moving around so I jogged in place. I was doing okay until a gust of wind caught me off guard and I fell into the snow and the oil lamp went out.

It took all my strength, physical and emotional, to keep from hysteria. I told myself I'd be okay, that Jon would find me, that Matt would get home, that the lamp could be relit, that everything was going to be fine.

But for a moment there I felt as though I'd been thrown into a snow globe by some powerful giant, that I was a prisoner and would never be free. I felt as though the world really was coming to an end and even if Matt made it home, we would all die anyway.

There was no point getting off the ground. I sat there, holding on to the useless lamp, waiting for Jonny, waiting for

Matt, waiting for the world to finally say, "That's enough. I quit."

"Miranda?"

Was it Matt? Was it the wind? Was it a hallucination? I honestly didn't know.

"Miranda!"

"Matt?" I said, struggling to get up. "Matt, is that really you?"

"What are you doing here?" he asked and the question was so dumb but so reasonable I burst out laughing.

"I'm rescuing you," I said, gasping, which only made me laugh louder.

"Well, thank you," Matt said. I think he laughed then, also, but the wind and my madness made it hard for me to tell.

"Come on," he said, reaching down to pull me up. "Let's go home."

We began walking against the wind toward the drive. Matt walked his bike on one side and held on to me on the other. At one point the wind blew me down and I pushed him down and he pushed the bike down. It took us a moment to get back upright and by the time we had, we could see Jon's oil lamp bobbing in the distance.

There was no point calling out to Jon, but we used the lamp as a guide and slowly made our way toward it. When we reached Jon he hugged Matt so hard I thought he'd drop the lamp and we'd all be there in total darkness. But the lamp stayed lit and we forged our way back to the house.

We went in through the front door and when we did, Matt called out, "We're home!"

Mom came racing as fast as she could toward us. Of course she hugged Matt first, but then she embraced me like she'd been as afraid for me as she had been for him.

Mom made all of us dry off completely and change all our

clothes and then we sat by the woodstove to defrost. All our faces were red, but Matt swore he was okay and not frostbitten.

"I would have gotten home sooner, but I didn't want to leave my bike," he said as we sat by the fire. "It was just Henry and me at the post office, and for a while we didn't realize it was snowing. Finally someone came in and told us it had been snowing for a couple of hours and we'd better get home right away. I would have gone with Henry, but he lives nearly as far from the post office as we do only in a completely different direction so that didn't make any sense. I was afraid if I left the bike I'd never see it again. You know how things are. Besides I didn't know if it was going to keep snowing or if it was just a squall. I hoped I'd be able to bike some of the way home, but that was impossible."

"You're not going back to the post office," Mom said. "I won't have it."

"We'll talk about that next Friday," Matt said. "In the meantime I'm not going anywhere."

At first I thought Mom was going to put up a fight, but then she just sighed.

"I'm hungry," Jon said. "Isn't it suppertime?"

"I'll make some soup," Mom said. "I think we could all use some."

We had soup first and then macaroni with marinara sauce. A two-course meal, proof that this was a special-event day.

We spent the evening going to the front door and peering out at the snow with a flashlight. I'm going to go back there once I finish writing this and then I'll go to sleep.

I don't know if I want it to snow all night long or if I want it to stop. If it snows, that's more water for us. But there's something frightening about this storm, even though we are all safe at home.

It doesn't matter. I can't do anything about it. It'll snow or it won't no matter what I want.

I just want this day to be over with.

It snowed all night and it's snowed all day.

The recycling bins are full of snow so Jon and Matt brought them in and we moved the snow into bottles and jars. Then we put the bins back out.

The garbage can was half full of snow. We figure there's been close to two feet of snow and it doesn't look like it's letting up any.

"We'll be okay for water now," I said, just to make sure. "The snow will last outside for a long time, so we can just bring it in and boil it when we need water. Right?"

"I don't see why not," Matt said. "I don't think we'll worry about water for a while. Besides, maybe it will snow again."

"Thanks, but no thanks," Mom said.

"It doesn't have to be a blizzard," Matt said. "But a few inches now and again could come in handy."

"And we're okay for wood?" I asked. I was in the mood for reassurance.

"We should be fine," Matt said.

I've decided to believe him. It's not like we can go to the Wood 'n' Water store if we need any.

Now that I think about it, I'm not sure we can go any-where. The roads won't be plowed, and I doubt anyone is going to shovel 4 miles of snow.

It's a good thing we still like each other.

When we got up this morning we found it had stopped snowing during the night. We couldn't see anything from the sunroom (which is really dark from the snow covering the sky-lights), but we went first to the living room and then to the front door and checked things out.

Because of the wind, the snow had drifted around. There were some stretches of land that hardly had any snow at all and other places where the snow was close to 5 feet high. I've never seen snow that high and I couldn't decide whether to be excited or scared.

We went back into the house. Mom took some of last night's snow and made us hot cocoa. Chocolate with an ashy taste is still better than no chocolate at all.

"Well," Matt said when we were all warm and cozy. "Are we ready for some problems?"

I would have said no but what good would that have done?

"We need to clear the snow off the roof of the sunroom," he said.

"Why?" Jon asked.

"Just a precaution," Matt said. "Snow can be heavy and we don't know if this is the last of it for the winter. We don't want the roof caving in on us."

"I don't want you on the roof," Mom said. "It's too dangerous."

"It'll be a lot more dangerous if the roof caves in," Matt said. "That could kill us. It WILL kill us actually because if we lose the sunroom, we lose the woodstove. I'll be careful, but it has to get done."

"You said 'problems,'" Jon said.

"The ladder is in the garage," Matt said. "So are the shovels."

"Let's see if there's snow in front of the garage," Mom said. She went to the sunroom door and tried to open it. But no matter how hard she pushed, the door stayed shut.

"There must be snow against it," Matt said. "But we can get out through the front door."

So we did. But instead of being able to look out the sunroom door to see how the garage was, we had to walk over to the driveway to get a look.

Just walking a couple of feet was exhausting. You had to lift each leg high to get it onto the snow, like exaggerated giant steps, and then the snow was so soft your leg sank right through it.

"It should be pretty easy to shovel," Jon said.

"That's good," Matt said. "Because we're going to have a lot to do."

We made it to the sunroom door. The snow was 4 feet high. No wonder Mom couldn't open it.

"Well, that's on our list to shovel," Matt said. "Now let's see how the garage is."

The garage was real bad. The snow had drifted higher than the padlock.

"We need the shovel," I said. "Are you sure it's in the garage?"

Matt and Jon both nodded. Mom took a deep breath and then she coughed. "We'll have to move the snow away by hand," she said. "The garage doors open out, so we don't have a choice. I think pots and pans will make the job go faster, and we'll all work on it. Jon, go to the house and put the pots and pans in a garbage bag and bring them back here. We'll do what we can by hand until you get here."

Jon began the long trudge back to the front door. Once he was out of hearing range, Mom turned to Matt and said, "How bad is it really?"

"Well, we're certainly isolated," Matt said. "I saw Dad's old pair of cross-country skis in the garage once. The shoes that go with them, too. They'll give us some mobility. Bikes will be use-less. Forget driving. I hope you don't mind my saying this, but it's a relief Mrs. Nesbitt is gone."

"I thought the same thing," Mom said. "Do you think the roads will be cleared at any point?"

Matt shook his head. "There aren't enough people left to shovel the roads out, and there isn't enough gas for the snow-plows. Maybe the townspeople will clear the main streets out, but that's going to be it. We're on our own."

"I'm thinking about the hospital," Mom said.

"I've been thinking about that, too," Matt said. "We can't get there. Peter can't get to us. And I don't think the snow is going to melt before April or May. And there's the risk of more snow."

"I like Peter," I said. "But it's not the end of the world if we don't see him for a few weeks. Or even a few months."

"That's not it," Matt said. "What if one of us needs a doctor or the hospital? What happens then?"

"We'll just be careful," Mom said. "So we won't need a doc-tor. Now come on, let's see how much of this snow we can re-move by hand before Jonny discovers all we've been doing is talking."

The snow got inside all our gloves, and our pant legs grew wet, too. We were relieved when Jon returned with the pots and pans. We each took one and used it as a minishovel. The pans speeded the process, but it still took a long time before the garage doors looked like they could be opened.

Then Mom realized the key to the padlock was in the house so we had to wait until Matt went back, got the key, and re-turned. Even when he did, it wasn't that easy to get the garage doors opened. But we cleared some more and we all pulled to-gether and much to our relief the door finally opened.

There were two shovels right by the door. There was also a 20-pound bag of rock salt, which claimed it would melt ice in below-zero temperatures.

"If it doesn't," Mom said, "we can always demand a refund."

This struck all of us as so funny we couldn't stop laughing until the coughing took over.

"Two shovels," Matt said. "One for me and one for Jon. Let's get started."

"No," Mom said. "I want us all to go to the house first and eat something. And we should take some aspirin."

"We'll be fine," Matt said. "You don't have to worry."

"Worrying is what I do," Mom said. "Occupational hazard of motherhood. Now everybody back to the house for food and aspirin."

"What's the aspirin for?" I whispered to Matt as we made our way to the front door.

"Our hearts," Matt said. "I guess Mom thinks we have the hearts of sixty-year-olds."

"I heard that," Mom said. "I just don't want you taking any more chances than you have to. Besides, you'll be aching all over by the time you're finished. You might as well start on the aspirin now."

Mom was certainly right about the aching all over. Just shoveling the snow out with a pot made my shoulders and upper back hurt. And I loved the idea of lunch (which turned out to be soup and spinach—I guess Popeye did his share of snow shoveling).

Once we'd eaten, Matt and Jonny went to work, first clearing out the sunroom door, then creating walkways from the house to the garage and from the front door to the road. Then they got the ladder and cleared off all the snow from the sunroom roof. It took them a long time, but they seemed to enjoy it.

"While they're shoveling, let's do some laundry," Mom said to me. "I'll boil down the snow and you do the washing."

"Women's work," I muttered, but the truth is much as I don't care for washing Jon's underwear, I sure don't want him washing mine.

If I thought my back hurt from the shoveling, it was nothing compared to how I felt after doing all the laundry. On the one hand it was exciting actually having water to wash clothes with. We had done a little with Mrs. Nesbitt's water, but we haven't since then and that was about a month ago.

But laundry is hard, hard work. For starters, snow melts down into not very much water, so Mom was constantly having to refill the pot on the woodstove. And of course the water was gray toned, which makes it harder to believe that the clothes are actually clean. Then I'd overcompensate with laundry detergent, and it would take forever to rinse it out. The water was really hot from the woodstove and the kitchen really cold, since it has no heat, and my poor body didn't know what to feel. My hands and face got steamy hot and my feet and legs stayed ice cold. Then once each sink load was washed and rinsed, I had to squeeze all the clothes dry, which took even more energy than the washing and rinsing. All this for clothes that are permanently dingy.

Mom strung up a clothesline in the sunroom because if we hang wet clothes in any of the other rooms they'll freeze. So now the sunroom has the smell of wet laundry to go along with everything else. At least the clothesline is nowhere near the mattresses. I don't want clothes dripping on my face while I'm sleeping.

Matt and Jonny did the roof clearing and while they were at it, they cleared the snow off the skylights, so whatever light is out there we now get.

I'm too tired to be scared. I wonder how I'll feel in the morning.

December 5

Mom told us to get back to our schoolwork.
"Snow day," Jonny said.
Mom didn't argue.
I almost wish she had.

December 7

We've been cooped up in the sunroom for almost a week now. I thought it was bad before, but this is ridiculous. At least before Matt and Jonny could go out and chop wood all day long. Now they're stuck inside, too.

Sometimes one of us invents an errand to take us away from the others. I'm still in charge of bedpans and chamber pots so I have to walk about 50 feet from the house for that lovely job. Jon cleans out Horton's litter so he has to go outside at least once a day (besides, he and Matt use the outdoors as a bathroom, poor guys). Matt brings in snow for our water needs. Only Mom never leaves the house.

But we'll all suddenly remember something we have to get from our bedrooms or the pantry, and no matter how cold the rest of the house is, it feels like heaven just to get by yourself for a few minutes.

Tomorrow is Friday so Matt went out with the cross-country skis to see if he could make it into town. Much to Mom's great relief, he came back and said he couldn't. He never really liked cross-country skiing and the snow is very light and powdery and he doesn't have the skill and probably not the strength to manage 4 miles.

On the one hand I'm kind of glad to know there's something

Matt refuses to try. On the other hand, much as I love him, it might have been nice not having him around for a few hours.

If it's only December, what are we going to be like by February?

December 10

Jon was making himself a can of green peas for lunch when all of a sudden he turned to us and said, "How come none of you eat lunch?"

It's funny. We haven't in ages, but Jon was always outside with Matt and I guess he figured Matt ate a big breakfast or something. He didn't know what Mom or I were doing. But now that we're breathing the same air constantly, Jon finally noticed.

"Not hungry," Matt said. "When I'm hungry, I eat."

"Same here," I said with a big false smile on my face.

"We all eat when we need to," Mom said. "Don't let what we do stop you, Jonny."

"No," Jon said. "If you're all just eating one meal a day, then that's what I should do, too."

We all said, "No!" Jonny looked absolutely horrified and ran out of the room.

I remember a few months ago how angry I was that we weren't eating as much as Jonny, how unfair that seemed. But now I feel like Mom was right. It is a possibility only one of us is going to make it. We have fuel and we have water, but who knows how long our food will last. Mom's so thin it's scary and Matt certainly isn't as strong as he used to be and I know I'm not. I'm not saying Jon is, but I can see how he might have the best chance of making it through the winter or spring or whatever.

Probably if only one of us really is going to survive, Matt would be the best choice, since he's old enough to take care of himself. But Matt would never let that happen.

I don't want to live two weeks longer or three or four if it means none of us survive. So I guess if it comes to it, I'll stop eating altogether to make sure Jon has food.

Matt started to go upstairs to talk to Jon, but Mom said no, she'd do it. Her limp was pretty bad, and I worried about her getting up the stairs, but she insisted on going.

"This is awful," I said to Matt, just in case he hadn't noticed.

"It could be worse," he said. "We may look back on this as the good time."

And he's right. I still remember when Mom sprained her ankle the first time and we played poker and really enjoyed ourselves. If you'd told me three months before then that I'd have called that a good time, I would have laughed out loud.

I eat every single day. Two months from now, maybe even one month from now, I might eat only every other day.

We're all alive. We're all healthy.

These are the good times.

December 11

I went outside to do chamber pot duty and Jon followed me out with kitty litter brigade. I was turning to go back in when he grabbed hold of my arm.

"I need to talk to you," he said.

I knew it had to be important. If Jon talks to anybody it's Matt.

"Okay," I said, even though it was 12 degrees below zero and I really wanted to get back in.

"Mom said I should keep eating lunch," he said. "She said she needs to know one of us is going to stay strong, in case the rest of us need him."

"Yeah," I said. "She's told me that, too. And you're the one we need to stay strong."

"Is that okay?" he asked. "Don't you mind?"

I shrugged.

"I don't know if I can be the strong one," Jon said. "Matt practically had to drag me into Mrs. Nesbitt's."

"But you went," I said. "You did what you had to. That's what we've all been doing. We do what we have to. You're a lot more mature than you used to be, Jon. I have so much respect for you, the way you handled your birthday. And I'll tell you something else. When we went for Matt, I fell and my oil lamp went out, and all I could think was, Jon will get me. Jon's stronger than I am and it'll be okay. So to some extent it's already happening."

"But what if you die?" he cried. "What if you all die?"

I wanted to tell him that was never going to happen, that we'd be fine, that the sun was going to be shining tomorrow and the roads would be plowed and the supermarkets would be open, full of fresh fruits and vegetables and meat.

"If we all die, you'll leave," I said. "Because you'll be strong enough to. And maybe someplace in America or Mexico or somewhere things are better and you'll manage to get there. And then Mom's life and Matt's and mine won't have been a waste. Or maybe the moon's going to crash into the earth and we'll all die anyway. I don't know, Jonny. Nobody knows. Just eat your damn lunch and don't feel guilty."

I'm sure the queen of pep talks. Jon turned around and went in. I stayed outside awhile longer and kicked the snow for lack of a better target.

December 13

"I think we've been doing this meal thing backward," Matt said this morning. For one gleeful moment I thought he meant he and Mom and I should be eating two meals a day and Jon only one, but of course that wasn't it.

"None of us eats breakfast," he said. "We're hungry all day. We eat supper and stay up a little while and then we go to sleep. The only time we're not hungry is when we're sleeping. What good does that do us?"

"So should we have our big meal at breakfast?" Mom asked, which was pretty funny since our big meal is our only meal.

"Breakfast or lunch," Matt said. "Maybe brunch like Miranda used to do. I think I'd rather be hungry at night than all day long."

"What about me?" Jon asked.

"You'd eat something at suppertime," Matt said.

I had to admit it made sense. Especially if Jon ate his second meal when we'd already eaten. There've been a couple of days when I've wanted to take his pot of whatever he was eating and pour it over his head. I'd probably feel less jealous if I wasn't as hungry.

"Let's try it," Mom said. "I liked supper because that was the time of day we were together. But now we're together all day long, so that doesn't matter anymore. Let's try eating at eleven and see if we like it."

So we did. And now it's 4 in the afternoon (or so Matt tells me) and I don't feel particularly hungry. And doing the laundry is easier too since I'm not hungry.

Life just improved.

December 16

"Are you still keeping your journal?" Jon asked.

"Yeah," I said. "I just don't have an actual journal anymore. I use notebooks. But that's what I'm writing. Why?"

"I don't know," he said. "I just wondered why. I mean who are you writing things for?"

"Well, not for you," I said, remembering how Mrs. Nesbitt

had burned all her letters before she died. "So don't get any ideas."

Jon shook his head. "I don't want to read about any of this stuff," he said. "Do you reread it?"

"No," I said. "I just write it and forget about it."

"Okay," he said. "Well, don't worry that I'll read it. I got enough problems."

"We all do," I said.

It's funny how sorry I feel for Jon these days. I'm 2½ years older than him and I feel like I got those extra 2½ years to go to school and swim and have friends and he got cheated out of them. And maybe he'll live 2½ years longer than me, or 20 years, or 50, but he'll still never have those 2½ years of normal life.

Every day when I go to sleep I think what a jerk I was to have felt sorry for myself the day before. My Wednesdays are worse than my Tuesdays, my Tuesdays way worse than my Tuesday of a week before. Which means every tomorrow is going to be worse than every today. Why feel sorry for myself today when tomorrow's bound to be worse?

It's a hell of a philosophy, but it's all I've got.

December 19

Lisa's baby was due about now. I've decided she had it and it was a girl. I've named her Rachel.

Somehow that makes me feel better. Of course I have no idea if she's had the baby and if she has, whether it's a boy or a girl or if it's a girl what her name is. Technically speaking, I don't know if Lisa is still alive, or if Dad is, but I really prefer to think they are. I've decided they made it to Colorado, and Dad got Grandma out of Las Vegas and they're all living together: Lisa and Lisa's folks and Dad and Grandma and baby Rachel. When the weather improves, somehow he'll come back for us and we'll all move to Colorado and I'll get to be baby Rachel's godmother, just like I was supposed to be.

Sometimes Colorado becomes like Springfield used to be for me, this fabulous place with food and clean clothes and water and air. I even imagine that I'll run into Dan there. After I've cleaned up, naturally, and eaten enough so that I don't look like a walking corpse. Also my hair has grown out. I look great and I bump into him and we get married.

Sometimes I speed things up and Rachel's our flower girl.

I bet Mom and Matt and Jon all have fantasies of their own, but I don't want to know what they are. They're not in mine, after all, so I'm probably not in theirs. We spend enough time together. We don't need to hang out in each other's fantasies.

I hope Dad and Lisa are okay. I wonder if I'll ever meet Rachel.

December 21

Mom put her foot down (her good one) and we're back to doing schoolwork. At least it gives us something to do besides laundry and playing poker.

Right now I'm reading about the American Revolution.

The soldiers had a tough time of it at Valley Forge.

My heart bleeds for them.

WINTER

EIGHTEEN

December 24

Christmas Eve. And the most wonderful thing happened.

The day was just like any other. We'll have a big meal to-morrow. (And of course, though Mom and Matt and Jonny don't know it, they're all getting presents. I am so excited at the thought of giving them things.) No laundry, though. We draped the clothesline with tinsel and hung ornaments on it. Matt called it a horizontal Christmas tree.

Okay. That means today wasn't just like any other.

We sat around this evening and started talking about Christmases past. At first you could see Mom didn't know if that was a good idea. But she didn't stop us and we all had sto-ries to tell and we were laughing and feeling great.

And then in the distance, we could hear singing. Actual caroling.

We put on our coats and gloves and boots and went outside. Sure enough, there were a handful of people singing carols down the road.

We immediately joined them. Thanks to the path Matt and Jon had shoveled we didn't have too much trouble getting to road level. (There were some icy patches and I wasn't crazy about Mom coming along, but there was no stopping her.)

The road itself is still covered with 3 feet of snow. Nobody's been traveling on it, so we created our own paths.

It was thrilling to be outside, to be singing, to be with people again.

I recognized the Mortensens from about half a mile down. The other people I didn't know at all. But our road is funny. Even in good times we didn't socialize with most of our neighbors. Mom says when she was growing up she did, but so many of the old families have moved out and new people have moved in and neighborliness has changed. Now being a good neighbor means minding your own business.

As we trudged and sang (loud and off-key), another family joined us. We ended up with 20 people acting the way people used to. Or at least the way they used to in the movies. I don't think we've ever had carolers before.

Finally it got too cold even for the most dedicated among us. We finished with "Silent Night." Mom cried and she wasn't alone.

We hugged each other and said we should see more of each other, but I doubt that we will. We don't want anyone else to know how much food we have or firewood. And they don't want us to know, either.

Still it was a wonderful Christmas Eve. And tomorrow is going to be even better.

December 25

Absolutely the best Christmas ever.

We woke up in great moods and we talked all morning about how much fun it had been to go caroling the night before. We don't even like the Mortensens, but seeing them last night, knowing they were still around and healthy, was so incredibly reassuring.

"We made a joyful noise," Mom said. "It's good to remember what joy feels like."

And lunch. What a feast. First we had beef broth with oyster crackers. Our main course was linguini with red clam sauce and string beans on the side. Mom even pulled out the bottle of wine Peter had brought ages ago, so we had wine with our dinner.

For dessert, Mom served the lime Jell-O I'd gotten at the free-food handout last summer. I don't know when she made it, but somehow she'd slipped it past us, and it was an incredible surprise.

So much food. So much laughing. It was great.

Then we all kind of hemmed and hawed and harrumphed and excused ourselves. I went up to my bedroom to get everybody's presents, and much to my surprise, Mom and Matt and Jon also went upstairs to their rooms.

When we met back in the sunroom, we were all carrying presents. Only Mom's were wrapped with real gift wrap. I'd used magazine pages for my presents and Matt and Jon used grocery bag brown paper.

But we were all surprised. So many presents.

It turned out there were two presents for each of us and one for Horton.

Horton opened his first. It was a brand-new catnip mouse.

"I got it at the pet supply store," Jon said. "I didn't tell anybody because I figured I was just supposed to be buying food and litter. And then I figured at least Horton should get a present for Christmas so I held on to it."

It was actually a present for all of us. Horton immediately fell in love with the mouse and licked it and jumped on it and acted like a kitten. I thought about how scared I'd been when he'd run away. But he knew what family was, too, and he came back and we were all together, the way we were meant to be.

Mom told us to open our presents from her next. "They're nothing special," she said. "Peter got them for me from the hospital gift shop before it closed."

"That makes them more special," I said and I meant it. "I wish Peter could be here with us."

Mom nodded. "Well, open them already," she said. "Just don't count on their being anything fancy."

My fingers trembled when I carefully removed the gift wrap. It was a brand-new diary, a really pretty one with a pink cover and a tiny little lock and key.

"Oh, Mom," I said. "I've never seen anything so beautiful."

Jon's present was a handheld battery-run baseball game.

"Don't worry," Mom said. "Batteries are included."

Jon's grin was so bright he could have lit up the whole room. "This is great, Mom," he said. "Something for me to do."

Matt's present was a shaving kit. "I figured you were due some new razor blades," Mom said.

"Thanks, Mom," Matt said. "I've been feeling a little scraggly."

I insisted Mom open my present next. She unwrapped it, and when she saw it was a box of actual chocolates, her jaw dropped.

"They're probably a little stale," I said.

"Who cares!" Mom cried. "They're chocolates. Oh, Miranda! Of course we'll share. I can't eat the whole box by myself." She stopped and covered her mouth with her hand. "Oh, I didn't mean that the way it came out!"

I burst out laughing. Jon kept asking what the joke was but that only made me (and Mom) laugh louder.

So I told Jonny to open his present from me next. He ripped into the paper and then flung the top off the shoe box. "I don't believe this!" he shouted. "Matt, look at these cards. Look at them. There are hundreds. And they're old. They're from the '50s and '60s. Look, Mickey Mantle. And Yogi. And Willie Mays. I've never seen a collection like this before."

"I'm glad you like them," I said, relieved he didn't ask where they came from. "Matt, you go next."

Matt opened my present to him. "What?" he said at first. "I mean, this is really nice, Miranda, but I don't think I understand."

"Oh," I said. "I know the pictures are all colored. But the pencils were in great shape and I thought you could draw on the back of the pictures. You used to draw really well and I thought maybe you'd like to do it again."

His face lit up. "That's a great idea," he said. "You keep your journal and I'll draw pictures of all of us. Thanks, Miranda. I'm going to love these pencils."

If I'd known he was going to draw us, I'd have looked for gray pencils. But he seemed excited and that made me happy.

"Open our present next," Jonny said so I cheerfully did.

It was a watch.

"How did you know I needed one?" I asked.

"You keep asking what the time is," Matt said. "It wasn't too hard to guess."

I almost asked where the watch came from, but then I really looked at it and saw it had been Mrs. Nesbitt's. It was an old-fashioned watch, the kind you have to wind every day. Her husband had given it to her and I knew how much she cherished it.

"Thank you," I said. "It's a beautiful gift. I love it. And now I'll stop pestering you."

"I guess this present is the last one," Mom said. "But honestly this whole day has been such a gift. I don't need any more presents."

"Open it," Matt said, and we all laughed.

"All right," Mom said. She took off the grocery bag paper and fell silent. "Oh, Matt," she said. "Jonny. Wherever did you find this?"

"What is it?" I asked.

Mom showed me what she was holding. It was an old black-and-white photograph of a young couple holding a baby. It was even in a frame.

"Are those your parents?" I asked.

Mom nodded and I could tell it was all she could do to keep from crying.

"And that's Mom in the picture," Jon said. "She's the baby."

"Oh, Mom, let me see," I said, and she handed it over to me. "It's beautiful."

"Where did you find it?" Mom asked.

"In a box at Mrs. Nesbitt's," Matt said. "I saw it was old photographs and I brought it back here. She labeled all the pictures on the back. It was Jon's idea to go back and find a picture frame it would fit in. I didn't remember ever seeing the picture before, so I thought maybe you didn't have it."

"I didn't," Mom said, taking it back from me. "It's summertime and we're on the back porch. How funny. We're in the exact same place, only now it's been enclosed. I must be about six months old. I guess we were visiting my grandparents. Mr. Nesbitt probably took the picture. I think I can make out his shadow."

"Do you like it?" Jon asked. "It isn't like it cost anything."

"I love it," Mom said. "I have so few memories of my parents and so little to remember them by. This picture—well, it takes me back to a different time. I will cherish it always. Thank you."

"I think I'll start sketching," Matt said. "I'll do some preliminary sketches before using my pencils." He grabbed some of the paper bag, pulled out the black pencil, and began drawing.

Then Mom did something that made me even happier. She opened up her box of chocolate and read the diagram very carefully. Then she took the top off the box and placed 12 of the chocolates in it and passed it over to us. "You can all share this," she said. "The rest is mine."

I loved that I was going to get to eat some chocolate but that Mom respected the fact it was my gift to her and not to all of us.

The Christmas after Mom and Dad split up, they both went crazy buying us presents. Matt, Jonny, and I were showered with gifts at home and at Dad's apartment. I thought that was great. I was all in favor of my love being paid for with presents.

This year all I got was a diary and a secondhand watch.

Okay, I know this is corny, but this really is what Christmas is all about.

December 27

No Christmas vacation for us. I'm back at history, Jon at algebra, Matt at philosophy, and Mom at French. We share what we learn, so I'm getting a refresher course in algebra and keeping up with my extremely minimal French skills. And we get into some really heated discussions about philosophy and history.

Also Mom decided that while Texas Hold 'Em has its good points, it isn't enough. She dragged out our Scrabble and chess sets, and now we play them, too. We play Scrabble together (so far Mom's on a winning streak), and anytime two of us are in the mood, we play chess.

Mom got it in her head that even though none of us can sing, we should do a <u>Sound of Music</u> thing and sing together. If Julie Andrews ever heard us, she'd probably jump into the first available volcano. But we don't care. We bellow show tunes and Beatles songs and Christmas carols at the top of our lungs and call it harmony.

Mom's threatening to make us darling little matching outfits out of the drapes.

Winning all those Scrabble games is definitely going to her head.

December 31

Tomorrow I'm going to start using my new diary. It has a three-year calendar in it, so I'll know what the date is. For some reason that makes me very happy.

Matt has been sketching every chance he gets. He even goes outside and sketches our desolate winter landscape.

When he was outside this afternoon, I decided the time had come to decorate the sunroom. Jon and I put nails in the plywood windows and hung up the paintings that Mrs. Nesbitt had left to him and Matt.

Then I asked Mom where Matt's sketch of me skating was. It took her a while even to remember it and then a while longer to figure out where it must be (back of the shelf in her closet). I put on my coat and gloves and went upstairs and found it. I also took a photograph of us kids, one of those Sears studio things that Mom had hanging in her bedroom, and brought it down as well.

The sunroom always used to be my favorite room in the

house, even more than my bedroom. But lately with the ply-wood, and four mattresses on the floor, and a clothesline that almost always has wet clothes hanging from it, and the smell of cooked canned food, and most of the furniture pushed out into the kitchen, and everything else in the room shoved to one side or another—well, it's not going to win any decorating awards.

When Matt came in and saw we'd hung all the pictures up, he burst out laughing. Then he saw the picture he'd drawn and looked it over carefully.

"That's really bad," he said.

"It is not!" Mom and I both said, and cracked up.

We outvoted him so it's staying up. Now I look at it and I don't see some idealized version of me. I see a skater, any skater, at a moment of perfect beauty.

I see the past the way I like to think it was.

"I wonder if they're dropping the ball at Times Square tonight," Jon said. "It's already New Year's in a lot of places on earth."

I wondered, and I think we all did, if this would be our last New Year's.

Do people ever realize how precious life is? I know I never did before. There was always time. There was always a future.

Maybe because I don't know anymore if there is a future, I'm grateful for the good things that have happened to me this year.

I never knew I could love as deeply as I do. I never knew I could be so willing to sacrifice things for other people. I never knew how wonderful a taste of pineapple juice could be, or the warmth of a woodstove, or the sound of Horton purring, or the feel of clean clothes against freshly scrubbed skin.

It wouldn't be New Year's without a resolution. I've resolved to take a moment every day for the rest of my life to appreciate what I have.

Happy New Year, world!

January 1

Matt informed us that he had made a New Year's resolution.

"You know something," Mom said. "This is the first year I didn't. I'm always resolving to lose weight and spend more time with you kids, and this year I actually lived up to those resolutions. I am now officially retired."

"That's fine, Mom," Matt said. "But I've resolved to master cross-country skiing. Jon and Miranda should learn with me. We can take turns with the skis. It'll get us outside and give us some exercise. How about it?"

Standing around in below-zero weather with the wind howling and falling into snowbanks didn't sound like all that much fun. But Matt gave me one of those looks and I realized this wasn't about fun and games. It was about being able to escape from here if one of us needed to.

"Great idea," I said. "And while we're talking great ideas, I have one of my own."

"Yes?" Matt drawled, skepticism practically oozing out of him.

"I think I should do Mom's and my laundry, and you and Jon should do your own," I said.

"No!" Jonny yelped. I guess he has some idea of what hard work doing the laundry is. "Mom?" he whined.

"It makes sense to me," Mom said.

"Then Miranda should do the dishes," Jon said.

"Okay," I said. "If we take turns with the dishes. I'm not going to do them all the time."

"Fair's fair," Matt said. "We rotate the dishes, and Jon and I do our own laundry. At least until we can start chopping wood again. Now let's go skiing."

I put on four extra pairs of socks so Dad's boots would stay on my feet and out we went. We ski about as well as we sing, and I spent entirely too much time in snowdrifts on the road. But it got Jon out of his whiny mood, and by the time we finished we could all manage a little.

"We'll do some more tomorrow," Matt said. "It's good for us and it's good for Mom to have some quiet time."

"Do you think I could ski to the pond?" I asked. "I'd love to do some more skating."

"I don't see why not," Matt said.

It felt great to expand my world again. The idea of not being stuck in the sunroom cheered me up almost as much as seeing the sun would have.

New Year. New hopes.

That's the way it should be.

January 3

We're definitely getting better with the skiing. Since it's one pair for the three of us, we don't travel great distances. Mostly we ski back and forth, but each time we increase our distance if only by a few feet.

I can't wait until I'm good enough at it to go back to the pond. I know Matt has us working at it in case there's an emergency and we need to get help, but I've set my goal as getting to the pond for some skating.

Even Jon's gotten into it. Matt pointed out to him that cross-country skiing is good aerobic exercise and he should think of it as wind sprints, which he'll need to do when the baseball season starts.

In a funny way the same thing is true for Matt. He was a miler back in college, and the skiing is helping him stay in shape. I'm not sure the air quality is so great for us, but at least our hearts are getting a workout.

We ski after lunch. It would be too hard in the morning on empty stomachs. There's a part of me that wonders if it's a good idea for us to be burning off calories, but I guess if I starve to death at least I'll have good muscle tone.

And it gets us out of the sunroom.

January 5

Something very weird happened this afternoon.

We'd done our skiing and were sitting around the sunroom doing schoolwork when we heard someone knocking at the front door. Smoke comes out of our chimney all the time so there's obviously people living here. But no one ever comes by.

"Maybe it's Peter," Mom said.

Matt helped her up off her mattress. We all went to the front door to see who it was.

Jon recognized him first. "It's Mr. Mortensen," he said.

"I need help," Mr. Mortensen said. He looked so desperate, it was frightening. "My wife. She's sick. I don't know what it is. Do you have anything, any medicine? Please. Anything."

"No, we don't," Mom said.

Mr. Mortensen grabbed her hand. "Please," he said. "I'm begging you. I'm not asking for food or wood. Just medicine. You must have something. Please. She's burning with fever. I don't know what to do."

"Jonny, get the aspirin," Mom said. "That's all we have. I'm sorry. We'll give you some aspirin. That should lower her fever."

"Thank you," he said.

"How long has she been sick?" Mom asked.

"Just since this morning," he said. "Last night she was fine. But she's delirious. I don't like leaving her alone, but I don't know what else to do."

Jon came back and handed over some aspirin to Mr. Mortensen. I thought he was going to cry, and I felt relieved when he left. We went back into the sunroom.

"Mom," Jon said. "Is Mrs. Mortensen going to be all right?"

"I hope so," Mom said. "Remember, Peter told us there'd be illness. But she could just have a cold. None of us is at full strength. It could be one of those twenty-four-hour things."

"Maybe he just wanted some aspirin for a headache," Matt said. "Mrs. Mortensen could be out right now building a snow fort and he just used her as an excuse."

Mom smiled. "That's probably wishful thinking," she said. "But I'm sure she'll be all right. Now it seems to me we're all behind on our schoolwork. Miranda, tell me what you've been learning in history."

So I did. And as the day went along I thought less and less about Mrs. Mortensen.

But now she's all I can think about.

January 6

I know this is silly but when we woke up this morning I was relieved that we were still alive and well.

When Matt suggested we do our daily skiing, I leaped up. I skied farther than I have before. I made it practically to the Mortensen house, but when I realized where I was, I turned around and set a record for how fast I made it back to Matt and Jon.

When we got home, I was relieved to see Mom perfectly okay. Matt and Jon and I didn't say anything about it, but we'd all worked harder on our skiing than we had before.

And Mom didn't say anything about how we'd stayed out too long.

January 7

It snowed last night. Our skylights are covered again and the sunroom is back to total darkness.

Matt says it wasn't snowing when he and Jon went out last night for their bathroom break. I guess it must have started right after that because by this morning there were already 4 or 5 inches of fresh (well, gray fresh) snow on the ground.

It was still snowing after lunch and Mom said we should stay in. Instead of skiing, we did our going-to-the-front-door-and-looking-to-see-what-it-looks-like-outside routine.

The snow stopped sometime this evening, so it was nothing like the blizzard last month. Matt figures we got 8 to 10 inches, not enough to bother cleaning the roof.

"The heat from the woodstove will melt the snow off the skylights," he said. "We should expect snow in January. Fresh snow means more water and that'll come in handy later on."

All of which sounds perfectly fine, but the more snow on the ground, the harder it is to get out of here. I'm not that good at cross-country skiing, especially since Dad's boots are way too big for my feet.

There's nothing I can do about it so there's no point complaining. But I miss the extra light in the sunroom.

January 8

Skiing was a lot harder on the extra 8 inches of snow. We all fell over and over. Of course Jonny and Matt were extra tired from having to shovel the walkways and a path to the road.

I did their laundry for them.

We're all on edge. I guess it's the snow. There were flurries again today, maybe an inch more.

I know it didn't snow for almost a month and Matt's right. It snows in January. But if it snows 8 inches every couple of weeks in January and February and it doesn't melt for months, then how much snow are we going to end up with?

We still have tons of firewood, but what if they can't cut any more?

What if our food supply runs out?

I know I'm doing this to myself. We've made it through so far. There's no reason to think we won't survive some more snow. But I have that scared feeling in the pit of my stomach.

It's dumb. I know it's dumb. But I wish Peter would walk through the door, or Dad and Lisa and baby Rachel. I wish Dan was here. I wish I had a postcard from Sammi making fun of me for being stuck in boring Pennsylvania.

I wish the snow was off the skylights.

I wish it was still Christmas.

NINETEEN

January 10

They're sick.

It started with Mom. She tried to get off her mattress this morning and couldn't. "Something's the matter," she said. "Don't let anyone come near me."

Matt and I went over to the side of the room and whispered so Mom wouldn't hear us. "We can't move her out," he said. "She'd freeze in the kitchen. We'll just have to take our chances."

But then Jonny screamed. It was the most horrifying sound I've ever heard. We ran over to him and saw he was delirious, crazed with fever.

"Aspirin," I said, and I ran to the pantry to get the bottle. Matt put a pot of water on the stove to make tea.

Mom was close to unconscious when the tea was ready, but we lifted her head up and forced the tea and aspirin down her throat. I was afraid she would choke on it, but after we saw her swallow, we put her head back down. She was shivering terribly, so I took one of the blankets off my mattress and draped it around her.

Jon was harder. His arms were swinging around so wildly that he hit me in the jaw and knocked me over. Matt got behind him and held his arms down while I pushed the aspirin into his mouth and poured the tea down his throat. Then I ran to the bathroom and got the rubbing alcohol. Matt turned him over and pinned him down while I gave him a back rub. He was burning with fever and kept tossing off his blankets.

"We need help," I said. "I don't know if I'm doing this right."

Matt nodded. "I'll go," he said. "You stay here and look after them." But as he got up he began to sway. For one awful moment I thought he was going to grab onto the woodstove to keep from falling, but he came to his senses and sank onto Jon's mattress instead.

"I can do it," he said and he crawled from Jon's mattress to his own. "Don't worry."

I didn't know if he meant he could make it to his own mattress or to get help, but it was obvious he wasn't going anywhere. I handed him a couple of aspirin and poured another mug of tea.

"I need you to stay here," I said when he gestured that he could get up. "Mom and Jon are helpless. You have to make sure the fire doesn't go out and Jon stays covered. Can you do that? I don't know how long I'll be gone."

"I'll be okay," he said. "Go. Peter will know what to do."

I kissed his forehead. He was hot, but nowhere near as bad as Mom or Jon. I put a couple of pieces of wood in the stove, and put on my coat, boots, scarf, and gloves. The skis were in the front hallway, so I got them, then closed the front door behind me.

The weather wasn't bad, but I'd forgotten to put on the extra socks I need for Dad's boots to fit, and I fell a dozen times as I made my way to the hospital. I fell into snow on top of snow, so I never bruised myself, but of course I got soaking wet.

It didn't matter. Each time I fell I got back up and started again. No one else was going to rescue us. It was all up to me.

I don't know how long it took me to reach the hospital. I remember thinking I should have eaten something before I'd left, so it was probably close to noon when I got there. But it didn't matter. Nothing mattered except getting help.

Unlike the last time I'd gone there, the outside of the hospital was completely deserted. No guards to prevent me from entering. I had a moment of pure terror that I'd find no one inside, but I pushed the front door open and could hear sounds in the distance.

The lobby was empty so I followed the voices. I'd never heard a hospital so quiet before. There weren't any lights on, and I wondered if their generator had finally stopped working.

If the hospital wasn't functional, what chance did any of us have?

Eventually I found the source of the noise. It was two women—nurses, I assumed—sitting in an empty room. I charged in there, relieved to see them, terrified of what they were going to say.

"I need Dr. Elliott," I said. "Peter Elliott. Where is he?"

"Elliott," one of the women said, and she scratched the back of her neck. "He died on Saturday, didn't he, Maggie?"

"No, I think it was Friday," Maggie replied. "Remember, Friday we lost ten people and we thought that was the worst of it. Then Saturday we lost seventeen. But I think he was on Friday."

"I'm pretty sure it was Saturday," the first woman said. "Doesn't matter, does it? He's dead. Just about everyone is."

It took me a moment to realize they were saying Peter was dead. Peter who had done all he could to protect us and care for us had died.

"Peter Elliott," I said. "Dr. Elliott. That Peter Elliott."

"Dead just like everyone else," Maggie said, and she kind of laughed. "I guess we'll be next."

"Nah," the first woman said. "If we're not dead yet, nothing's going to kill us."

"Flu," Maggie said. "Past couple of weeks. It's flying through town. People kept coming here, like we could do something, and all the staff came down with it, except for Linda here and me and a couple of others. We'd go home except we're scared of what we'd find and besides we'd just make our families sick. Funny, isn't it? We've survived so much and it's the flu that's going to kill us all off."

"My family has it," I said. "Don't you have any kind of medicine? There must be something."

Linda shook her head. "It's the flu, hon," she said. "It just runs its course. Only thing is no one has any strength left to fight it off."

"It's a bad strain," Maggie said. "Like in 1918. The kind that would kill you anyway."

"But my family," I said. "What should I do for them?"

"Make them comfortable," Maggie said. "And don't bring them here when they die. We're not taking any more bodies."

"I gave them aspirin," I said. "And an alcohol rub. Was that the right thing to do?"

"Honey, listen to us," Maggie said. "It doesn't matter. Maybe you'll be lucky. Maybe your family's stronger. Aspirin won't hurt. Alcohol rubs won't hurt. Pray if it'll make you feel better. But whatever's going to happen is going to happen. And it'll happen fast."

"You can try fluids," Linda said. "If you have any food, try to make them eat. They'll need all the strength they can get."

Maggie shook her head. "Save the food for yourself, hon," she said. "You look healthy enough. Maybe you're like us and you're resistant to this strain. Your folks would want you to live. Take care of yourself. Your family's going to live or die no matter what you do."

"No!" I said. "No. I don't believe you. There has to be something."

"There were how many people here last week?" Maggie asked. "A hundred, maybe more. We lost half of them the first day. Go home and be with your folks. Give them whatever comfort you can."

"Sorry," Linda said. "I know it's a tough break. Sorry to tell you about Dr. Elliott. He was a nice man. He worked until the end, then he just collapsed and died. We've lost a lot of staff that way, working until their last breath. But maybe your family will make it through. Some people do."

There was no point staying. I thanked them and started the journey home.

The wind had picked up and was blowing against me for much of the walk. I stumbled as much as I skied, and it was all I could do to keep from bursting into tears. Peter was dead. For all I knew Mom and Jon were, also. Matt might die, too.

I remembered how Jon had asked me what he would do if he were the only one of us to survive and how flippant I'd been. And now I was facing the same thing.

Yesterday everything was fine. By tonight I could be completely alone.

I told myself over and over again that I wouldn't let that happen. We were strong. We ate, we had heat, and shelter. We'd been lucky so far. We'd stay lucky. We'd stay alive.

The sky was darkening when I finally made it home, but it looked like a snow sky, and I was sure it was still daytime. It took all the courage I had to open the door. But when I got to the sunroom I saw things were pretty much as I'd left them. Mom was so quiet I had to kneel by her side to make sure she was still breathing, but she was. Jonny was delirious, but he was covered and not flailing around so much. Matt was lying on his mattress, but his eyes were open, and he turned around when he saw I'd come in.

"Peter," he said.

I shook my head. "We're on our own," I said. "It's just the flu. We'll be fine."

"Okay," he said, and closed his eyes. For the most horrible moment of my life, I thought he'd died, that he had stayed alive until I got back and then felt he could die. But he'd just fallen asleep. His breathing was shallow, but he was definitely alive.

I put some wood in the stove and collapsed onto my mattress. That's where I am now. I don't even know why I'm writing this down, except that I feel fine and maybe tomorrow I'll be dead. And if that happens, and someone should find my journal, I want them to know what happened.

We are a family. We love each other. We've been scared together and brave together. If this is how it ends, so be it.

Only, please, don't let me be the last one to die.

Sanuary 11

We've made it through the night.

Mom and Jonny don't seem any better. It was harder getting the aspirin down Mom's throat. She coughed a lot and threw the pills back up, so I dissolved them in tea.

Jonny alternates between delirium and stupor. I don't know which is scarier.

Matt is the least sick of the three, and I really think he'll survive. He sleeps most of the day, but when he's awake he's Matt.

I gave all of them aspirin and cold remedies every 4 hours and sponge bathed them and gave them alcohol rubs. It's hard keeping the blankets on Jonny.

I heated beef broth and spoon-fed all of them. I had to hold up Mom's and Jonny's heads when I did. Matt was able to stay awake long enough to take a few swallows on his own.

That's got to be a good sign.

When I went out this morning to clean the bedpan, I discovered it was snowing again. It probably started right after I got in yesterday. It was obviously dying down by this morning, but we probably got another 6 inches. Not that it matters.

I don't have a fever. I'm tired from staying up and it's hard to remember to eat, but I'm definitely not sick. Maybe I'm crazy, but I keep thinking if Mom and Jonny and Matt have made it this long, they're not going to die. Linda and Maggie made it sound like everyone at the hospital died the day they got sick.

Mom's moaning. I think I'd better check on her.

January 12

No change.

Matt's a little weaker. Jon's a little quieter. It's getting harder for Mom to swallow.

There was an ice storm last night. The tree branches are all covered in gray-tinged ice.

January 13

Horton woke me up. He was yowling. I didn't even realize I was asleep. I remember putting logs in the woodstove and lying down for a few minutes, and I must have fallen asleep.

Horton was yowling and I was coughing. Gut-wrenching coughing.

Then I realized the room was filled with smoke and we were all coughing.

I thought, The house can't be on fire because that would just be too funny. I managed to turn my flashlight on, like I needed it to see if the house was on fire, but I didn't see any flames.

I moved the flashlight around and saw the smoke was pouring out of the woodstove. It had backfired and was filling the room with smoke.

Smoke inhalation can kill you.

My first thought was to get the hell out of there, run outside, and breathe some real air. But everyone else was coughing, which meant they were all still alive and I had to get them out of there.

Mom and Jonny were far too weak to get up on their own. I didn't dare take them outside. The kitchen floor was going to have to do.

I took my blankets and grabbed one off of Matt's bed, waking him up in the process. I was half blind from the smoke, but I managed to get the blankets onto the kitchen floor. It took every ounce of courage I had to go back into the sunroom, but I did. Thank goodness Matt had enough strength left to help me pull Jonny first and then Mom into the kitchen. I told Matt to stay there, and I ran back in and got everyone's pillows and blankets. Matt helped get them in place. He was gasping so badly I was afraid he'd have a heart attack, but he waved me off.

Next I went to the thermostat to turn on the furnace, but I didn't hear anything go on. I remembered that Dad and Matt had jerry-rigged a battery cell to the furnace, and I would have to go to the cellar to turn it on. I went back to the kitchen where Mom, Matt, and Jonny were all still racked with coughing, and I opened the cellar door. At least the air was clear down there, but the temperature was probably close to zero and I regretted not having put my shoes on. I held on to the flashlight, and with it I raced to the furnace, took a moment to figure out what to do, and pulled the right switch. The furnace turned on almost immediately. We still had oil. I went back upstairs as fast as I could and put the thermostat at 65 degrees.

Horton had followed everyone into the kitchen so I didn't have to worry about him. I went to the bathroom and found the cough medicine with codeine that we'd taken from Mrs. Nesbitt's medicine cabinet. I gave Matt his first and his cough subsided enough that he was able to help me give the medicine to Jonny and Mom. I was afraid to take it myself in case the codeine put me to sleep. Instead I grabbed a washcloth and threw it into a water pot. Once it was thoroughly wet, I covered my mouth with it and went back into the sunroom.

Panic overwhelmed me. The room was filled with smoke and breathing was close to impossible. I couldn't think what to do next. We were all going to die and it would be all my fault.

I got really mad then and that pushed me into action. The first thing I did was open the back door to air the room out. There was one piece of good luck: The wind was blowing in the right direction.

I stayed outside long enough to get some air back into my lungs. Good thing I've been sleeping with my coat on, but even so I couldn't manage more than a minute since I didn't have any shoes on. Still that was enough air to get me back into the sunroom.

I tried opening the skylights but there was too much snow on top of them. I cursed myself for not having gotten on the ladder to clear them off when the snow had started, but it was too late now. I pulled the plywood off one of the windows opposite the door and opened the window. The crosswind worked and I started to see the smoke lessening.

I knew what I had to do next and that was get rid of the piece of wood that had caused the backfire. I went to the door, took a few deep breaths, then came back in and opened the woodstove.

The smoke was overwhelming. I raced back outside and grabbed a handful of snow to rub against my burning eyes. I swallowed some of the snow. Mom'll kill me, I thought, drinking unboiled snow.

The thought made me laugh, and that got me coughing again. I laughed and cried and coughed and choked. But in spite of it all, I was damned if I was going to die and I was double damned if I was going to leave Matt and Jon and Mom like that.

So I went back into the sunroom. The smoke was still incredibly thick and I thought I'd cough my lungs up. I crawled over to the stove and put on the mitts. I reached in and pulled out the smoking log.

Even through the mitt, I could tell the log was wet. Hot and wet and steaming and smoking. I juggled it between the mitts, crawled to the door, and threw it out.

The log shouldn't have been wet. We hadn't had that problem with any of the wood Matt and Jonny have cut up until now. I realized the stove had to be wet. Snow or ice must have fallen through the chimney and made the entire stove damp.

I had to make sure the stove was dry or else the same thing would happen again. And that meant I had to get another fire going just to dry out the stove, and that meant more smoke.

My whole body began to shake. It was stupid, but I kept thinking how unfair it was. Why did I have to be the one? Why couldn't I be sick and Matt take care of me? Or Jon? He's the one who gets to eat. Why did he have to get sick? He should be healthy. He should be the one choking to death and I should be in the nice warm kitchen, all drugged with codeine.

Well, it was useless to dream. I looked around the sunroom to see what I could burn. A log wouldn't do. It would just get wet and start the whole business over again. I needed to burn lots and lots of paper.

My first thought was the textbooks, but I knew Mom would kill me. If we all got well and she found we couldn't keep studying, she would kill me. But I felt like if I had to go through all this, I should be rewarded by burning a textbook.

I left the sunroom and made my way through the kitchen. Everyone was still coughing, but not the way they had been. Matt looked feverish, but he waved me away when I tried to hover.

"I'm okay," he whispered.

I didn't have much choice but to believe him. I went upstairs and got a couple of the textbooks I'd taken home my one day at school. While I was up there, I changed into dry clothes and put on shoes. Just doing that helped.

I went back to the kitchen and freshened the washcloth. Then I crawled back into the sunroom. The smoke had lessened but once I reopened the woodstove, it poured out again.

I tore page after page from the textbook. With a shaking hand I lit a match and threw the burning paper into the stove. The smoke grew stronger and I wasn't sure I'd be able to bear it. But I shoved as many pieces of paper as I could in there, and when I was sure the fire would last at least a minute, I let myself go to the back door and gulp in some air. Then I went back, tore more sheets out, and burned them.

I don't know how long I burned paper, but I know I killed

one and a half textbooks. If the school wants them back, they can just sue me.

Finally the stove stopped smoking. I tore some more textbook then piled on some of my kindling. When the fire was going good and strong, I put a couple of logs in and everything was fine.

I took a pot and filled it with snow and put it on the top of the stove to get some moisture back in the room. I waited about half an hour and then I closed the window. I waited another half hour after that, watching the fire and making sure it was burning clean before I closed the door.

I wanted more than anything to curl up on the kitchen floor and go to sleep. But I didn't dare leave the woodstove untended. So I stayed awake and only left the sunroom to go into the kitchen a couple of times to check on Mom and Matt and Jonny.

The window I took the plywood off of has an eastern exposure. I can see the sky lightening, so I guess it's dawn. It really isn't January 13 anymore.

I'm going to leave everyone in the kitchen for the time being. I'll give them their aspirin and let them go back to sleep. It's taken hours for the house to get from below freezing to 65 degrees and they might as well enjoy it. Besides, the sunroom still stinks of smoke, and I really should open the window and the door and air things out. We'll be sleeping on smoky mattresses for weeks to come.

Because if this didn't kill us, nothing will. It's January 14 and I can see the dawn and we're all going to survive.

January 14

We're all still alive.

I'm scared to leave everyone in the kitchen and I'm scared

to move them back. What scares me most is I don't think Matt has the strength to help me get them into the sunroom.

I'm just going to hope we have enough heating oil to make it through the night.

I stink of smoke and it hurts to breathe.

January 15

After I gave Mom her morning aspirin, I bent over her and kissed her forehead. It was just like <u>Sleeping Beauty</u>. Mom opened her eyes, stared straight at me, and said, "Not until you finish your homework."

I burst out laughing.

"Don't laugh at me, young lady," Mom said.

"Yes, ma'am," I said, trying with all my strength not to.

"Very well," she said. "I'll make supper now." She struggled to get up.

"No, that's okay," I said. "I'm not hungry."

"Nonsense," she said, but she fell back asleep. Her breathing was steady and I could tell her fever had broken.

She woke up a few hours later and seemed puzzled to be in the kitchen. "Is everyone all right?" she asked.

"We're fine," I told her.

She looked over and saw Jon and Matt sleeping on the floor. "What are we doing here?" she asked. "What's going on?"

"There was a problem with the woodstove," I said. "So I turned the furnace on and you've been sleeping in here."

"You look terrible," she said. "Are you eating properly?"

"No," I said.

Mom nodded. "Well, none of us are," she said, and went back to sleep.

When she woke up this evening she was just about normal.

She managed to sit up, and she asked how each of us was doing. I gave her the rundown.

"How long have we been sick?" she asked.

"I don't know," I said. "I've lost track. A few days."

"And you took care of us all that time?" she asked. "By yourself?"

"Matt helped," I said. I wanted to collapse by her side and weep and have her hold me and comfort me. None of which, of course, could I do. "The real problem was the woodstove, but that's okay now. Maybe tomorrow you'll move back to the sunroom."

"When did you eat last?" she asked.

"I haven't been hungry," I said. "I'm okay."

"You need to eat," she said. "We can't have you getting sick. Get yourself a can of mixed vegetables and eat all of it."

"Mom," I said.

"That's an order," she said.

So I did. And when I finished the can of vegetables I realized I was famished. I went back to the pantry and made myself a can of carrots and ate all of that. I probably haven't eaten in a couple of days, so I guess I'm entitled.

Then I realized Mom was well enough to eat, so I heated up a can of soup and gave her some. Matt woke up and he ate along with her.

"I'm worried about Jonny," Mom said when she finished her soup. "Do you think you should get Peter and have him check him out?"

"I've already been to the hospital," I said. "I went the first day you all got sick. It's the flu and the only thing we can do is wait it out."

"I'd still feel better if Peter could see him," Mom said. "I know you've been doing everything you can, but Peter's a doctor."

"It's too late for me to go anyplace today," I said. "Let's see how Jonny is tomorrow, okay? Now go back to sleep."

Thank goodness, Mom did. With everything that's happened, I haven't even thought how to tell her Peter died.

January 16

Jonny woke me this morning. I was sleeping in the doorway, head in the sunroom, feet in the kitchen.

"I'm hungry," he said.

He was weak but he was Jonny.

"I'll get you some soup," I said. I got up, went to the pantry, pulled out a can of soup, and heated it on the woodstove.

He was able to sit up and eat most of it. While he was eating, Mom and Matt both woke up. I heated more soup for them and soon they were all sitting up, eating, and even talking.

"Shouldn't we move back to the sunroom?" Mom asked.

"Later," I said. "Let me change the sheets on your mattresses first."

I went upstairs and got fresh sheets. I would have liked to flip all the mattresses over, but I didn't have the strength, so I told myself it wouldn't matter.

Once I got the clean sheets on the mattresses, I helped everyone get up. First Matt, then Mom, and finally Jonny. They all collapsed onto their mattresses. The walk from the kitchen to the sunroom took a lot out of them.

But after they'd napped, they woke up and I could see the difference in all of them. I heated up some vegetables and they all ate.

I gave everyone sponge baths, and then I took all their dirty sheets and pillowcases and spent the afternoon washing them.

Since the house was still warm, I hung them all up in the kitchen and the living room. When the laundry felt damp, I turned the heat off. I probably shouldn't have kept it on as long as I did, but it was so luxurious doing the wash in a warm kitchen.

Mom didn't ask about Peter.

January 17

Everybody was crabby and demanding. Get me this. Bring me that. I'm hot. I'm cold. It's too bright. It's too dark. Why did you do that? Why didn't you do that?

I swear I hate them all.

January 19

I can see how much better everyone is. I'm worried most about Matt. He was never as sick as Mom or Jonny, but he's still very weak.

I worry that when he helped me pull Mom and Jonny out of the sunroom he might have strained his heart.

Mom and Jonny both walked a few steps today.

January 21

I'm feeding everybody three meals a day. It's probably suicidal, but it's just so wonderful to see them eat.

Mom says tomorrow she's going to be strong enough to do the cooking.

Jon asked for his baseball cards and he stayed up all afternoon organizing them. Matt asked me to bring him a murder mystery and he spent the day reading it.

This evening Matt told me not to worry about the fire. He'd make sure to keep it going during the night. I should just get a good night's sleep.

I'm going to take him up on that.

I guess I slept for two straight days. I feel real groggy and hungry.

Mom's making me a cup of tea. Matt and Jon are playing chess.

Even Horton is sleeping on my mattress.

I think we're going to be okay.

January 26

I climbed onto the roof today and cleared the snow off. It's been on my list of things to do since that awful night, but I wanted to make sure someone would be strong enough to rescue me if I got into trouble.

Jon's getting stronger faster than Mom or Matt. By this afternoon, I figured I could take my chances. It was hard work, and I can't imagine how much harder it must have been after the blizzard when there was so much more snow.

I'm actually doing everybody's work these days: snow removal and all the laundry, etc. But tomorrow Jon'll start doing the dishes. He's eager to do stuff, but we all agree it's better for him to take things slow and make sure he recovers fully. Mom wasn't crazy about his being outside all the time I did the roof cleaning, but I worked as fast as I could and Jon doesn't seem any the worse for it.

I'm more tired than I used to be, but I think that'll pass. The important thing is I didn't get sick and we all think if I didn't then, I'm not going to now. Me and Maggie and Linda. I hope they had as good luck with their families as I did with mine.

January 27

I was in the kitchen doing laundry when Mom joined me. "You shouldn't be here," I said. "Go back to the sunroom."

"I will in a minute," she said. "But this seemed like a good time to talk."

There was a time when that tone would have meant I was in trouble. Now it just means she wants some private conversation. I smiled at her and kept scrubbing.

"I want you to know how proud I am of you," she said. "There aren't words to say how grateful I am. We would have died without you and we all know that. We owe you our lives."

"You would have done the same for me," I said, staring at the dirty underwear. I knew if I looked at Mom I'd start crying, and I didn't want to do that because I worry if I start crying I'll never stop.

"You're a very special girl," Mom said. "No, you're a very special woman, Miranda. Thank you."

"You're welcome," I said. "Is that it? Because if it is, you really should go back to the sunroom."

"There is one other thing," she said. "I'm confused about something. Those first few days—well, everything is hazy in my mind. Was Peter here? I think I remember you going to get him, but I don't remember seeing him. Did you get to see him? Did he know we were sick? I know it's close to impossible to get from here to the hospital, so I don't even know if you made it. But did you try? I'm sorry. I'm just trying to put all this together and make sense of it."

This time I looked away from the laundry. I dried my hands off and turned to face Mom. "I made it to the hospital," I said. "That first day. Matt was too sick to go, so I went. Basically I was told what I already knew, that you all had the flu and you should be kept warm and given aspirin and made comfortable until you got better. So I came back and did all that."

"Did you see Peter?" Mom asked.

"No," I said. "I spoke to two women there, nurses I think."

I turned away from her and willed myself to be brave. "Mom, Peter's dead," I said. "The nurses told me. The flu decimated everyone at the hospital, patients and staff. You got sick on Tuesday and he'd died the weekend before. I don't know for sure, but I think a lot of people in town died. Maybe people all over the country. It was that kind of flu. We were incredibly lucky you all pulled through. Well, not completely because of luck. You've seen to it we've had food and water and shelter and heat. Even Matt making us move into the sunroom when we still had heating oil probably saved your lives because when we needed the oil, we still had some."

Mom stood there stone-faced.

"I'm sorry," I said. "I haven't wanted to tell you. The nurses said he worked to the end. He was a hero."

"I wish we didn't need so damn many heroes," Mom said, and went back to the sunroom.

Me too.

January 30

Matt remains weak, which is really annoying him. Mom keeps telling him that people recuperate at different speeds and he should just not rush things.

But I think he's never going to be 100% again.

Jon's regained most of his strength and he's impatient to be doing things, but Mom's keeping him on a limited schedule. Except for that one day when I cleared off the roof, he's stayed in the sunroom. Since he can wash the dishes in the old basin we found in the cellar, he doesn't even have to leave the sunroom to do that.

Mom isn't as strong as I'd like her to be, but I know she's also sad about Peter. After I told her, she had me tell Matt and

Jonny, too, so now everybody knows, but of course it's Mom who feels it the worst.

Now that it's been a couple of weeks since the fevers broke, I figure I can do some stuff on my own. This afternoon I took the skis and went back to the road to practice.

It was glorious being alone and outside and doing something other than nursing and housework. And since my trek to the hospital, I've been thinking how I really should get better on the skis. I don't know when Matt will be strong enough to go any distance, and one of us needs to be able to get around. That leaves Jon and me, and I have a head start.

This is my time. I've earned it.

February 2

Mom must be getting better. She asked if I'd forgotten about schoolwork.

"It hasn't been my highest priority," I said.

"Well, we need to change that," she said. "For all of us. Jonny, there's no reason why you can't go back to algebra. Matt can help you. And I'm going to forget all my French if I don't start working on it. We don't want our brains to rot away."

"Mom," I said, "I'm doing all the housework and I'm skiing. What more do you want from me?"

"I don't want back talk from you, I can tell you that," she said. "Now open up that history textbook and get to work."

It's a good thing I didn't burn it. Or maybe it's not such a good thing!

February 4

Matt needed something from his bedroom.

It's hard for Mom to get upstairs since she fell the second

time, so I go to her room if she needs something from there. Jon only started going upstairs last weekend. Up till then, I got whatever he needed, and of course I've been doing the same for Matt.

"Do you think you're ready?" Mom asked him.

"Sure," Matt said. "I wouldn't do it if I weren't."

Mom exchanged glances with me, but when I started to get up to go with him, she shook her head ever so slightly.

Matt made his way out of the sunroom, through the kitchen, down the hallway to the staircase. I don't think any of us breathed as we heard his lumbering steps on the staircase.

Then the sounds stopped.

"Go," Mom said to me.

I ran to the staircase. Matt was standing 4 steps up.

"I can't do it," he said. "Damn it to hell. I can't get up the stairs."

"Then stop trying," I said. "Just come down and try some other time."

"What if there isn't another time?" he said. "What if I'm a useless invalid for the rest of my life?"

"You may be an invalid, but you'll never be useless," I said. "Matt, has it occurred to you that the reason you're so weak is because you pulled Mom and Jonny out of the sunroom that night? That maybe you sacrificed your health to save their lives and that's something you should be proud of? They wouldn't be alive if it weren't for you. You have no idea how much you give to us every single day. You think I liked nursing all of you? I hated it. But I'd think of how you do things, without complaining. You just do what has to be done, and I tried to be like you. So walk down those stairs and get back to bed and if you stay exactly the way you are now, you'll still be the strongest person I've ever known."

"It takes one to know one," he said.

"Great," I said. "We're both the bestest people ever. Now tell me what you want upstairs and go to the sunroom before Mom gets hysterical."

So he did. I watched to make sure he made it down the stairs, then I ran upstairs and got what he needed in the first place.

It's going to kill us if Matt doesn't get stronger. But he doesn't need to know that.

February 7

Mom's birthday.

Christmas, when Mom had shared her candy with us, I ate 2 of the 4 pieces I took, and saved the other 2.

So Mom's birthday present was 2 pieces of candy.

Jon let her beat him in chess.

And Matt walked to and from the staircase 3 times.

She said it was the best birthday she'd ever had.

TWENTY

February 9

Jon's strong enough to demand time on the skis and I've run out of excuses to keep him from using them.

Every morning I go out and ski by myself for an hour or so. It keeps my mind off food, and that's good, too.

Then after lunch I go out with Jon and watch while he skis. Mom won't let him be outside alone yet. He doesn't last more than 15—20 minutes, so it's really not that bad.

Matt walks to and from the staircase 3 times every morning and 4 times after lunch. I think he's going to try climbing the stairs next week, just a couple at first, and then build up, however long it takes.

Mom isn't ready to do laundry, but she's making our lunches again. Somehow everything tastes better if Mom's the one who prepares it.

At my insistence (and I love that I actually won an argument) we kept the plywood off the one window. Most of the snow is gone from the skylights, so there's a little more natural light in the sunroom. I don't think the air quality is much better, but I can tell the days are getting longer.

There's a lot of stuff to worry about, but I've given myself a holiday. I can always worry next week instead.

February 12

I came home from my morning ski and found Mom frying something in the skillet.

It smelled wonderful. We haven't had any fresh vegetables in so long, and there's no point frying canned spinach or string beans. We were practically jumping with excitement by the time Mom served lunch. I couldn't figure out what we were eating. The texture was kind of like an onion, but the taste was a little bitter.

"What is it?" we all asked.

"Tulip bulbs," Mom said. "I pulled them out of the ground last summer before the ground froze. I've been saving them for a nice treat."

We all stopped chewing. It was almost as though Mom had sautéed Horton.

"Come on," Mom said. "We won't be the first people to eat tulip bulbs."

It was a comforting thought. That and hunger pushed us through lunch.

February 14

Valentine's Day,
I wonder where Dan is.
Wherever he is, he's probably not thinking of me.

February 15

Matt walked up 6 steps.
We all pretended like this was no big deal.

I stayed in this morning. I said it was because the book I was reading was so interesting, but of course that was a lie.

We had lunch and then Jon and I went out while he did his skiing. I thought he'd never get tired, but after a half hour or so he was ready to go back in. I think by next week Mom'll let him go out on his own.

We went back to the house together. I ran in, got the skates, took the skis and the shoes and the poles from Jon, and said I'd be home in a couple of hours.

And then I did what no other athlete has done before. I won 2 Olympic gold medals in 2 different sports in the same afternoon.

First I won the cross-country ski race. I went from home to Miller's Pond and won by so much I couldn't even see my competitors.

But that was just a warm-up. When I got to the pond, I skated my legendary gold medal—winning long program. I could hear the thousands of people in the stands cheering my every move. My crossovers, my Mohawks, my spiral, my spins. My breathtaking single toe loop. My Ina Bauer. The brilliantly choreographed, seemingly spontaneous footwork sequence.

The ice was showered with flowers and teddy bears. The TV commentators said they were honored to be in the arena to see such a performance. I wiped away a tear or two in the kiss and cry. Every one of my competitors came up to me and congratulated me on the skate of the century. I stood proudly on the podium as the American flag went up. I smiled and sang along to "The Star Spangled Banner."

America's darling. The greatest athlete in American history. And a shoo-in for 8 gold medals in swimming at the next Summer Olympics.

"Did you have a good time?" Mom asked when I got back from the pond.

"The best," I told her.

February 20

"Jonny, why haven't you eaten any supper?" Mom asked him this evening.

"I'm not hungry," he said.

That's the third day in a row he hasn't been hungry at suppertime.

I guess he went into the pantry when none of us were looking. I guess he knows now what the rest of us figured out already.

I wonder if he's noticed that Mom's hardly eating anything.

February 22

We were all asleep when suddenly noises woke us up. Noises and light.

I think we all woke up disoriented. The only noise we ever hear is each other and the wind. And light comes only from the woodstove, candles, oil lamps, and flashlights.

This was a different kind of noise, a different kind of light.

Matt figured it out first. "It's electricity," he said. "We have electricity."

We leaped off our mattresses and ran through the house. The overhead light was on in the kitchen. A long-forgotten radio was broadcasting static in the living room. The clock radio was flashing the time in my bedroom.

Mom had the good sense to look at her watch. It was 2:05 AM.

By 2:09 the electricity was off.

But we all can't help thinking if it came on once, it'll come on again.

"You know," Mom said at lunch today. "That little burst of electricity got me thinking."

"Me too," I said. "About washing machines and dryers."

"Computers," Jon said. "DVD players."

"Refrigerators," Matt said. "Electric heaters."

"Yes, all of that," Mom said. "But what I was really thinking about was radio."

"All we got was static," Matt pointed out.

"But if we have electricity, maybe other places have it, too, and radio stations are broadcasting again," Mom said. "And we don't need electricity to find that out. We should turn on a radio and see if we can get any stations."

For a moment I wanted to tell Mom not to try, that the whole world had probably died from the flu and we were the last ones left on earth. I think that sometimes.

But then I realized someone had to have done something to give us those four glorious minutes of electricity.

The thought of our not being alone was thrilling. I ran into the living room and got the radio.

Mom's fingers actually trembled as she turned it on and tried to get a station. But all we got was static.

"We'll try again tonight," she said. "After sundown."

And we did. We waited all day for the sky to go from gray to black.

When it finally did, Mom turned the radio on again. At first all we heard was static. But then we heard a man's voice.

"In Cleveland, Harvey Aaron," the man said. "Joshua Aaron. Sharon Aaron. Ibin Abraham. Doris Abrams. Michael Abrams. John Ackroyd. Mary Ackroyd. Helen Atchinson. Robert Atchinson . . ."

"It's a list of the dead," Matt said. "He's reading the names of the dead."

"But that means people are alive," Mom said. "Someone has to be reporting who died. Someone has to be listening."

She played with the dial some more.

"In other news today, the president said the country has turned the corner. Better times are predicted for the weeks to come with life being back to normal by May."

"The idiot's still alive!" Mom cried. "And he's still an idiot!"

We burst out laughing.

We listened to that station for a while, until we figured out it was broadcasting from Washington. Then Mom found a third station, out of Chicago. It was broadcasting news, also. Most of the news was bad, the way it had been last summer. Earthquakes, floods, volcanoes, the litany of natural disasters. There were a few things added to the list, though: Flu epidemics and cholera. Famine. Droughts. Ice storms.

But it was still news. There was life going on.

We aren't alone.

February 25

Matt figured if the radio stations were back on, maybe we had phone service and just didn't know it. So he picked up the phone, but it was still dead.

The only person who might be trying to reach us is Dad. Other than that, it doesn't matter.

February 26

Electricity again.

This time at 1 in the afternoon, and it lasted for 10 minutes.

Jon was outside skiing so he missed it.

"We're going to start a laundry next time," Mom said. "Whatever gets done gets done."

It's so glorious to think there could be a next time.

February 27

12 minutes of electricity at 9:15 tonight.

Mom changed her mind about the laundry. "We'll give it a try in daytime," she said. "Maybe tomorrow."

February 28

6 minutes of electricity at 4:45 AM.

Big deal.

I know I should be excited because we've had electricity 3 days in a row, but we need food more than we need electricity. A lot more.

Unless electricity can make us some canned vegetables and soup and tuna fish, I don't know what good it's going to do us.

I wonder who'll read our names on the radio after we've died of starvation.

March 3

No electricity for the past 2 days.

We were better off without any electricity. Why did they have to give us the taste of it just to take it away?

Mom listens to the radio for half an hour every evening. I don't know why. She goes from station to station (we're up to 6 now) and all they broadcast is bad news.

No, that's not true. They broadcast bad news and the president saying things are looking up. I don't know which is worse.

It scares me a little that Mom is willing to burn up batteries just to listen to the radio. I think it's her way of accepting that there's no point in the batteries outliving us.

March 4

Matt had been up to 10 stairs and I was sure by the end of this week he'd be climbing the whole staircase.

But today he only did 6 stairs. I know because I tiptoed behind him and peeked through the living room door. Mom knew that's what I was doing and she didn't tell me not to. Jon was outside, but even he's down to 20 minutes skiing.

I don't think Matt knows I was spying on him. I got back to the sunroom before he did and I was real quiet.

Mom hardly spoke all afternoon. Matt got back on his mattress and slept for 2 hours. Not even Jon walking back in woke him.

Sometimes I think about everything I went through when they were all sick and it makes me so angry. How dare they die now?

March 5

It snowed all day. At least we could watch it through the window in the sunroom.

I don't think we got more than 4 or 5 inches, and Matt pointed out it was good to have fresh snow for drinking water.

Mom's told me not to bother washing the sheets for a while. I guess I should be glad, since the sheets are my least favorite things to wash (they're just so big). She says it's because if we get electricity back for good, it'll be so much easier to wash the sheets that way, but I think it's because she's worried I burn up too much energy washing things that bulky.

I finally figured I should know the worst and I checked out the pantry.

I wish I hadn't.

March 6

Jon was outside and Matt was sleeping this afternoon. Mom gestured to me and we went into the living room.

"I hate to ask this of you," she said. "But do you think you could skip lunch a couple of times a week?"

Mom's been eating every other day for a couple of weeks now. So she was asking less of me than what she's doing herself.

"Okay," I said. What was I supposed to say?

"I want Matt and Jonny to still eat every day," she said. "Can you live with that?"

I burst out laughing.

Even Mom grinned. "Bad choice of words," she said. "I apologize."

"It's okay," I said. I even kissed her to prove I meant it.

I think Mom figures Jon still has the best chance of surviving. And I think she can't bear the idea of seeing Matt die.

Neither can I. Better Mom should go first, then me, then Matt. Matt will see to it Jon makes it through.

March 7

This is so stupid. I started looking at this diary and all its empty pages. I was so excited when Mom gave it to me at Christmas. I even worried I'd finish it up by April and have to go back to the blue books.

So many empty pages.

March 8

Electricity again. This time for 16 minutes around 3 this afternoon.

I don't know what that means.

March 12

Mom fainted this afternoon. I don't think she's eaten in 3 days.

I made some soup and forced her to eat it. I'm not ready for her to die yet.

I did another inventory of the pantry. There's so little in there, it didn't take much time for me to check. There's maybe 2 weeks worth of food if only Jon and Matt eat. With Mom and me eating occasionally, we'll run out of food in 10 days. If after we die Matt stops eating, then Jon gets another few days, which could give him enough time and strength to get out of here. Matt can tell him who to go to so he can barter any leftover firewood for food.

I wonder what Jon will do with Horton.

March 13

The four of us shared a can of tomato soup for lunch. Then Mom insisted Matt and Jon share the last can of mixed vegetables.

It might be easier for Mom and me if we stopped eating altogether. We only had a couple of sips of soup anyway, just enough to remind me what food tastes like.

My birthday's next week. If I'm still alive, I hope Mom will be, too.

March 14

Nearly an hour of electricity this morning.

I stupidly looked at myself in a mirror when the lights were on.

For a moment, I actually didn't recognize myself. Then I remembered what I look like.

Not that it matters. Who cares what a corpse looks like.

I dreamed last night that I went into a pizza parlor. Sitting there were Dad, Lisa, and a little girl who I knew right away was Rachel.

I slid into the booth. The smells—tomato sauce, garlic, cheeses—were overwhelming.

"Is this Heaven?" I asked.

"No," Dad said. "It's a pizza parlor."

I think the dream gave me an idea. But it's hard to tell what's an idea and what's nonsense when you can't even tell the difference between Heaven and a pizza parlor.

TWENTY-ONE

March 17

By the time I fell asleep last night, I knew what I was going to have to do today. The only question was would I have the strength.

But when I woke up, I saw Mom struggle to get off her mattress, as though she needed to be up and around to do things for us. And that made up my mind for me.

After Matt and Jon rose and we all pretended like today was just another day, no harder than any we've been through, I made my announcement.

"I'm going into town," I said.

They stared at me like I was truly crazy. They were probably right.

"I'm going to the post office," I said. "I want to see if there's any word from Dad."

"What difference does it make?" Jon asked. "You think he sent us food?"

"I want to know if Lisa had her baby," I said. "I need to know that. I need to know that life is continuing. I'm going to town and find out."

"Miranda, can we talk?" Matt asked. I nodded, since I knew someone was going to question me about this and it might as well be him. We left the others in the sunroom and went to the living room to talk privately.

"Do you really think you have the strength to make to town and back?" he asked.

I wanted to say, No, of course I don't and we both know it and that's one reason why I'm going. I wanted to say, Stop me, because if I'm going to die, I want to die at home. I wanted to say, How could you have let this happen to me? as though it was Matt's fault and he could have saved us somehow. None of which I said.

"I know it's crazy," I said instead. "But I really need to know if Lisa had the baby. I feel like it's okay for me to die if she did. And maybe the post office is open and maybe there is a letter. How much longer can I last anyway? A week? Two? I'm willing to lose a few days for peace of mind. You understand that, don't you?"

"But if you can, you will come back," he said after a long pause.

"I hope I can," I said. "I'd rather be here. But if I can't, that's okay, too."

"What about Mom?" he asked.

"I've thought about that," I said. "I think this is actually better for her. If I don't come back, she can always have hope that I'm okay. I don't want her to see me die and I don't know that I can outlive her. This is really best, Matt. I thought about it a lot, and this is the best."

Matt looked away. "I'm sorry," he said. "But what about the skis? Jon's going to need them after we're gone."

Well, that was it, wasn't it? I was leaving home to give Jonny just a little better chance. We were starving ourselves to give

Jonny just a little better chance. If I really wanted him to have that chance, then I'd better accept that this casual stroll to town was meant to kill me. In which case, I didn't need the skis.

"I'll leave them behind," I said. "Tell Jon they'll be behind the oak tree and he should get them right after I leave. But don't tell Mom unless she asks. Let her think I'm coming back, okay?"

"You don't have to do this," Matt said.

"I know," I said, and kissed him good-bye. "And I love you and Jonny and Mom more than I ever knew. Now let me go in and say good-bye while I still have the nerve."

So I did. Mom was so weak I don't think she really understood what was going on. She just told me to get back before dark, and I said I would.

Jon looked like he had a thousand questions but Matt wouldn't let him start. I kissed him and Mom and told them to leave a light on for me, like that had any meaning. I rammed a pen and one of the blue books into my coat pocket. Then I went to the front door, picked up Dad's shoes, skis and poles, and walked to the road. When I got to the oak tree, I carefully placed everything where no one from the road could see them. Then I started the walk to town.

I wanted desperately to turn around, see the house, say good-bye, but I didn't let myself. I was scared that if I allowed myself that moment of weakness, I would race back in, and what good would that do any of us? Did I really need to be alive on my birthday? Did I even want to be, if Mom died between now and then?

So I kept my eyes straight ahead and began the journey. For the first mile footing wasn't too bad, since Jon and I had skied there and compacted the snow. Sure I fell a few times, where the snow was icelike, but I managed. I told myself the rest of the trip wouldn't be too bad, and there was hope I could get to town, maybe even find a letter from Dad, and get home again.

I liked telling myself that.

But the next 2 miles were brutal. I don't think anyone had walked on it since Christmas. I found I couldn't walk after a while, so I sat on the snow and pushed myself forward, half rowing, half sledding. It took all my strength to go a few feet, and the harder I worked, the more I yearned to give up and let myself die then and there.

But I pictured the pizza parlor and Dad telling me they weren't in Heaven. If there was a letter, I wanted to know. Death could wait a few more hours.

I felt a lot better when I got to a spot where I could walk upright again. I was soaking wet by that point, and freezing cold, but being on my own two feet gave me a sense of dignity and purpose. It made me feel human again and that gave me some strength back.

One of the scariest things was seeing how very few houses had smoke coming out of their chimneys. It wasn't like I could go to any of them and say, Rescue me, feed me, feed my family, because all they'd do was throw me out. We would have done the same if anyone came to our door.

But to see so many houses with no signs of life. Some people I knew had simply left while that was still possible. But others must have died from the flu or the cold or the hunger.

We were all still alive, Mom and Matt and Jonny and me. And I'd left a record. People would know I had lived. That counted for a lot.

The closer I got to town, the easier it was to walk. But the closer I got to town, the fewer signs of life I saw. It made sense. The people there lived closer together, so they shoveled their snow at least in the beginning. But they were also less likely to have woodstoves and more likely to have frozen to death. The closer they lived, the faster the flu would have spread. Our isolation had saved us, given us weeks, maybe even months more life.

By the time I got near enough to see the post office, I was starting to feel like I could make it back home. I knew that was madness, that the road was uphill and I had no strength left for that part where I wouldn't be able to walk. It's one thing to push yourself downhill, but pushing yourself uphill would be impossible. My heart would give out and I'd die a couple of miles from home.

But I didn't care. I'd made it to town and that was all I planned for. I'd go to the post office and find word from Dad that he and Lisa and baby Rachel were alive and well. Then it wouldn't matter where I died or how. Jonny would live and so would Rachel and that was what counted.

It was eerie standing on the main street of town, seeing no one, hearing no one, smelling nothing but the stench of death. I saw the carcasses of dogs and cats, pets people had left behind that couldn't survive in the cold without food. I bent down and clawed at one to see if there was any meat left, but what little clung to the skeleton was too frozen to pry off. I threw it back down onto the snow-covered street, and felt relieved I didn't see any human bodies.

Then I got to the post office and saw it was dead, too.

I felt such despair. It was probable the post office had never reopened since that last day Matt had worked there. Any fantasy I'd had that the reason I'd left the sunroom was to find a letter from Dad floated out of me.

I'd gone to town to die. There was no point going home, forcing the others to watch that happen.

I sank onto the ground. What was the point? Why should I

even try to get back to the house? The kindest thing I could do would be to stay where I was and let the coldness kill me. Mrs. Nesbitt had known how to die. Couldn't I learn that from her?

But then I saw a glimpse of yellow. My world has been nothing but shades of gray for so long that the yellow almost hurt my eyes.

But something was yellow. I remembered yellow as the color of sun. I'd seen the sun last July. It hurt to look straight at it, and it hurt to look at this new burst of yellow.

It wasn't the sun. I laughed at myself for thinking it might be. It was a sheet of paper dancing in the crosswinds down the street.

But it was yellow. I had to have it.

I forced myself to stand up and chase the sheet of paper. It taunted me with its dance, but I outwitted it and with all my remaining strength, put my foot over it and pinned it to the sidewalk. I bent down and felt the world swirling around me as I picked it up and stood straight. Just holding it made me excited. There were words. This was a message. Someone sometime had said something and now I would know what it was.

CITY HALL OPEN FRIDAYS 2—4 PM

There was no date, no way of knowing when it had been posted or why. But the words told me where to go. I had nothing to lose. Any dreams I might have had died with the post office. If City Hall were closed, also, it made no difference.

So I began the walk to City Hall. It was only a couple of blocks away from the post office. I looked at my watch and saw I had half an hour before it would close, assuming it was even open.

But when I got there, the door was unlocked and I could hear voices.

"Hello?" I said, proud of myself that I remembered the word.

"Come on in," a man said. He opened an office door and waved me in.

"Hi," I said, like this was the most normal thing in the world. "I'm Miranda Evans. I live on Howell Bridge Road."

"Sure," he said. "Come in. I'm Mayor Ford and this is Tom Danworth. Pleased to meet you."

"You too," I said, trying to believe that this wasn't a dream.

"Come here to sign up for your food?" Mayor Ford asked.

"Food?" I said. "I can get food?" It had to be a dream.

"See?" Mr. Danworth said. "That's why we're not getting many takers. Nobody knows."

"Lot of death up Howell Bridge way," Mayor Ford said. "No reason to go out there. How many in your family, Miranda?"

"Four," I said. "My mom and brothers had the flu but they all lived. Can I get food for them, too?"

"We'll need a witness they're still alive," the mayor said. "But everyone's entitled to one bag of food a week. That's what we've been told and that's what we're doing."

"Program's been going on for four weeks now," Mr. Danworth said. "So this young lady is entitled to at least four bags."

If it was a dream, I didn't want to wake up.

"Tell you what," the mayor said. "Wait until four when we officially close and Tom here will take you home on the snowmobile. You and your four bags, that is. And he'll check out your story and if what you say is true, then next Monday we'll send someone out to your home with food for the rest of your folk. Monday's delivery day. How does that sound?"

"I don't believe it," I said. "Real food?"

The mayor laughed. "Well, not gourmet," he said. "Not like we used to get at McDonald's. But canned goods and some boxed stuff. Nobody's been complaining."

I didn't know what to say. I just walked over to him and hugged him.

"Skin and bones," he said to Mr. Danworth. "Guess she got here just in time."

We waited around for the next 15 minutes but no one showed up. Finally the mayor told Mr. Danworth to get the 4 bags from the storage room and take them to the snowmobile.

I longed to go through the bags, see what kind of wonders were inside them, but I knew that would only slow things down. Besides, what did it matter? It was food. 4 bags of food. For a whole week, we wouldn't be hungry.

What had taken me 3 hours was a 20-minute trip in the snowmobile. It felt like flying watching the houses whiz by.

Mr. Danworth drove the snowmobile right to the sun-room door. The noise had obviously startled everybody, because they were all standing by the door when I knocked.

"Well, I guess you were telling the truth," Mr. Danworth said. "I definitely see three people here and they all look mighty hungry."

"I'll help you bring in the bags," I said. It was incredibly important to me to do that, to be the one bringing in the food that was going to save us.

"Fair enough," he said. "But let me help."

He ended up carrying in 3 bags to my one, but it didn't matter. Then he gave Mom a piece of paper to sign saying there were 4 of us in need of food.

"We'll be back on Monday," he said. "I can't guarantee you'll get all twelve bags you're entitled to, but we should manage seven, three for this week and four for next. After that you can count on four bags a week, at least until you hear otherwise."

Mom was sobbing. Matt managed to shake Mr. Danworth's hand and thank him. Jon was too busy poring through the bags and holding things up for all of us to see.

"You take care," Mr. Danworth said. "The worst is over. You made it this far, you'll make it all the way."

"Can we have supper tonight?" Jon asked after Mr. Danworth left. "Please, Mom. Just this once?"

Mom wiped away her tears, took a deep breath, and smiled. "Tonight we eat," she said. "And tomorrow and Sunday we'll eat."

We had sardines and mushrooms and rice for supper. For dessert (dessert!) we had dried fruit.

The electricity came on for the second time today while we were eating.

This may be a fool's paradise, but it's paradise nonetheless.

March 18

The electricity came on while we were feasting on chickpeas, lentils, and carrots.

"Come on," Mom said. "Let's try a laundry."

And we did. It was kind of a challenge because we don't have running water, so we had to pour water into the machine for the wash and rinse cycles. But even so it was still much easier than doing it by hand. We washed all our sheets and the electricity stayed on for most of the clothes-dryer time.

We celebrated by washing our hair. We took turns shampooing everyone else. Mom's insisted we sponge bathe daily, but shampoos are a real treat.

Then tonight the electricity came back on. Only for 10 minutes or so, but we didn't care. We made supper in the microwave.

Supper in the microwave. The most beautiful words I've ever written.

March 19

We still have three bags of food in the pantry, but I can tell Mom's nervous about tomorrow. It's like the electricity. It comes and goes but you can't count on it.

Still, even if the food's that way, we can make sure Jon's strong and well fed and that will give Mom peace.

March 20

My birthday.

I'm 17 and I'm alive and we have food.

Mr. Danworth himself showed up this morning with 10 bags of food.

"We know you're owed more, but this'll have to do," he said. "See you next Monday with your regular four bags."

There was so much and it was all so wonderful. Powdered milk. Cranberry juice. Three cans of tuna fish. Well, I could write it all down, but it doesn't matter. It was food and it will get us through for weeks and there'll be more food to come.

Because it was my birthday, Mom let me decide what we were going to have. I found a box of macaroni and cheese. It was as close to pizza as I could get.

There's still so much we don't know. We can only hope Dad and Lisa and baby Rachel are alive. Grandma, too. Sammi and Dan and all the other people we knew who left here. The flu was all over the U.S., probably all over the world. We were lucky to survive that; most people weren't.

The electricity comes and goes, so we don't know when we'll be able to depend on it. We have firewood for a while yet, and Matt is getting stronger (he walked up 10 stairs today and only Mom's insistence kept him from climbing them all). There's plenty of snow outside, so we're okay for water. The sky is still gray, though, and even though the temperature's been above zero for a week now, 20 degrees still feels balmy.

But today isn't a day to worry about the future. Whatever will happen will happen. Today is a day to celebrate. Tomorrow there will be more daylight than night. Tomorrow I'll wake up and find my mother and my brothers by my side. All still alive. All still loving me.

A while ago Jonny asked me why I was still keeping a journal, who I was writing it for. I've asked myself that a lot, especially in the really bad times.

Sometimes I've thought I'm keeping it for people 200 years from now, so they can see what our lives were like.

Sometimes I've thought I'm keeping it for that day when people no longer exist but butterflies can read.

But today, when I am 17 and warm and well fed, I'm keeping this journal for myself so I can always remember life as we knew it, life as we know it, for a time when I am no longer in the sunroom.